GODDESS ASCENDING

JANEAL FALOR

Goddess Ascending
by
Janeal Falor

Copyright © 2016 Janeal Falor

To learn more about this author, please visit: www.janealfalor.com

ISBN: 978-1946860019

Cover Image from ShutterStock by tugolukof

BOOKS BY JANEAL FALOR

Mine Series

Mine to Tarnish (Mine Prequel)

You Are Mine (Mine #1)

Mine to Spell (Mine #2)

Mine to Fear (Mine #3)

Sacrifice of Mine (Mine #4)

Darkening Light

Ever Darkening (Darkening Light #1)

Savage Light (Darkening Light #2)

Elven Princess

Bound by Birthright (Elven Princess #1)

Bound to Endure(Elven Princess #2)

Bound by Love (Elven Princess #3)

Death's Queen

Death's Queen (Death's Queen #1)

Death's Queen (Death's Queen #2) Coming Fall 2017

Standalones

Goddess Ascending

A Genie's Heart

To Sotia
For all that you do and the caring you show

EPISODE ONE

Episode One

CHAPTER 1

THE THIN BAND of iron locks around my neck with a *click*. This is the first time a goddess has ever been captured. Or a god, for that matter. Of course, I have to be the one locked up. I've failed in so many ways, I can't begin to make up for it. Despite it all, I hold my head high. They will not see how much this brings me down.

"Are you sure this will hold her, Norhe?" a man asks.

The man referred to as Norhe runs a finger across the metal on my neck and attaches a chain to it, which he uses to yank me forward. "It'll hold her, all right. Have you ever seen such a thing of beauty?"

Is he talking about me or the collar? Either way, I give him a glare.

"Never," the other man says. "Who is she?"

Norhe leans in close, his beady eyes trained on mine. "I'm not sure exactly. She was delivered to me by—" He turns around, but my deliverer is already gone.

That fiend Ramco, god of war, left the moment my collar clicked shut. I should have known better. I should have expected the betrayal. Instead, I thought he was taking me for a walk, my first foray into the human world. A foray supposed to be for friends. Seventeen years of life weren't enough for me to understand his cunningness; I still haven't figured out his plan. Being trapped is bad enough, but his betrayal makes it worse.

Norhe yanks the chain holding my collar, forcing me to walk. I pull against it, but it's no use. I fling into the bushes ahead of us and cry out when the bushes scratch me. Fortunately, my injuries heal, but I've never felt such pain before. Hardly felt any pain before.

I reach inside, ready to use my power of creation to make a soothing cream, but my power is stuck, forced to stay inside me by this treacherous collar on my flesh. The steel is cool against my neck, hard and unforgiving. I reach up to tear it from my neck, but the only thing it does is make my skin ache.

Norhe laughs. "Gentleman, our prisoner thinks she can escape." He pulls me closer—the closest I've ever been to a human. Just a few inches separate us.

I want to squirm, but I hold my ground. I'm not a goddess for nothing.

"You'll quickly learn there is no escape from us. Tell me your name," Norhe says.

I don't dignify the question with a verbal response. Instead, I give him the evil eye.

He tugs on my chain, jerking me toward him. "You'll learn your place soon enough."

I know my place. It's in the heavens, with the gods. I am Izlana, goddess of creation. I belong where I can make things for this world, not chained up like a dog. Though I do want to growl.

The way down the mountain I landed on is hazy. It's hard to pay attention when I'm under such stress. These men—what do they have planned for me? It can't be anything good. At least they don't know who I am. At least, I don't think they do

Time passes, and my legs grow weary of moving. I should start paying attention. I need to know the path we followed so I can get back home. Why didn't I think of that sooner? It's too late now. I lower my shoulders.

I take in the area, anyway. It's wooded with aspens, grass growing in tufts all around. A few flowers pop up here and there, but they're tiny little things. My white dress has grown dirty from the hike, its thin material not enough against the coolness of the world.

We walk a ways more before Norhe calls his men to a stop. We're in a clearing now, big enough for our group of five men and me. Norhe pulls my chain so I'm forced closer to him as he looks me over.

"With that white hair and those vivid green eyes," Norhe says, "you're going to bring us a pretty krat at the market tomorrow."

That's what I've been brought here for? To be sold on the slave market? Good thing they don't know I'm the goddess of creation; it'd likely make things worse. Still, who will buy me tomorrow? The thought makes me shiver with fear. I'm not sure I want to know the answer.

CHAPTER 2

THE AIR IS FILLED with the scent of sweat and dirt. The crowd, selling and buying wares, is loud. There are humans all around me tied up in some way by other humans. It's a disgusting sight that makes my already sick stomach worse. I'm the only one with a metal collar. It's hard against my skin, but not as bad as sleeping in it last night was.

The grounds are filled with dust from the barren terrain. If I had my power, I could grow grass and flowers to make this a better place than a slave market. But with my power taken, I'm as useless as a human. Maybe more so.

As I wait in the blaring sun, the first thing to be auctioned off is a horse. It's tied up like the humans, but unlike them, it goes for a high price.

Why did I never notice the slave trade before? I could have created something to stop it, though I don't know what. Why have none of my priestesses asked for help in ending such practices? My anger boils as such thoughts make my magic simmer beneath my entrapment. Curse this magic steel.

A man stumbles into me. I stagger, but my chain keeps me from falling all the way to my knees.

"What do you think you're doing?" Norhe asks.

The man, younger than I first thought—perhaps not much older than me—glances at me. "Are you all right?"

I give a jerk of my head in response. He's kind and looks right at me instead of around me, like everyone else here. His eyes are hazel.

"Get away from her," Norhe booms. "Unless you can afford to buy her at the auction, which I doubt, you have no business looking over my wares."

"Forgive me," Hazel Eyes says. "It was my mistake." Despite his words, he gives me one final look before getting lost in the crowd of people wearing homespun clothing.

"Cheapskate," Norhe mumbles.

I turn my back to him, focusing on the slave being sold now. A man, thick with muscles. Ropes are tied around both of his wrists with several men holding him back. He looks as if he would be worth a lot, except for his struggling on the tall tree trunk he's standing on. He's much too obstinate to be of much value. I approve wholeheartedly.

"We're next," Norhe says. "Don't you go fighting like this slave is doing, or I'll cut off your pinky finger."

How dare he threaten me? Still, I clasp my fingers together, trying to keep them all in one piece. It's degrading enough to be locked up like an animal. Imagine if I returned to the heavens with no pinky. What would the other gods think of me then?

The obstinate slave is pulled from the trunk, sold for very little to a burly, sour-looking man. Norhe pulls on my chain, and we move forward toward the area. It's the last place on this planet I want to be, but I don't have a choice if I want to keep my finger.

"Get on the block," Norhe says.

I glance at the stone that's as tall as my knees. It's rectangle and smoothed out, so I can stand flat if I get up there. The crowd is watching with eager eyes. People push forward to get a better look at me. It's tempting to try to run, but I wouldn't get anywhere.

"On the block. Now." Norhe gives my back a shove.

With one more look at the crowd, I climb onto the tree trunk. The wood is warm beneath my feet, having sat in the sun all day. At least it's smooth and not jagged, unlike the ground I've been walking on all day. My feet ache from the treatment. The heavens are so much softer. The reason for the smoothness though, is probably the plethora of humans they've sold from this very spot. The thought makes me ill.

"This fine specimen is regal in bearing," Norhe yells, disrupting my thoughts. "She is soft like satin and more beautiful to look at than a sunset. Her long white hair and emerald eyes will bring class to your dwelling and make all your friends jealous as she serves you. Let the bidding begin."

The sun is blinding as the price for me goes up and up and up. I wonder what the bidding would be like if they knew me for what I truly am. The Ramco may have wanted to get rid of me, but he didn't want them to know what I am. I don't know if that's good or bad.

"One thousand krats," a man bellows.

The crowd hushes. He's a thin, wiry man, with graying hair and beard. What uses he has for me, I do not want to know.

"One thousand krats," Norhe says, greed evident in his voice. "Any other takers?" When the crowd remains silent, he slaps his hands together. "Sold to the man with the staff."

And like that, I am owned.

CHAPTER 3

I WAIT IN THE SUN, skin tightening with what I think is a burn. I never had a sunburn before, so it's hard to know for certain, but it doesn't feel normal. Norhe is giddy, rubbing his hands together and giving little glee-filled laughs. I want to shove a horse down his throat. Of course, that would be cruel to the horse.

The man who bought me approaches. He's watching me with an expression that has me itching to get out of my own skin. I hate to think what he could have planned for me. What thoughts are running through his head.

If he takes off this collar, it won't matter. I'll be powerful enough to get away. I'll have to concentrate all of my energy on getting it off.

"Name's Pennington," the gray-haired man says. He's using a knobby staff at his side as a cane.

"I don't care what your name is," Norhe says. "I just want my money."

Pennington smiles like he's indulging a child. "Here's half your payment." He hands Norhe a massive bag. By the way Norhe staggers under its weight, it's heavy too.

"Where's the rest of it?" Norhe asks.

"You'll get it from the bank, after the girl is in my possession."

"Fair enough." Without hesitation, Norhe hands my chain over to Pennington.

Pennington strokes the metal of my chain like it's a prize. "Do you have any idea what you sold me?"

The way he says those words leaves me wanting to shiver. Instead, I focus my whole being on acting like I couldn't possibly care.

"Of course," Norhe replies. "An exotic new pet. What plans do you have for it?"

"Plans you'll hear of after they happen, I'm sure."

Norhe shrugs as if he doesn't care. I suppose he doesn't, after he's gotten so much money for me. It's one thing I've learned from creating things—humans love their money.

"I'm going to get the rest of my payment," Norhe says. "If it's not there, be assured I'll be coming after you, together with every official I can find."

"It's there, all right," Pennington says. "Off with you. I have a lot of work to do now."

Norhe hurries away like he doesn't care about anything except finding the bank, while staggering under the weight of his new money.

As soon as he's out of earshot, Pennington turns to me. "I never thought something like this would come to pass." He leans closer, until he's whispering in my ear, sending a chill through me. "Welcome to my service, Izlana."

CHAPTER 4

HE KNOWS WHO I AM. It can't possibly get any worse. If he knows who I am, he knows how much I'm truly worth. No wonder he was willing to pay a large amount for me. I can't let my fear show, though. He'll only have more control over me if he knows how much I fear him.

"It's time to take you home."

His words lift my spirits enough to almost make me talk, until he says, "You like the idea of going to my home, don't you?"

He's not talking about returning to the heavens. He probably doesn't even know the way. Though the fact that he knows who I am does give him some credence. I turn my head away so he won't see the tears forming in my eyes. I work to blink them away.

"Ah. Not what you were hoping for, after all. Don't worry. I plan on treating you better than that last imbecile. Only a fool would ill-treat a goddess. Let's start with getting you shoes."

I've never worn shoes in my life. I don't want to start now. But my feet hurt. Leather or fur would be welcome to protect them from the harshness of this planet. I wish I didn't have to accept something from him.

Though he holds the chain, he doesn't force me around, like Norhe did. He says, "Come on," and slowly walks away.

I follow. I don't have a choice, and getting yanked around hurts. I try to stay a few steps behind him, but he keeps slowing so I walk even with him. We wind our way past the slave trading, where people are still being sold. I vow to do something about it. But I have to get myself free first.

We make our way to the market, through the dust road. It's louder than the slave trading was. People are yelling for different objects they're buying, costs are being called out, and groups are chatting. It's mass chaos, but somehow no one is trampled.

The wares are out on the street. There are so many objects I'd love to stop and look at. Humans are a creative people. The only things I have like these back home are relics from when my ancestors visited the humans and were given gifts. I've always been drawn to them. Mother said I refused to calm with a heavenly cloud blanket; I had to have a human one. Sure, it felt coarser, but it had a certain charm to it that couldn't be found among the clouds.

People stare at me as we go by. I'm not certain if it's because I'm a slave or because I look so different than the rest of them, at least from this area, with their dark hair, dark skin, and dark eyes. Whatever it is, I try to pay them no attention. It's easier said than done.

In the heavens, I'm worshiped by humans, not a spectacle.

"Here we are," Pennington says. He leans against his staff while he looks over many pairs of shoes. Some are covered while some are sandals. All are made of fine leather. "Pick out a pair you like."

A pair of shoes I like? As much as I enjoy human things, I don't enjoy these shoes. I don't want my feet constricted. I don't want them bleeding either.

"Your slave seems to be having a hard time deciding," says a young woman with a raspy voice. "Should I pick a pair for her?"

"The finest you have," Pennington says. "I want her to be comfortable."

The woman lifts an eyebrow at this, but she goes on to pick a pair of sandals. She helps me strap them on, and they come up to my knees, beneath my long white dress. Or, I should say, *once* white. It's now covered in dirt. Heavens' clothing is not practical for earth.

As if reading my mind, Pennington pays for my shoes and leads me to a stall selling clothing. Lots and lots of clothing.

"Go ahead and choose three outfits," he says. "You'll need clothing more practical in these parts."

This time, I don't hesitate to choose. The shoes may be tight against my feet, but the clothes are things of beauty. It's hard to decide on three, but eventually I pick two green dresses and a blue one. They seem like pieces of wonder. Though I can create anything with my power, these people create them with their hands.

"Now, I need to get you a servant, and we'll be off."

"Why are you getting me a servant?" I ask.

"So you do talk," he says. "I was beginning to wonder."

I shrug.

"I'm getting you a servant because of who you are. You deserve one."

"If you think I deserve one, why don't you unlock me from these chains?"

"We can't have that. I have big plans for you. Plans you'll go along with, or you'll feel just what it's like to be beaten."

The way he's looking at me with a gleeful expression makes me wonder what plans those are. I shiver, not wanting to know.

We stroll over to yet another stall, this one with lots of people in the background.

"How may I help you?" a middle-aged man asks.

"I've come to buy time from a servant," Pennington replies.

The man whistles, and the group of people behind him form a straight line. "Who would you like?"

Pennington looks to me. "Your choice."

Mine? Why is it mine? I'm not sure I care. These people may not be slaves, but they're working off a debt, which is almost as bad. I wish I could pay off all their debt and free them, but there are too many consequences for me to do that. Or so my mother always told me. I wish she was around now. She'd be appalled at the state I'm in.

The line of people consists of men and women of all ages. There's even a girl that looks to be about ten. It sickens me. What parent would send their child off to be a servant?

As I'm looking over the group, someone catches my eye. It's the young man with the hazel eyes who tripped over me earlier, when Norhe still had me. Something about his face and the way he holds himself makes me want to get to know him better. He's got broad shoulders and is well built, but mostly it's those eyes that get me.

"That one." I point to the man.

"Are you sure you wouldn't prefer a woman?" Pennington asks.

I glare him down. "You said I could pick. Are you taking that back?"

"Nope. If he's who you want, he's all yours." Pennington plops down another bag, presumably filled with money.

The owner looks through the bag and gives a nod. "Very well. Marric is his name. He's not working off a debt, but is paid one krat a month in exchange for his work. And he's all yours. Marric, you now take orders from this man."

Marric steps out from the group, ignores Pennington, and gives me a nod.

"He knows his place, but just in case." Pennington slugs him right in the eye, making Marric fall back several feet. "That's the least of what you'll have to deal with from me if you get out of line. Now, may as well get started. Carry her."

"No. You don't have to do that," I say.

But it's too late; Marric already has me up in his arms, one arm beneath my legs and another around my back. He's stronger than he looks, which is quite the feat. He smells of woods and sunshine. I squirm in his arms—no one is to touch me. His expression is flat, his eyes giving away nothing.

"Get used to it," Pennington tells me. "We have a long way to go, and you wouldn't handle the journey if you were to walk. I was going to hire someone to carry you, but he'll do just as well."

With that indignity, Marric marches after Pennington to what I expect to be my new prison.

CHAPTER 5

My head lolls on something soft but firm. I readjust it, snuggling in the softness. The scent is familiar, but not deep within my memories. Woods and sunshine.

I'm being carried by Marric. I forgot. I squirm.

"Whoa," he says. "It's not time to get down yet."

Embarrassed that I fell asleep, but grateful for the rest, I ask, "When are we getting there?"

It's Pennington who answers from ahead of us. "We're there. The creak of the gate must have woken you."

I scramble to get down, and thankfully, Marric lets me.

"Welcome to your new home, for the rest of forever," Pennington says.

I scoff. Humans know so little about gods and goddesses. I may be immune to sickness and heal faster than a person, but that doesn't mean I'll live forever. Neither will this be my home.

It's a stately house, something I'd predict from a man who can afford to pay so much for me. It's a white home with two floors and lots of windows. A few bushes line the walk to the door, but the rest of the vast yard is rundown.

The door opens before Pennington can reach it. A woman with graying hair opens it and bows as we pass.

"Send dinner up to my office," Pennington barks at her.

He leads us up a flight of stairs, down a hall, and into a room filled with books. Without a word, he goes straight to a shelf, pulling me along with him. It's the most forceful he's been with the chain since he got me.

He goes from one book to another, to another, scanning each of them through. I exchange a glance with Marric. He seems to be as confused as I am. Not what I expected when Pennington brought me to his house. He's searching for something. I wonder what it could be.

Time passes as the search continues. My stomach growls, but I ignore it. There's no point in eating, except maybe to keep up my strength.

"Sir," Marric says, "is there a book I could help you look for?"

"Nothing you can do to assist except keep quiet," Pennington replies with a snap.

I exchange another look with Marric. Whatever Pennington is searching for must be important.

A while later, a servant comes up with a tray. She takes one look at Pennington's wild state and sets the tray on a small coffee table before hurrying out of the room.

It takes a while, but Pennington eventually notices the food, now growing cold. "Go ahead and eat, you two."

I head for the tray, grateful my chain is long enough to reach it.

"What about you, sir?" Marric asks.

Pennington waves. "I've got more important things to do. Make sure she's fed." He suddenly shifts his attention to me. "If you eat, that is."

"I do."

"Very well." With that, he goes back to his search.

Ignoring him, I take a seat at the table and take a plate. Marric is next to me, grabbing a spoon of what looks like pillows of bread and gravy.

"Would you like some?" he asks.

"Looks good." Though it won't be as tasty as the food in the heavens. It's not possible.

He dishes me some, along with some vegetables. I eat, and while it is yummy, I was right. It's not as delectable as food from home.

After Marric and I finish eating, there's more waiting. Only I've had enough "Excuse me, Pennington."

He turns and gives me his attention.

"I need necessary."

He gives a heavy blink. Blinks again. "You what?"

My face heats. "I need to use the bathroom."

"I didn't know you did that."

Marric looks back and forth between us, a crease between his eyebrows.

How daft can Pennington be? He knows I eat; he should realize I function like a normal human. At least in most ways. "Well, I do," I say. "So where is it?"

He sighs like I'm causing him a lot of work. "I'll take you."

He leads me there but stays outside the door while I use the premises. Another thing not as nice as in the heavens—it's basically a pot set in a hole in the floor. Gross.

When we return to the book room, Marric is where I left him, but there's something different about him. Something I can't figure out.

Time passes slowly. I wonder about starting a conversation with Marric, but I wouldn't know what to say. I ignore him and study my fingernails. I want to sleep, mostly, but I don't dare with these men around going to do who-knows-what.

Hours later, Pennington squeals with delight, three different books open in front of him. "I've got it. I've got it."

"Got what?" Marric asks.

Pennington swivels around, eyes shining bright as he stares right at me. "I know how I can control the great goddess, Izlana."

I gasp.

Marric chuckles. "You'd have to find her first."

It's my turn to stare at him.

"You don't know?" Pennington asks. "You're sitting right next to her, and I'm going to be the first one ever to harness the power of the gods."

CHAPTER 6

I'm SITTING in the middle of the room, on a cushioned chair. Pennington fiddles with my chain, not far off. The more he fiddles, the more nervous I become. Marric watches from the couch we ate lunch on. I'd trade places with him if I could.

Pennington lays the chain down in a straight line. He stands and calls out loud words I can't understand. It sounds like he's muttering nonsense to himself. He reaches down and runs his hands along the length of the chain.

The chain glows a faint blue. My magic feels different, too. Like it's trying to bubble up to the surface but the collar still blocks it. It aches to not be able to use my power when I'm accustomed to applying it so frequently. But it's not only the ache of not being able to use it but a niggling worry about what Pennington's done to it. What's made it so different than before?

A stab of fear jolts through me. My muscles stiffen, or I'd scramble back.

"It's time to see if it works," Pennington booms. "Izlana, goddess of creation, make me a krat."

My power springs forward, jumping at the chance to obey someone, even if it's not me. My hand moves of its own accord, lifting until my arm is out ninety degrees from my body and my palm points upward. My magic rushes to one spot on my palm and releases all at once, making a golden krat appear.

"Yipee," Pennington howls.

Marric's face has gone as white as mine feels. How can Pennington make me do this? I don't understand how he has this power over me. It shouldn't be possible. Whatever magic he performed is tainted by evil. I should have known, but I didn't expect it to work. Not one bit.

"You shouldn't be playing with this," Marric says. "The power of the gods is not to be taken lightly."

Pennington's happy mood evaporates. "Quiet, boy. Say something like that again, and you won't have to worry about finding another job, because you'll be dead."

Marric's lips thin. Pennington may be scolding him, but I'm cheering him on. There's nothing I'd like more than for Pennington to let me go. To take off these chains and return me to the heavens. But this keeps getting worse.

"What are you going to do with my power?" I ask.

Pennington smirks. "Whatever I want."

CHAPTER 7

TWO DAYS LATER, I've made more krats than I've ever made of a single object before. Pennington is now richer than any one person should be. Not only that, but also—since he has power over me—his dominion will soon be complete.

For the first time since he bought me, he leaves me alone for more than using the necessity. Though I'm not by myself; Marric is with me. I'd think this was a bad thing if it wasn't for the comment he made to Pennington, but I know there's someone here who isn't completely crazy. Someone I'm going to have to confide in if I ever hope to make it out of this place.

I've barely slept these two days. My eyelids are heavy, but I don't want to give into exhaustion until I know where things stand with this man I've been left with. I wish he was given his own room so I could sleep without interference, but he doesn't seem able to leave my side.

No one else is around. Just these plain walls, closing in on me.

"So, Marric"—not the beginning I was going for, but I'm making some conversation—"tell me a little about yourself."

He widens his eyes at this. "What is it you want to know?"

Anything that will help get me out of this place. "Where do you come from?"

"Excuse me if I'm being impertinent, but what does a goddess want to know about my little life?" He brushes his thumb against his chin. His hands are shaking ever so slightly.

Good question. What answer is there that doesn't sound as if I'm trying to use him? "It looks like we're going to be spending a lot of time together. I figured maybe we should get to know each other."

He laughs. Then he laughs harder, an almost hysterical sound.

"What's so funny?" I ask.

That simmers him down. "I'm sorry if I'm being rude. It's only that I never thought I'd be in a position to have a goddess wanting to know me. You see, I don't pray to any of the gods or goddesses. Truth be told, I didn't even believe in them until two days ago, when Pennington made you create that first krat."

It's my time to laugh. He turns red, and I stifle my chuckles. "I'm definitely real, and I can vouch for the other gods and goddesses. I've met them all. We're real."

"Now I feel silly. What god am I going to end up with when I die if I claimed not to believe in you my entire life?"

With me. Wait. Where did that thought come from? He's not someone I would consider taking as a mate. Not that I'm ready to take a mate, but if I was, it wouldn't be him. It would be a devoted follower, and then after he dies, one of my souls, the way it should be. If he was to come with me after he died, it would be to serve me. "I wouldn't worry too much, where you're going. You'll either change your life, follow the god or gods you want, and end up in their kingdom, or you'll be picked up by one of the gods that needs followers."

"What gods would that be?"

"There's Tybalt, the god of pain, or Aella, the goddess of sleep. They are such dears, but more people prefer Beazle, the god of festivals."

"I can understand why," he mutters.

"What was that?"

"Nothing."

Remembering my plan of getting him to help me escape, I get back on track. "Tell me about yourself. Where are you from? What are your people like? I know you don't believe in the gods, but what do you believe in?"

"I believe in myself," he says with a defiant set of his chin, like I'm going to be disgusted at that.

"That's good. Nothing will get you further in this world than having confidence."

He widens his eyes, as if he doesn't believe I said that. I'm a god after all; People rely on me. But as much as I love my followers, I enjoy people who have confidence. Not boastfulness—nothing like that—just genuine belief in one's self.

"Yes, well... I believe you exist now," he says.

I laugh. "That's a wonderful thing."

"Are there really more of you?"

This has nothing to do with anything that will help me escape. Still, I can't help but answer. "There are lots of us. Over twenty. There used to be more, but—" I can't tell him the rest. I don't know why I started.

"But what?"

Not all gods and goddesses find a mate to continue their line with. Usually those who are less believed in don't. I can't tell him that, though. It's a well-kept secret among the gods that we're not eternal. Like the humans, we die of old age, and a new god takes over, though with the same name. "We aren't as many as we used to."

He gives me a funny look, but doesn't pursue it. "To answer your questions, I'm from all over," he says. "I never spent more than a year in one place. We were constantly on the move because that was what my father wanted for us—to get to know many people and customs."

"You're a gypsy." It's a statement more than a question.

"If you'd like to think of it that way."

It's strange, but the idea fits him. "What were your parents like?"

"They're very giving." His response is sarcastic.

"You sound like you don't believe your own words."

He leans back, crossing his ankles out in front of him. "I've never told anyone this before, but it's true. While I believe they're generous people, I don't believe they're thoughtful to their own children. They weren't cruel or anything like that; they were never around. They served others before they were there for us. I practically raised my younger brothers and sisters, among other things."

"That must have been hard for you."

He shrugs. "It was life."

"Where are they now? Are they okay without you?"

"My sister is watching over them. I needed to make money, so I've been working as a servant. They need food, clothes, and a roof over their heads, no matter what my father thinks."

"That's generous of you."

"Honestly, it feels selfish. As much as I love my siblings, I was ready to be on my own and not have them as responsibilities any longer."

"But you're working to provide. Doesn't that make them a responsibility?"

"In a different way. It's easier to make money for them than it is to take care of them."

"I see." Though I'm not sure I do. Maybe if I had siblings, I'd understand. But of course, gods don't have siblings. There's only one of us born for each god and their mate, and each child is the same gender as the divine parent. I'll never know what it's like to have siblings or mother more than one child.

Pennington comes charging in the room. "I need more krats." He unlocks and unhooks my chain from its place and starts demanding krats from me. Whatever he's planning takes a lot of money. I wonder what he's going to do with it all.

Pennington wasn't gone near long enough. I didn't learn what I was hoping to from Marric. Then again, perhaps I learned more than I thought. Marric believes in himself, works hard for others, and questions Pennington. Maybe he can help me escape, after all. Not that I'll trust him. Humans have proven themselves to be vile, untrustworthy people, no matter what.

CHAPTER 8

PENNINGTON'S HOUSE is richly dressed. Where before it was nice, now it's fit for a god. I fear Pennington is beginning to think himself as one. I'd feel a lot better if all those krats I created were going to something useful, like feeding hungry children. Pennington is a self-serving creature I don't want anything to do with. But as long as my chain remains under his control, I can't go anywhere. Plus, I'm being constantly watched.

Except for right now.

Marric fell asleep.

I couldn't have hoped for anything better. Now's my chance to bolt. I hurry quietly to the hook on the wall, where Pennington puts the end of my chain when he's not lording it around. The iron metal glows a faint blue.

I curse that blue. It's what gives Pennington control over me, and I'd do anything to get rid of it. Unfortunately, gods only have power over so much. I know of nothing I can create to get rid of this blue. What's more, thanks to this blasted collar, I don't have my powers anyway. I'm not sure if the collar has something about it that contains my powers, or if it's because it's made of iron. I think the former.

If I escape back to the heavens, I can try to jimmy the lock or maybe one of the gods will be able to help me with it. Then Ramco will pay for what he's done to me.

I put my hand on the last link of my chain, the one hanging on the hook. I glance at Marric. Still asleep on the couch. As silently as I can, I lift the chain from its place. Or rather, I try. It doesn't budge. Doesn't wiggle at all within its locked place.

I pull harder. Nothing. It's not going to move. Pennington never has to do anything special to move it. What am I doing wrong?

Maybe it will still work, despite my not being able to move it, only being able to hold it. I whisper the words to get me a key to unlock it from its place. Nothing happens.

When I look around the room again, Marric hasn't moved, but he's watching me, eyes wide open. If I'm correct, he hasn't been asleep at all this whole time. He's been waiting for me to escape. Or maybe, he wanted to catch me in the act, to get in better with Pennington. I narrow my eyes at him.

He stands and hurries over. "What's wrong with it?"

"You aren't going to turn me in?" I ask, baffled.

"I've been waiting for a chance for you to escape. No man should have power over the gods." His eyes look sincere.

Something deep inside me warms. Maybe I can trust him, judging by his eyes. People might be vile, but not all of them. A few are good. Like my followers, of which I think Marric could be one. Someday. "It won't move."

"Let me try." He reaches up and wiggles the chain without a problem.

"My life is now in your hands."

He straightens, and a more serious look comes into his eyes than I've ever seen before. I'll be safe with him. Unless, of course, that look is him getting ready to use my power for himself and he's going to create a key that will unlock my chain from the hook.

He opens his mouth to speak. Can he utilize the power too, or can only Pennington? A squeak comes from the hall outside. He shoves the chain back to its place, and we both race away from it.

A moment later, Pennington enters the room. My cheeks burn. He's going to know I tried to escape or that Marric held the chain. But Pennington has eyes for nothing but that end link, hooked to the wall. I relax. I may not be safe, but at least I don't have to deal with Pennington's wrath at my trying to leave him. I can't imagine how angry he'd be, or what exactly he would do.

Instead of demanding I create him krats, Pennington looks at me with a smirk. "It's time to make something a little different. I should have asked for something more than money to begin with, but I was thinking like a human."

More like a greedy human.

"Goddess Izlana, create me a throne made of pure gold and the finest jewels, with the softest of seats."

A throne? He has to be kidding me. I'm not about to make him king. But my magic is already moving to comply with his request. It's time I see how much control I have over this. Though I know he means a chair fit for a ruler, I'm not going to make it for him.

As my magic starts to create the gold, I form it differently, smiling when I realize I do have some control after all. I make only two jewels, since he didn't specify how many, and give him the softest seat imaginable, only I leave a hole with a removable pot in the middle of it.

He goes from from glowing to glowering with anger. "I did not ask for a chamber pot."

Despite the danger I may be putting myself in, my smile grows. "You asked for a throne. I gave you a throne fitting you."

He picks up the chamber pot and hurls it against the wall. "You've behaved yourself so far. Don't go playing games with me now. I've treated you well, haven't I?"

"You locked me to your wall and took away control of my power. I wouldn't say that's *well*."

"I haven't beaten you, like is done to most slaves. I've given

27

you the finest foods and clothing. I've taken care of you, and this is how you repay me?"

A golden cage is still a cage. I hold my head high. "I am not a slave. I am a goddess."

He comes at me and smacks me across the face with enough force to knock me to the ground. My face stings. It won't last long, but it still hurts—the humiliation more than the pain.

Next thing I know, Marric is at my side, helping me to my feet. "Are you all right?" he whispers.

"Fine." I'm anything but. It's not like I'll admit otherwise. Saying something would mean Pennington wins, and I can't have that.

"You will do as you're told," Pennington says. "But I see I'm going to have to be more specific.

I don't give him the benefit of a reaction, but if he is more specific, I won't be able to do anything about it.

"Izlana, goddess of creation, make me a chair fitting for a king," he says. "A throne most beautiful, made of pure gold, with many precious gems lining the top and sides. It will be a most comfortable chair, soft and fine. Not a chamber pot." His last words are sharp.

As soon as he finishes, my power enlivens. This time there's nothing I can do about the final product. He didn't leave room for misinterpretation.

The creation of the chair ends with my hand touching a magnificent throne, fitting the highest king of kings—none of which exists. I have a feeling Pennington means to change that.

CHAPTER 9

PENNINGTON COMES at least once a day to have me create things. A scepter. A crown. More money. A few times he takes me to different areas of his house, to make them bigger and grander. I wonder what his neighbors think of such sudden and drastic changes, though it's unlikely I'll ever meet them.

The time he's not around, I spend lounging and being bored. Nothing to read or do. Sometimes I talk to Marric, but mostly I long for home.

When Pennington enters my room today, I feel like tackling him to the ground. I could never do so. I'm not weak, but nor am I strong. Pennington is stronger than his old body indicates from the way he's smacked me and Marric around. Plus, he has magic and a staff on his side. I only have me.

He picks up my chain and leads me out of the room, Marric following behind. Poor Marric. I'm sure having to babysit me constantly isn't what he had in mind when he signed up to be a servant. Especially not with a man like Pennington for a boss.

We twist through hallways I've created and out a side door. The grounds are not befitting such a grand house. They are sparsely planted, mostly a flat terrain filled with dirt. There's a lot of land though, more than I remember seeing when I first came here—but then, I was rather distracted on that first day.

For a moment, I'm hopeful Pennington will let me go. That he realized the folly of his ways, or at the very least, is done with me.

Instead, he says, "Izlana, goddess of creation, make me a beautiful garden that thrives all year round, with flowers of every kind except those that are poisonous. Make walkways through them and water features. Make this a refuge for weary souls."

A refuge for weary souls sounds nice, but knowing him, he has an ulterior motive.

Against my will, my hand goes to the ground, and power flows through me. Grass springs up in curving lines, making paths everywhere. In the midst of the paths, all sorts of vegetation pops up. Flowers of many varieties. Bushes and trees want to come, but I hold them back. He didn't say anything about them, and I'm not about to make this any better for him than it already is.

I feel a natural spring in the ground. It's too easy to tap it, to create an unlimited supply to a water fountain. The fountain wants to be made of the most beautiful white marble, but I trade it for plain stones. Not much of a tradeoff—it's still a sight to behold—but not like it could be.

Pennington rubs his hands together, my chain jostling between them. "This is perfect," he says. "Soldiers."

Out comes a group of burly men in tattered rags. There has to be at least a dozen of them.

Pennington moves over to me and whispers in my ear so only I can hear, "Izlana, goddess of creation, turn these men's rags into armor fitting battle, tough and strong. Forge them mighty weapons that can cleave their enemies in two."

Fear streaks through me. What is he making me do? This isn't who I am. This isn't what I stand for. This is making war. Ramco would be proud, but I'm just sick.

Still, I have no control over my feet, as they wander to each man and in turn give them armor and weapons.

"How does she do this?" one man asks.

"Simple magic," Pennington replies.

A second man says, "I've seen magic, and this is nothing simple at all."

"Maybe not," Pennington replies. "She is quite powerful. But she's also under my control, as you can well see. She will do whatever I ask of her."

The men look at him with awe, then one by one, they kneel to him.

What have I done?

CHAPTER 10

LATER THAT NIGHT, Pennington drops me off at my room and hooks my chain onto the wall, locking it as he goes.

"You've done well," he says. "I'll see that you're rewarded."

The only reward I want is to be free of him. Praise be, he leaves. Of course, Marric is still here. He's always here. He eats with me, sleeps in the same room, and guards me night and day. Heavens only know when he uses the necessary.

"Another day done," I mutter, flinging myself onto the bed.

Marric shuffles over to the couch, where he spends most of his time when we're in this room. It's not a bad room, though it doesn't compare to home. It has a bed large enough for two of me; the couch, which is soft but firm; some books, though all are on benign subjects; and a very small window on the second floor. Another tiny room with plain walls, and my clothes sit off to one side.

"Can I ask you a question?" Marric sits on the couch.

"You did, but go ahead and ask another."

"Is there no consequence to all these things you create?"

"Oh there's a consequence, all right," I reply. "My wrath."

I shouldn't say such things to him. He could report back to

Pennington and cause problems. But then, maybe I want him to report it. I don't care what Pennington thinks. I want to go home. To have my power back. To keep the world together. Who knows what it's turning into without me?

I have priestesses still doing my work, but I don't know how long they'll be able to do it without my assistance. Hopefully, long enough for me to escape.

I close my eyes, willing myself to wake up from this nightmare. A noise echoes through the night.

I spring upward. "What was that?"

"Just an owl," Marric says. "Don't you know what an owl sounds like?"

Though his voice is calm, I don't appreciate being questioned. "Of course I do. I created owls." Still, I look out the window, expecting to see a hideous monster coming for me.

There's none. Only an owl sitting in one of the trees I created earlier this day after Pennington decided to add a few.

"What is it like to be a goddess?" Marric's question pulls me from my fears.

I sigh and settle back onto the bed. It's the most glorious thing ever, and I have no idea how to describe it to a mere mortal. "It is what it is."

"That's not very helpful."

"And your remarks are impertinent."

"Forgive me. I'm trying to understand you better."

I sniff and readjust my position. "You're forgiven. But being a goddess isn't something I can describe. It's my state of being. How would you describe being a human?"

"Um… Well, I can think."

Maybe he's getting it. "And so can I. And so can the birds in the trees and the fish in the oceans. Many, many things can think. That's not what makes you human."

He ponders that a moment. "Let me ask you this. What makes a god different than a human?"

"The belief people have in us, and the power we hold."

He lifts an eyebrow. "Those are all the differences?"

Almost. But I can't let him know. "There are more. Those are the ones we focus on."

"What about the ones you don't focus on? What are those?"

He's persistent; I'll give him that. "Those are things we do not disclose."

"Not even if I promise to keep them a secret?"

"Not even then."

"Do any humans ever get to know?"

I think of the gods' mates, those few select humans who get to know everything, who are one of our secrets. They live in the heavens with us and never return to this world, so they can't disclose anything they shouldn't. "It depends."

"On what?"

"On what they are willing to give up."

He looks more confused than ever. "What would they have to give up?"

I say nothing further. I've already said more than I should have, anyway. "Isn't it time to sleep?"

"You're avoiding my question."

"If you don't want to sleep, you don't have to, but I'm tired." I go into the private chamber to change into my night clothes. I don't know what compelled me to tell him so much. I'll have to be more careful in the future, though I'm going to have to trust him if I want him to help me escape.

CHAPTER 11

THERE'S A RUMBLING OVERHEAD.

"Someone's angry," Marric says. It's been raining all day.

I look to the ceiling of my room. "Probably Ramco or Venza."

"The god of war and the goddess of rage?" He lifts an eyebrow.

"The very ones. They are the two who usually cause lightning and thunder." When he continues to look skeptical, I add, "The god of death and the god of pain usually cause rain."

"Then why does it rain and lightning at the same time?"

"It doesn't always." As if to prove my point, the rain lets up.

"Hmm."

The thunder continues making a ruckus. I wonder which god is so angry. Probably the goddess Venza. Ramco has me right where he wants me; he must be happy. It makes me wonder if any of the gods are looking for me. If anyone even misses me. Maybe the chain is hiding me from them if they are looking.

"What are you thinking so deeply about?" Marric asks.

"How I was betrayed."

He sits up and scoots closer to me on the couch we're sharing. "You were betrayed? Is that how you came to be here?"

I nod, cursing the tears forming in my eyes.

"What happened?"

Should I tell him? The heavens probably know my folly. What difference does one mortal make? "I thought Ramco cared for me as a friend. I thought he wanted to show me the world."

"The god of war? Why would you think that?"

Because I was a dunce. "It was wrong of me. He's never cared for anyone." None of his ancestors did either, according to stories. Not even their mates. "But he showed me attention. Spent time listening to me. Spoke of the human world, which he knew I had a great desire to visit."

"Why would you want to come to this world when you have the heavens?" He sounds genuinely curious.

I give a half-smile devoid of joy. "I know it sounds silly, but there are many great treasures to be found in this world. I helped create it, after all." Or my predecessors or the other gods did. "I wanted to see those creations, not from my home, but up close and personal."

"I see."

Thunder sounds, closer this time. I jump.

Marric puts a hand on my shoulder, warmth blossoming where he touches and spreading outward. "Do storms always scare you this much?"

"Believe it or not, they aren't as loud at home."

"That seems backwards."

"Maybe. But lightning is a human-world thing. In the heavens, we're not as close to the clouds. We can see and hear it, but it's like looking through a crystal ball. Here, I'm actually experiencing everything."

Experiencing a lot more than I ever expected.

His hand is still on my shoulder, comforting me. I want to lean into him and gain all the comfort I can. This is unlike any feeling I've had before.

"I like hearing you talk about home," Marric says.

"I like talking about them to you."

We're moving closer together, and I'm feeling something heated. Something peaceful yet exciting. Something wonderful.

The door opens, and we burst apart. Marric's hand leaving my shoulder makes me feel cold.

"What's going on here?" Pennington demands.

"The thunder scared me," I say.

He gives me a quizzical look but doesn't comment on it further. "I need you, Izlana."

Of course he does. He always needs something. More money?

I share a glance with Marric. There's a glimmer in his gaze I don't understand. A light I want to explore. But I'm not my own person down here. I'm chained and collared. There's nothing I can do to follow my own wishes.

CHAPTER 12

TODAY, Pennington has me in what he calls his throne room. There have never been kings in this land. Only the gods rule over the people, but glancing at him right now, I know that's changing for the worse. He sits on his throne, wearing the finest red velvets, scepter in hand, crown on head, and there are people lined up to see him.

This is not how things should be. Not at all. The priest and priestess are over the land, under the gods' guidance. Seeing him turning himself into a ruler, realizing that someone I know has evil intentions, makes me sick.

It's a grand affair, with Pennington at the head of everything. It won't be long before they start actually calling him king. With everything I've created for him, he has more than enough tools to become one. He needs a royal guard, which he's working on, with a collection of servants he's having trained into soldiers.

Is this what Ramco wanted? To create a king? I see how that would lead to war, but how could he foresee such a thing? How could he have even known I'd end up in Pennington's hands? It's not likely. I wish I knew what Ramco's plan was, so I could fight against it. Not that I can do much fighting from here.

The crowd stays mostly silent, though in between people asking things of Pennington, whispers arise. Nothing that I can make out.

A woman comes before Pennington, clasping her hands together. "Please help me. My children are starving. I can't provide food for them since my husband passed away."

Pennington glances around the room, as if he's debating something. "Go to my kitchens and get you and your children some food."

"Thank you. Oh, thank you," she says before hurrying off.

I wonder how long she and her children will be fed for. Food is a good start, but if he really wanted to help her, he'd find a way to have her bring in an income so she could continue to provide for her family.

What is he playing at? Why does he help these people but demand nothing but money and things from me? Why does he keep me locked up? What plans does he have? Is he really good to everyone but me, or is there more going on here? Is he not as evil as I thought? I think of the time he hit Marric. That doesn't seem like the action of a benevolent ruler. Neither does demanding things from a god.

"Most gracious Pennington," a middle-aged man says.

I share an eye-roll with Marric. At least he understands.

"May I ask who this beauty is that you have by your side?" the man asks. "Is she your betrothed or a slave? For she's beautiful enough to be by your side, but I see you have her chained up."

His words whip an icy chill through me. Pennington's wife? Never. A goddess never marries, and he's certainly not the type of man I would take for a mate.

But Pennington has a new look in his eyes as he peruses me. A look of calculation.

"As a matter of fact," Pennington says, "she is a slave. But I've grown so fond of her that I think I will marry her. And all of you are invited."

A cheer goes up in the crowd. My stomach roils. The only thing keeping me from being sick is the look on Marric's face. He's just as disgusted as I am, if not more so. At least someone is on my side.

CHAPTER 13

As soon as Marric and I are alone that night, he says, "We can't wait any longer. We have to get you out of here before Pennington does anything more stupid."

"But how? I've had to make his home more of a castle fortress these past few weeks. Not only that, but he's training soldiers. How will we be able to get past it all?"

He puts a hand on each of my shoulders, and the touch is more comforting than it should be. "We'll figure a way out. I'm more worried about Pennington himself. If he gets a hold of your chain, there's nothing that can stop him. At least he's leaving you alone more and more often."

Alone with Marric, that is. I'm grateful that Marric won't let me despair. Without him, I don't know what would happen.

"What is your plan?" I ask.

"I don't know yet. It's hard, because I can never leave your side. Not that it's a bad thing." He gives me a tentative smile, which I return with full force.

"Can we sneak out in the middle of the night?" I ask. "I think that might be our best chance."

"Maybe. But it may be better to do it in open daylight. Act like we belong there. Then, if we're stopped, we can claim that Pennington sent us out there. I doubt we could claim that past nightfall."

"What if they send for Pennington, though? Then we'd be in trouble for certain."

"We have to think of something. We can't let him go through with marrying you." The passion in Marric's words makes me want to hug him. The only person I ever hugged in my life was my mother and mortal father. They were good people until they died. They passed away way too early. We don't know why.

"I still think we should try and get out at night," I say, pulling myself from my thoughts.

"Maybe. What excuse will we have if we get caught outside?"

"Caught outside doing what?" Pennington asks, making me jump.

I rein in my nerves, so as not to give myself away. "We were thinking of holding you a party."

"A party?" He narrows his eyes at us.

"Yes, a party," Marric says, thankfully catching on to my plan. "It was going to be a surprise, but we couldn't figure out how you wouldn't catch us. We figure all those people who were in the throne room with you would enjoy a party in your honor."

"You two thought of this?" Pennington asks.

"That's right." I hope he believes it.

"I thought you'd be upset about my announcing our engagement," he says.

I will never marry, but I can't let him see how much the thought does upset me. "Of course not. I've become your slave. I'm getting used to you getting whatever you want."

He stares me down, and I do everything in my power to not look away. I wiggle my toes, the only outlet I have for my nerves. "My wife you will be, and a party we will have," he says. He backs away, heading for where my chain is hooked on the wall. "It is only fitting that we celebrate all I've accomplished. Besides, a party will make the people like me even more. Have them more likely to accept my rule over them. Once I have that, I can get everything I've ever wanted."

I was right. He isn't kind to the people out of the goodness of his heart. He wants to rule over them, something no man should ever do. I'm beginning to think gods shouldn't either, not with the way that things are down here with slavery and people vying for power. There has to be a way to have a leader, a voice for the people, without one person having all the control.

These aren't things I can be thinking on. I need to find a way to get Marric and me out of here.

CHAPTER 14

Pennington plans the party without us. He says he doesn't want me distracted from anything other than creating what he needs me to. Most of what I make now is for the party. Fireworks—lots of them. Instruments of the best quality, though I don't know who is going to play them. I suppose he has people in mind. Flowers and more flowers. I want to tear them all up, though I'd never ruin their beauty.

The day before the party arrives, and I make food, food, and more food. It's everywhere. I wonder if such extravagance will make the people like him more or turn them against him. I'd like to think they'll turn against him, but chances are they won't.

"Izlana, creature of beauty," Pennington says, making me want to gag. "I think that is all for now. Marric, take her to her room. Her dress is waiting for her, along with a suit for you."

"Yes, sir." Marric gives a little bow, like everyone has started to do in the past few days. Everyone, that is, except me. I refuse to bow even the tiniest bit to a man who'd use me this way.

For the first time ever, Pennington hands Marric the chain. I suck in a breath. He's letting go of his control of me.

Pennington laughs, as if something is funny, though I don't see what. "You are more than you seem. Aren't you, Marric?" He turns and walks away.

Despite the oddness of it all, this is a step toward me getting freedom. Until I notice a guard following us.

I turn to him. "Can I help you?"

"Pennington has asked that I keep an eye on his future bride, for your safety."

This has to be a joke. I can't have him following me everywhere. We'll never escape this way. "I can assure you I'm as safe as can be."

"That may be, but I'll be here just in case."

We continue walking, and I exchange a glance with Marric. His expression gives nothing away, but he has to be as upset about this new development as I am.

We enter my room, and to my great relief, the guard locks up my chain before stationing himself outside the door. Once the door is closed, I sigh.

Marric holds one finger to his lips. He moves next to me, putting him mouth beside my ear. "He may still be able to hear us."

I shiver, though it's more to do with his closeness than with thoughts of the guard. I tilt my mouth towards his ear, enjoying the warmth emanating from him. "How are we going to escape now?"

"I don't know."

Both of us remain silent, but we don't part. I wonder if my nearness is affecting him as much as his affects me. He smells of that woods-and-sunshine scent I've come to enjoy. It fills me, and I commit it to memory. I commit everything to memory—his presence, his proximity, his heat. It's better than anything I ever experienced in the heavens.

I wonder if this is what it's like for gods, when we meet our mate. It seems too soon to meet him. It has to be a different feeling.

It's hard to imagine anything better than this, but then, I never imagined I could feel so good to begin with. Excitement and nervousness and joy are all mixed together with emotions I can't identify.

The more I stay near him, the more I want to be closer. To be touching him. To feel his arms around me. This can't be good. I step away, missing his presence the moment it's gone. But still, I'm grateful for the distance. I need some space to think properly about what I felt.

Marric clears his throat. "There's the dress Pennington sent up for you."

I glance around until my gaze lands on the bed. A dress I didn't make waits for me, along with a simple black suit. The suit itself is fine, but the dress is the most hideous thing I've ever seen. It's puce, smothered with dark yellow-green lace.

That's all I need to see. I glance away. "What was he thinking?"

"Maybe they're his favorite colors," Marric says.

"It would go along with the rest of his personality," I mutter. "Guess that's what I'm wearing tomorrow."

"Lucky you."

I give him a gentle shove.

He laughs. "Sorry you have to wear it. Maybe you can suggest creating your own gown next time you see him?"

"With my luck, I won't see him until the party, and I'll be wearing it by then. Knock on the door. Maybe the guard will let me contact him."

Marric does as asked, but the guard promptly turns him down. "We're not to disturb Lord Pennington." He slams the door closed.

Lord Pennington, is it? That makes me more disgusted than the dress.

Silence follows. Neither of us are chatty like we usually are. Whether it's because of circumstances or the guard outside, I'm not sure. Whatever it is, I don't feel like talking. I don't feel like doing anything. I haven't been so despondent in my life. It's a depressing feeling.

"Well…" I say.

"Well." He looks just as at a loss as I feel.

"I guess I should get ready for bed."

"Yeah," he says. "It's a busy day tomorrow."

"Yes, it is." A party for the man who owns a goddess. A busy day, indeed.

CHAPTER 15

TOMORROW COMES ALL TOO SOON. I find myself wearing the hideous puce dress and standing next to Pennington. I was right. I didn't see him until after it was time to wear the dress. I didn't dare question him, with how edgy he's been over everything.

"The band isn't playing well enough," he says to the conductor.

"Forgive me, sir. We didn't have enough time to practice with these new instruments. They are lovely, to be sure, and we appreciate you gifting them to us. We are playing them the best we can."

Pennington yanks me closer with the chain and grumbles in my ear, "Isn't there something you can do about this?"

"No." It's a lie. I could create instruments that played beautifully no matter what talent was using them.

Pennington storms off, dragging me after him. I run to catch up so the collar doesn't pull against my neck. Marric looks murderous. We hurry off outside, through the gardens, past several people putting together the party, and to the end of Pennington's property, where they are setting up fireworks.

"Where are the rest of the fireworks I sent you?" Pennington demands. "You should have more."

The woman working with the fireworks bows quite low. "I'm so sorry, but this is all you sent us."

"Then I demand more." He turns to me and whispers, "Izlana, goddess of creation, make fifty more fireworks, the grandest ever seen."

He left that more open than he has left an order since I made him a chamber pot. The power is moving through me, and I push it out in a big burst. Big fireworks he wants, big he'll get. It'll be just perfect for my new idea.

The pile of fireworks when I finish is huge, with all sorts of giant ones.

Pennington smiles. "Very good work, my dear. Let's get you to the party. Our guests should start arriving soon."

Just what I want. I follow him around, hoping the next few hours pass by quickly. I don't think they will, though. Not at all.

Marric gives me a quizzical glance. I shrug and smile. As much as I'd like to tell him my plan, there's no doing it with both Pennington and my guard around.

We make our way to the throne room. Pennington takes his place at the throne, with his crown and scepter. I want to rip the scepter out of his hand and smack him across the head with it. Instead, I settle on the floor beside his throne, pretending this is where I want to be.

"This was a good idea," Pennington tells Marric and me. "Thank you for thinking of it. You'll both be rewarded."

If all goes to plan, we'll be gone long before the party as over.

CHAPTER 16

THE NIGHT GOES as slow as I expected, my impatience making time even crawl more slowly. Still, it's almost time for fireworks. Now to put my plan into action.

"Pennington," I say, "I've got a terrible headache. Would you please excuse me to my rooms for the evening?"

"You can't go now. The best part is about to start."

I put a hand to my head and squeeze my eyes tight. "It's really bad."

"Very well, if you must. Marric, take her to her room and make certain she rests. I can't have my prized possession coming down sick."

Sing praises, he believes me.

Marric takes the end of my chain from Pennington and leads me through the crowd in the throne room. They'll soon be headed outside, and I want to be in my rooms by the time they do. My guard matches our pace, the biggest concern I have at the moment.

We wind our way through the people, until we break from them. It doesn't take long to make it to my room. We shut the door behind us, leaving my guard outside.

Marric puts his mouth to my ear. "Are you really sick, or is there something else?"

"We're going to escape tonight, during the fireworks. I figured the noise will help mask any sound we make."

He grabs both my arms. "Brilliant."

"All I need is some type of disguise. I certainly can't go dressed like this, and my hair and eyes are recognizable."

"That's true." He runs a hand through my hair. Once is enough to make me want more.

"I have another idea. What if you use my chain to call on my power? I'm not sure if you can or only Pennington can use it, but it's worth a shot. All I need is a hooded cloak."

He takes a step back and whispers, "I don't know."

"Why don't you like the thought?" I keep my voice low.

"I don't like the idea of using your power like Pennington does. It seems evil."

His reply makes me like him all the more. "But it'd be my wish. I'd do it myself if I could," I say.

He sits on the couch and puts his head in his hands. As much as I want to follow him, I give him time to think. It isn't an easy thing I ask of him, though I have no problem with him using my power for this. It's a step in the direction Pennington has taken, though, and Marric clearly doesn't want to be like him.

After some time, he stands and comes back to me to whisper, "Are you certain you're okay with this?"

"More than okay. I want you to do this. It's our chance to escape."

"And what about the guard?"

"We'll have to lure him in and knock him out." The thought of doing that to a human makes me sick, but it's either that or stay here and forever be Pennington's slave.

Marric nods. "Let's do this."

He motions to my chain. "Why don't you at least try holding it one more time?"

"It's worth a go."

I try to pick it up from the locked hook, but it won't budge. Also, I try whisper the words to produce a key, but nothing.

Marric picks up the chain again, letting it dangle inside the lock. "It's weird that you can't hold it."

"It's frustrating," I reply. "Now, this is what I want you to say, and we'll see if it works. *Izlana, goddess of creation, make me a black cloak with a hood and a key that will fit this lock.*" That should give me plenty of leeway to make it how I want.

He says the words, and my power moves through me. I create a cloak that's neither the finest material nor thread bear. Something that would fit in with most people I saw at the party. Granted, most of them weren't wearing cloaks, but it's better than leaving my hair down for everyone to see. A key also appears.

The cloak and key appear in my hand. "Success."

"I can't believe that worked." He takes the cloak from me and wraps it around me, tying it at my neck. After that, he quickly unlocks me from my place, taking the end of my chain in his hands.

"One more thing," I say. "Do you know how to use a sword?"

"I don't."

"That's all right. I can make one that works for you."

"We're going to make me a sword?"

"Yup. And one for me as well."

Both his eyebrows lift at this. "Let's get to it, then."

"Say, Izlana, goddess of creation, make me two swords that will always hit their target."

Again, he says the words, and the power courses through me. I create the blades of the swords sharp enough to easily cut through metal and create the pommel to adjust to the person using it.

One in each of my hands, the two swords are a sight to behold. I hand one to Marric, who takes it with his free hand.

"This is a thing of beauty, more than a weapon," he says.

I shrug. "I like making beautiful things." There's nothing else to do. It's time. "Let's lure in the guard."

CHAPTER 17

I LAY ON THE COUCH, my sword hidden beneath my cloak in case I need to use it. Though Marric should have that part of things covered. I give Marric a nod and then close my eyes.

A moment later, the door creaks open.

"You have to come quick," Marric says. "She's fainted."

There's a rustle of movement. I let my eyes flutter. Next thing I know there's an *ufgh*.

I open my eyes, to find my guard on the ground. Marric succeeded. I jump to my feet. "Let's go."

As we hurry out the door, I pull the hood of the cloak over my head. There's a problem, though. My shackle is obvious, trailing from my neck to Marric's hand.

"What about the chain?" I ask.

Without hesitation, he takes my hand, and in the same hand, he's holding the last link. The chain can still be seen, but it's not as noticeable.

"Is this all right?" he asks.

I try not to smile as big as I want to at the way his hand feels in mine, even if there is a chain alongside it. "It's fine." More than, actually.

We hurry down the halls to the door that leads outside. Once there, we're surrounded by a crowd. The further we get into them, the more I dart my gaze around, looking for Pennington or one of his soldiers. My heart races, and I wish I could do something to calm it, but I'm stuck with it.

Fireworks blast, booming louder than the noise we're making and keeping most people's focus. I glance at the sky to find I did a good job with them—better than I thought I did. They're enormous and bright, in a multitude of colors.

The crowd jostles me as we hurry through, elbows poking me and several people bumping into me. Marric pushes them back, giving me space, but it keeps happening. There are too many people here.

As we near the end of Pennington's property, the crowd thins. We're almost there. We have to make it out, and then we'll go... Well, I don't know where we'll go, but it'll be better than here.

We burst out of the group of people and keep a calm, but fast pace. Once we get past this street, we'll be able to hide around the corner. Until then, I feel exposed, like gazes are watching my back, but I don't dare turn around to see if someone really is watching or not.

Marric gives my hand a squeeze. "We'll make it."

"How can you be sure?"

"Because we're almost there. We've almost done it."

He's right. We're going to be free of Pennington and his abuse of my powers forever. I grin as we hurry toward the last few feet before we turn the corner. When we get to the end of the lane, I glance back. No one is following us. No one is even paying us any attention; everyone is focused on the fireworks.

We round the corner, and everything in me feels as if it drops to the ground.

Pennington, surrounded by what has to be all of his guards, except the one we hit on the head, maybe a good fifty of them.

"What are you doing here?" I ask, wondering how we're going to get out of this one. "Shouldn't you be watching the fireworks?"

"I know gods don't get sick, you fool," Pennington says. He glances at where Marric and I are still holding hands. "I see I should have been keeping a closer eye on the two of you, but I didn't think a goddess would fall for a human."

I want to withdraw my hand, but instead, I latch on tighter. Pennington can't scare me into anything. At least, I can't let him know he can.

"It's time to come back with me," Pennington says.

"I'm never going with you again. I'm done letting you abuse my powers." I put all my feeling into the words, letting them bite.

"Then I guess we'll have to take you by force." Pennington motions to the guards. "Kill the boy. Don't harm the girl, but get her restrained."

I pull out my sword, and Marric angles his toward the oncoming attack.

The guards come in fast and hard, trying to separate us. I lift my sword to the first man moving toward us. It hits his blade with a *clang* before moving of what feels like its own will. It circles around the attacker's sword and slices into his midsection. I cringe but know there's no other choice if I'm to make it out of here with my free will.

Marric and I continue to defend, the ground hard beneath my feet. Our swords make the fight easier, but the balance is still skewed in our attackers favor by their sheer numbers, not to mention their fine armor and swords. To think I created the very weapons we're fighting against. I try to think of something to create to help us, but the altercation is taking most of my attention.

The cries of the fallen echo through the night air, Marric and I still stand. One by one, the guards fall before us. As when continue to dominate, other guards flee before us.

Suddenly, I'm yanked from behind, a sword brought to my throat.

"Stop fighting or the girl dies," a burly voice says.

"You can't kill me. I'm immortal," I yell even though it's not true.

"I can injure you, though."

Everyone stops, but Marric doesn't put down his sword. "You won't hurt her," he says. "Your master wants her unharmed."

He's right. I thrust my sword behind me. It twists in my hand, changing its angle and heading for the man holding a sword to my throat. It connects, and the man is gone.

Marric takes out the last of the guards that haven't run away, so only Pennington is left. He takes several steps backward. "You'll regret this. One day, I'll get you back, and you'll rue the day you ever left me."

He turns and runs through the woods, toward his house, where a group of people will no doubt welcome him.

Marric and I hurry down the lane, not trusting that Pennington won't come back. But he doesn't. We've gotten away. He can no longer use my power as his own.

CHAPTER 18

MARRIC and I sit beside a well in the middle of a town miles away from Pennington. I'm exhausted beyond belief, but safe. That's what matters.

"Let me try to get your collar off again," Marric says.

He's tried many times since we left, but the collar and accompanying chain are stubborn as can be. Nothing is able to move them.

"I don't know if we should bother trying," I reply. "It doesn't seem like anything we do will get it."

"I had a thought about that, but it may be dangerous."

"Dangerous I can handle. What is it?"

He hesitates. "I was thinking maybe I could use my sword. It's supposed to slice through its target. If my target is your collar, but not you, it might work."

Might is risky, but— "Do it."

"Are you sure? What if I accidentally cut your neck?"

"It'll be worth trying to slice through to get this thing off. Besides, I trust you." And it's true. I do trust him. More than that— I care about him. And I think he cares about me too.

He shakes his head. "Well, here goes nothing."

He places the sword by my neck, and I can tell he's applying pressure. Nothing happens.

"What if you try to cut the chain?" I ask. "If it works, we'll know it can be broken, and we can try again on the collar."

"Good idea. And less nerve-wracking."

He lays my chain out on the ground in a straight line. Then he lifts his sword above his head and brings it down on the chain. A *clang* is the only response. He does it again and again. Still nothing, and the noise is starting to draw people to the well.

"I think that's enough," I say.

Marric glances around and puts down the sword. "You're right. We should probably be on the move again."

He helps me up, and we begin walking out of town, ignoring the spectators.

"Why do you think the sword didn't work?" Marric asks.

"I'm not sure," I reply. "It may have something to do with the magic Pennington used when he spelled it so he could harness my power."

"Could you create something that could break it?"

"I don't know. I'd like to try."

Without further prompting, Marric says, "Izlana, goddess of creation, make something that will break through or unlock the collar you're wearing."

My power bubbles to the surface like it normally does, but I don't feel a tug in any direction telling me what to make. My power pushes and shoves its way through me, but still nothing. It's wearing me out in a way I've never felt before. I'm tired and frayed.

I collapse to the ground as my power overwhelms me, but still no idea comes to mind of what to create.

"Izlana," Marric shouts. "Are you okay? What should I do?"

I shake my head. I don't know. If my power keeps pulling on me like this, it could over take me. Who knows what would happen then, but I have a feeling it would be something along the lines of my downfall.

"Izlana," Marric says again, "goddess of creation, I take back my comment. Make nothing."

My power simmers back to a normal range. I heave deep, gasping breaths.

Marric kneels beside me and puts a hand on my shoulder. "I'm so sorry."

Once I have enough breath, I say, "It's not your fault. It's this stupid collar with its stupid magic."

"What happened?"

"My power tried to create something but couldn't. I think it struggled and kept growing in the attempt."

"Has that happened before?"

"Never." And that scares me more than I'd care to admit.

I take another minute to gather myself before he helps me to my feet.

"Let's get going," I say.

"Are you sure you're up for it?" he asks.

I nod. "We need to in case the townspeople come looking for us. It's not every day you see a man trying to free a slave in the middle of town."

"Maybe next time we should go somewhere more secluded to try to get your collar off."

"Wise idea."

"What are we going to do now?" he asks.

"We'll find someplace safe." And someone who knows how to enter the heavens. I wish I knew, but I don't even know where in this world I am. I'm lost.

Marric smiles. Maybe I'm not entirely lost. I'm not sure where we're going, but we have each other.

EPISODE TWO

Episode Two

CHAPTER 19

THE IRON COLLAR around my neck chafes. I've had it on far too long, more days than I can count. Ever since Norhe put it on me and sold me to Pennington, who imbued my collar and chain with magic so I'm not able to take it off but others can harness my powers. It's odd being without them. I feel like I've lost a limb.

Marric hands me a full water skin he scrounged up earlier. At least I have him, even if the rest of my world is mixed up.

"Where do you think we should go?" he asked.

It's a question I've been puzzling out. I think I finally have an answer. "What if we go to one of the temples of creation? My priestesses would keep us safe."

"That's a good idea."

"Do you know where to find a temple? I'd recognize it if I saw it, but I don't know how to get to any of them."

"I know of one nearby. Definite benefit to traveling so much as a kid."

"Let's get started."

We stroll on the road, southbound. The day is barely dawning, but it's warm and fine. Birds are out, happily chirping away. The walk itself isn't too taxing, though a little difficult still because I'm not accustomed to it. My biggest worry is what to do if we get caught. I can't go back to living with Pennington misusing my powers. And I'm certainly not going to marry him. Gods don't get married.

"How does the collar feel?" Marric asks. "Is it bothering you much?"

"Not much." It's a lie. Not like he can do anything about it if I admit it's bugging me.

"I wish I could get it off of you."

"Don't worry. We'll figure something out." I hope.

There's a rustle up ahead. Without a word, Marric grabs my arm and helps me off the road. We hide in some bushes, and I understand why so many people pray to the gods. If I wasn't one myself, that's what I'd be doing right now.

I hear people approaching. I squeeze Marric's hand, and he squeezes back. This isn't the first time we've had to hide, but it's no less worrisome. So far, it's been harmless gatherings of people, but that doesn't mean they'd stay that way if they saw my white hair and emerald eyes. Thankful for the cloak I have, I pull it further over my head to make certain my hair doesn't show.

The group of people comes into view. They're soldiers that look an awful lot like the ones Pennington had. We were right to hide. Maybe they're looking for me. Pennington would do anything to get his hands back on me.

The closer they get, the more erratically my heart beats. Did we hide far enough back? Will they be able to see us? They get right up next to us, and I clench my jaws together. They pass. We're going to make it.

Something tickles my arm. I glance down and see a giant, hairy, black spider on it. Without a thought, I whip the spider off of me, just keeping from calling out.

The last two men in the group of soldiers stop. One of them says, "Did you hear that?"

I curse stupid spiders and my inability to let them crawl on me.

"I heard something," the second man replies.

They look around, and I duck so I'll be better hidden in the bushes. The sound of footsteps becomes closer. I hold my breath, my palms growing sweaty. What will happen if they find us? Will they drag me back to Pennington? I'm almost positive they will. I'll go kicking and screaming the entire way.

"What are you guys doing?" a male voice shouts from farther away. "We've got to find the girl, not lollygag."

"We thought we heard something," one of the men close to us responds.

"You hear lots of things. Now come on."

The footsteps shuffle away, and I can breathe again. I peek my head up to find they're no longer in sight. Still, Marric and I stay silent for a little longer. Neither of us wants to get caught.

After several minutes pass with no sight or sound of the soldiers, I relax.

"That was too close," I say.

Marric nods.

"Did you see that spider?" I ask.

His face is pale—whether from the spider or the encounter, I'm not sure. "It was huge. I would have screamed."

The thought of him screaming over a spider gives me the giggles, but they don't last long.

"Don't you have spiders in the heavens?" he asks.

"We do, but I still don't like them." One of the previous goddesses of creation made them. I can see how they're useful to eat other bugs, but I still can't bring myself to like them.

"Huh."

"That was dangerous," I say.

"Too dangerous."

"We can't risk running into more groups like that. It's too perilous. We need to get to the temple as soon as possible."

"We'll hurry." I'm the one slowing us down—I can't go as fast as I'd like to—but we have to try. There's much at stake if I'm caught and can't ever get my powers back.

CHAPTER 20

"The temple is up ahead," Marric says.

I'm exhausted from our two-day walk from escaping. "Thank the heavens."

He laughs. "Do you thank your home often?"

"As often as needed." I clutch my side and try to ignore the sweat collecting beneath my collar. It's disgusting and painful. I wonder if the priestess at the temple of creation will know how to get it off, or if I'll have to find a god who knows what to do. I hope the priestess can do something because I don't want to wait any longer.

Marric's been using the chain to carry out my desires of creation and our necessities, like food and water for us both, but it isn't enough. I miss being in full control of my power. I need it. If I don't use it on my own for too long, who knows what can happen? Maybe nothing, but maybe something bad.

"Do you think the priestess will be able to get it off?" Marric asks, as if reading my thoughts.

"It's possible."

"But?"

I sigh. "But I'm worried she won't. That I'll be stuck this way."

"I hope she'll be able to help."

"Thank you. Not only for your hope, but for all you've done. I've never known a person to be so selfless and helpful before." Not that I know many people, just my priestesses.

"Maybe it's not selfless," he says.

"Why do you say that?"

Before he can answer, we round a building to find ruins. A building toppled to the ground. White marble in a tall mound with chunks of it scattered around. Parts of the white have been marred with black char marks.

Tears form in my eyes. "I know this place. It was my temple. My priestess Telrua was here."

Marric puts a hand on my shoulder. "I am so sorry."

I cry harder now, not just for the loss of my temple, but the loss the people endured. They can't come worship me. My priestess can't fulfill wishes and hopes with part of my power she was imbued with. She can't pass those wishes and hopes she's unable to fulfill on to me.

I sink to the ground, unable to help the sobs coming out of me. Marric kneels beside me and wraps his arms around me. My heart feels as if it's being wrenched from me.

"Who would do this?" I ask when I calm down enough to talk.

"I don't know." His voice is calm and soothing. "I just don't know."

"There's never been a temple destroyed before when there was still a god alive to worship. What could have happened?"

He rubs my back. "I wish I had an answer for you."

I dry my tears and rise to my feet, chain clinking as a reminder of helplessness. I howl. "Whoever did this will pay."

CHAPTER 21

I MOVE to the ruins to give them a closer look, and Marric follows. Not that he has a choice. If he didn't want to come with me, I'd drag him around as long as he holds the chain. Of course, all he has to do is drop the chain, and I won't be able to go farther than it allows. That last link isn't in my control, no matter what we do.

The building is an utter wreckage. Nothing is left at all. The beautiful white walls have crumbled to the ground and are covered in black soot. It appears as if there was a fire. Maybe even an explosion.

"It looks like a war happened right in the middle of this building," Marric says.

Ramco, god of war. Somehow, this is his doing. I know it. It's not enough that he has me collared down here on the world, but he has to go to war with my temples and priestesses as well? I don't know how, but I'll exact my revenge.

"Excuse me," a female voice says.

I whip around to find a thin girl of about twelve. "Yes?"

"You're not from these parts, are you?"

"We're not," Marric replies.

"It's best if you leave," the girl says. "Soldiers come by every so often, checking the ruins for people."

Soldiers? Are they Pennington's men? Is he trying to send me a message? Or is it something else? "When was the temple destroyed?"

"Three days ago."

After we left Pennington's. So was it him?

"Thank you for your advice," Marric says. "We'll be on our way."

On our way where? This was supposed to be a place of safety, but clearly we can't stay here. The girl hurries out of the ruins, heading for a side street.

As we walk away, I ask Marric, "Where are we going now?"

"I know another temple, a day's walk from here."

"What if it's destroyed as well?"

He sighs, running a hand through his hair. "Perhaps we can try a temple of a different god?"

"It's riskier, but it may be what we have to do."

"This begs the question—who is going around destroying your temples and why?"

We pass a man on the road. Though he goes by without a problem, we both quicken our pace.

"I have a feeling Ramco had something to do with it. Though it could be Pennington," I say.

"It makes sense. Is he attempting to start a war with you?"

"Why would he? He had me locked up on this world, where there was nothing I could do about it."

"Maybe he's trying to get rid of you and your worshipers."

I think of the little girl who warned us to get away. I hope she's still a worshiper and doesn't have problems with the soldiers. What's more, I wonder what the other gods think of this. If they're worried about their own temples and followers. "Why would he want to get rid of me?"

"You are the goddess of creation. You're probably the most powerful god."

I want to deny it, but it's true. Who else is more powerful than someone who can create anything from nothing? "Maybe you have a point." Ramco has been out to get me after all.

Marric puts a hand on my shoulder. "I'm sorry. This can't be easy for you to deal with."

"Thanks. I'm definitely hurt, but I'm also confused."

"Let's focus on getting to the next temple of creation. Depending on how things are there, we'll decide what to do next."

"Sounds like a plan to me." Though all I want to do is stop Ramco and his minions.

CHAPTER 22

IF I THOUGHT the walk before was bad, it was nothing compared to the walk now. We hike up a mountainside filled with lush vegetation. My feet hurt. My legs hurt. My sides hurt. Everything hurts. I didn't know being on this world could be so strenuous.

With the mountain terrain around, I think I know which temple we're going to. It's a peaceful place. Probably the most peaceful of my temples. They're all pretty calm, but this one has an air about it. A welcoming vibe. It's a place of peace and joy. It's one of my favorites, though I shouldn't have any.

If it's destroyed, even in the slightest, my rage will rival that of Venza, goddess of rage.

We continue in silence for a while. It's nice being here with Marric and enjoying the fresh breeze. It'd be nicer if I knew all my temples were safe.

After some time, a thought occurs to me. "You can't come with me. What about your family? They need you to provide for them."

His silence says a lot more than a verbal response would.

"That's it." I stop. "Drop my chain. I'll stay here until the next person comes by, and I'll have them take me to the temple." If only I could take myself. Stupid magicked chain. "Then you can be free to go back to your siblings. To earn money for them or assist them however you need."

Marric grabs my hand. "I am not leaving you to any passerby who could use your power however they wanted."

"They'd have to know who I am for that to happen."

"But they'd at least think of you as a slave. At worst, they'd turn you back over to Pennington and they'll have no reason to take you to the heavens."

"I promise I'll be fine." Though his arguments make me doubt that's true. "Your family needs you."

"The best thing I can do for my family is get you back to safety."

"How is that going to help them?"

"You can figure out what's happening to all this destruction. You can create peace."

"Do you really believe that's something I can do?" I'm having doubts myself.

"I know it."

I look up to the sky. Its soft blue is calming. "If you're certain…"

"I'm positive. My sister will take care of them. Everything will be fine until I get back. Right now, you're my priority."

I blush. Sure, I've had people worship me, but it's nothing compared with the face-to-face contact with Marric. He's so sure everything will be fine. That this is where he needs to be.

"I guess we should keep walking, then," I say.

"Let's get to it."

I put one foot after the other up the hill, ignoring the burning in my muscles.

"You know," he says, "I can carry you."

"You've got enough to carry with that sword at your side and my chain in your hand."

"Those are nothing. It'd be easy."

"I'm fine." But my gasping gives away how much I'm struggling.

Without another word, he swoops me up into his arms, jostling my chain. As much as I don't want him to carry me, it feels good to not be hiking up the mountain.

"For a minute," I say. "And then I can walk again."

He holds me closer. "I've got you for as long as you need."

His words send my heart fluttering. "I don't want your muscles to wear out."

"They're more than fine. Just relax."

So I do. I rest my head on his shoulder, and it feels oh-so-good. I wish it was always this easy to get around, but it's not fair to him to carry me everywhere. If I ever come down to the world again, I'm going to make certain I exercise more beforehand. The heavens aren't nearly this exhausting. Though now that I can look around and really appreciate the nature surrounding us, I'd say it's well worth it.

The next thing I know, I'm blinking awake. When did I fall asleep? By how close the sun is to the horizon, I've been sleeping for some time. I squirm, to get down.

Marric sets me on ground that has leveled out. "I wondered when you'd wake up."

"I'm sorry. I didn't mean to fall asleep. I wanted to rest for a minute."

"Don't worry about it. It's completely fine."

I have a new appreciation for his muscles, though they're bound to be sore tomorrow. I'm grateful I'm not heavier.

"Where are we?" I ask.

"Almost there. I was actually going to wake you in another five minutes or so."

A jumble of emotions plagues me—excitement, fear, hope. A tangle of things I can't figure out. "Do you think we'll be safe?"

"I'd like to tell you *yes*, but I can't. There hasn't been anyone on the road since you fell asleep, though."

Which explains why he didn't have to hide. "But where is everyone?"

"That's why I'm not sure it's safe."

I quicken my pace, ignoring my body's protests. I have to know if my temple is still standing or not. Many yards later, the temple appears, seemingly out of nowhere. I stop, swaying with relief.

Its stone edifice is covered with moss and trees, like I expected it to be, but its beauty is so much more to behold in person. My symbol is on it, like all the gods keep on their own temples. The way the trees arc to the middle, where the door stands open is graceful.

Wait. Open door? This can't be good.

CHAPTER 23

I RACE FOR THE DOORWAY, startling poor Marric. The chain grows taut between us, and he hurries after me. I get to the doorway and pause. There is only darkness. I'm not sure I'm ready to see what's inside. What if it's in ruins like the last one, with only the outer walls left standing? What if they massacred my priestess?

The thought makes my chest tighten. I can't handle facing this. But I have to. It's my duty.

"We don't allow slaves here," a woman says, easing my fears.

I lift my head, letting the hood fall off my blinding-bright hair, and my eyes show. "I am no slave."

"Merciful heavens." Next thing I know, the woman rushes in sight and kneels on the ground before me, forehead touching the stone entrance. "Forgive me, goddess. I didn't expect to see you in such a state, or even on this world."

I glance at Marric, who's looking on with a confused expression. He knows people worship me, though maybe it's peculiar to see it. I know it feels different to be worshiped in person than it does from the heavens. I hurry to say, "Please rise, Priestess Luce."

She gasps, tilting her head up toward me. "You know my name?"

"We have talked several times. Of course I know your name."

"Izlana, goddess of creation, forgive your humble servant. I didn't know— I didn't expect—"

"It's fine. Please rise."

She scrambles to get to her feet. "Won't you enter your sanctuary?"

I follow her in the building, with Marric trailing behind. My collar and chain feel extra obvious and irritating.

The building is dark at first, like the entrance was, but as we follow Luce through the halls toward the middle of the building, the ceiling opens up and a courtyard is in the middle of the room. Natural light shines through the room. A statue of my likeness with real emeralds for eyes is in the middle of the courtyard. It's eerie to look at. That statue is where I usually join in communication with my priestess. Each temple has one.

"Why did you not allow a slave into the temple?" I question Luce.

"I hope you'll forgive me. There have been rumors of soldiers about, desecration to the temples, fighting, and all sorts of concerning things. I've been extra cautious with even slaves coming through. I've been praying to you about it. I thought that's why you came?"

"I'm sorry. It isn't."

She leads us into a room that still has some natural light but also has lit candles throughout. There's a table with one chair.

She motions for me to sit. "Please, be seated. I'm sorry we don't have better accommodations for you. If times weren't so trying and I knew you were coming, things would be different."

"Don't concern yourself over it. Do you have any food?"

She widens her eyes at this request. "For your escort?"

"For us both."

"I didn't know… But of course, I'll get something for both of you. Please wait here, and I'll be right back."

As soon as she's gone, I say, "What do you think?"

Marric hesitates.

"What is it?"

"I know you are a goddess," he finally says. "What I didn't know—or, I guess, didn't expect—was to see someone worship you like that. I also didn't expect her to recognize you."

"The statue we use to communicate looks more like me when I'm using it for conversing with my priestess. It would be strange if she didn't recognize me. Besides, my hair and eyes are unique. It's probably how Pennington realized who I was." When he says nothing further, I add, "Are you okay with this?"

"I need some time to absorb it all. Mostly, I'm happy this temple is still standing and we can find you a safe place to stay and hopefully get some answers."

This also means it's time for him to go to his family. Priestess Luce can take control of my chain and help me from here on out. The thought has me wanting to reach for Marric. To keep him close. But it's selfish. I can't keep him from his family. Oh, how I want to be selfish, though.

"Here we are," Luce says, putting some bread, cheese, and fruit on the table. "It's not much, I'm afraid, but it's all I have."

I reach for a slice of bread.

"As in, this is all your food?" Marric asks. "Or this is the only type of food you have?"

She looks at the ground. "It's all the food I have left." Her reply is faint.

I put the slice of bread down.

"Oh, no," she says. "Please eat it. It's an honor to have you at my table."

I pick it back up, not wanting to offend her. This won't do. I'll have either her or Marric make me create more food. And extra food, to send Marric on his way. My heart gives a painful squeeze at the thought.

"Why don't you have more food?" I ask.

"Like I said, times are hard."

The bread feels thick in my throat, but I remind myself that I can give her more. "What do you know of these rumors about the soldiers?" I ask her.

"Only what I've told you, but they keep people out of the temple. Make fear leaving the temple. I was hoping you could create some sort of protection for the building."

Marric and I exchange a glance. I can't create anything at the moment, but he can use my power. Or Luce could. It's frustrating, not being able to do it myself.

"What type of protection did you have in mind?" I ask.

"Guards, hopefully." The awe in her eyes makes me not want to answer her.

"Unfortunately, I can't create people, unless it's in the womb of a mother. Even then, the baby would take years to be a man full grown in order to guard the temple. And I would hate to make him if he didn't want to. He would, after all, have his free agency."

Her expression of awe doesn't dim like I expected it to. "We'll think of something. Mostly, I was worried about communicating with you, but now that you're here, I don't have to worry about that. Can you tell me why you've come?"

I exchange another glance with Marric. This isn't as easy as I thought it was going to be with her wanting my help when it's me that needs assistance. "As you can see, I've been chained," I say.

She furrows her eyebrow. "I thought that was for show, so people didn't know who you really were."

"I wish that were the case. This collar was placed on me the moment I came on this world. I don't know what type of magic or power is in it, but with it on, I'm unable to use my power." I almost tell her about the magic Pennington added to it, to allow the person holding the chain to access my power. Though I trust her — she is one of my priestesses— it's a weighty thing to share with someone. I'll have to share it anyway if Marric is to go home.

"I haven't heard of anything like that," she says.

"Neither have I. As far as I know, no god has ever been captured like this before."

"I'm sorry it had to be you."

It's my fault for trusting Ramco, but I don't tell her that. She needs to keep as much confidence and faith in me as possible. I can't afford to lose worshipers when I'm already in such dire straits.

"We need to know," Marric says, "if there's a way you can get it off of her?"

"I'm not sure. I've never seen anything like this," she says. "I can try." She takes a step toward me, which puts her next to me in this small room. "If I may?"

"Of course," I say.

She touches the collar. Explores it. I can't tell what she's doing, but she takes her time. When she pulls away, her mouth is turned downward. "I'm afraid there's a magic in this that I have no idea how to combat."

"You have magic?" Marric asks her.

"I don't. I have the power to read it, but that's all. You need someone with strong magical ability to get this off."

Pennington comes to mind, but he would never let me out of my collar. "Do you know anyone with magic?"

She shakes her head. "Not with strong enough magic to get this off."

Then I'm stuck with this thing.

CHAPTER 24

"I wish I could make you a nice, hot cup of chocolate," Luce says. "It'd be soothing at a time like this."

What would be soothing would be food from home. "Thank you for your thoughtfulness, but I'm fine. What I need is for you to take control of this chain so Marric can be on his way. Then you can help me get to someone who can help me." Though the thought of Marric leaving makes me want to grip his hand and hold on tight. To never let him go. But he has to go, and she has to be able to take her place. It's time for her to know this all.

"I suppose she's right," he says, though he sounds more hesitant than I'd expect him to. I thought he'd be eager to get back to his family.

"I'm happy to help," Luce says.

For that, I will reward her the best I can. If I ever get my powers back.

Marric doesn't move; he just looks at me. I don't know what he wants. Could he feel the way I do? Does he not want us to be parted? No. He has to want to go be with his siblings. They need him. I only want him.

He holds up the end of the chain, turning to Luce. "You have to promise me you'll treat her with the utmost respect and won't take advantage of her in any way."

Luce is solemn as she responds. "I promise."

He hands her my chain, only instead of staying in her palm, it slides out like it does for me.

"What is going on?" I ask.

"I don't know," Luce says. "It slipped from my fingers."

Marric glances at me. We knew that I couldn't hold it because it was my own chain, but maybe there's a difference reason. But then, how is Marric able to hold it when no one else that we've tried can? Does this have something to do with why Pennington laughed when he gave Marric the chain and Marric could hold it?

Luce bends down and tries to pick up the chain. She grips it, but no matter how hard she clenches her fist, her fingers turning white, she can't pick up the link.

"This is imbued with great magic," she says. "Only those who hold magic can pick it up."

My gaze sprints to Marric. "You have magic?"

"No." He shakes his head vehemently. "I've don't have any."

"I'd wager you do." Luce stands to her full height. "Otherwise, you'd never be able to pick this up and carry it around." She takes a step toward him.

He takes one back. "There must be some other explanation," he says.

"You can tell if someone has magic, can't you?" I ask Luce.

"I can, but I have to touch him." She lifts a hand. "If I may."

He backs up so he's against the wall. "I don't have magic."

"Luce," I say, "can I talk to Marric privately for a minute?"

"Of course. I'll be in the courtyard when you need me."

Once she's gone, I turn to Marric.

His eyes are wide, his face pale. "I can't have magic."

"What's so wrong with having it?"

"You've seen what it does. Pennington held power no man should ever have."

Fair enough answer, but it feels like there's more. "Is Pennington the only reason you don't want to have magic?"

With a sigh, he sits on the floor. "No. My father has magic." Which makes it even more likely that Marric has it too.

"Did he do something wrong with it? Something to make you not like it?" I ask.

He nods, going even paler.

"Do you want to talk about it?"

"I don't know. I've never talked about it with anyone before. I mean, my whole family knows he has it and how he uses it, but we don't talk about it. Don't bother with it at all."

I wish I was wiser at this moment. That I had more years behind me so I could know how to handle a situation like this. But I don't. I'm at a loss at what to do. If only my mother were here to talk to him instead of me. "Let me know if you decide you do want to talk about it. I promise not to judge you." That didn't sound too bad, did it?

He's silent, making me wonder if I should have kept quiet after all. The longer the silence stretches, the more I wish I didn't say anything. I never know the right thing to do. Awkward, for a goddess. People expect me to know. To have all the answers.

Sometimes I wish we would tell humans that gods are born like they are. Wish we weren't so secretive about how we live. Mistakes would feel more acceptable then. Humans make them all the time, but a god is expected to be perfect. I'm anything but.

I can't keep dwelling on these thoughts. It's not helpful. I'm getting ready to stand and ask Marric to take me to Luce, when he speaks.

"He would use it to torture us children. My father, I mean. It's one reason we would stay on the move so much. Whenever anyone started to question the way he treated us, we'd move."

I walk over to him and put a hand on his shoulder, like he's done to me so many times. "I'm so sorry. No child should have to live with that."

He squeezes his eyes shut and shudders. "It's done now. My family is safe from him."

"What happened to him?"

"The last time he tortured me, something went wrong with his spell. It backfired and killed him."

I put a hand to my mouth. If it hadn't backfired, Marric wouldn't be here now. I would have never met him and had his help. I would still be under Pennington's rule. But more than that, I wouldn't know Marric as a person. I wouldn't have come to care for him like I do.

What does a person say to that? I don't know, so I give his shoulder a squeeze.

"I never want to have magic. I can't end up like him," Marric says.

"You won't. Even if you do have it, you're not a cruel man. You would never do anything to harm someone like that."

He looks up at me, eyes desperate for answers. "Do you really believe that?"

"I do."

His shoulders slump forward like a great weight has been lifted off them. "Then I guess we should go see Luce and find out if I do have magic."

CHAPTER 25

LUCE BARELY TOUCHES Marric before saying, "Oh yes. He has magic. A lot of it, at that."

He clenches his jaw but otherwise doesn't give a reaction to the news.

"That's why he can carry my chain, then?" I glance at the end of my chain, which is currently on the floor.

"I'm guessing so."

"Then why can't I pick it up? As a god, I have more power than any human." Not to brag, but it's true.

"That's the key. You have power; humans have magic. There's an innate difference between the two. They don't work the same."

"How so?" Marric finally speaks.

"I'm not exactly sure," Luce says. "I only know that things which a god's power can do, magic cannot and vice versa."

"Is there anyone who'd know the difference?" I ask, wondering if it matters.

"There may be, but I don't know many people outside of the worshipers who come to the temple."

"What about your power?" I ask. "Where does it fit into all of this if you don't have magic?"

"I thought you of all people would know that." She gives me a funny look. "My power is a gift from you. I get it to carry out your will."

I know nothing of giving her my power. "When did you receive it?"

"About thirty years ago."

That explains it. My mother must have given some of her power to Luce. There haven't been any new priestesses since I was born. It's probably one of those things my mother needed to teach me but never got the chance to. I wonder how many more things out there are like this.

"Do you think Marric will somehow be able to undo my collar, since he has magic?"

He brightens at these words.

"It's hard to say. I know so little of magic."

"Where do we go from here?" Marric asks.

To that, no one has an answer.

"There has to be something," Luce says.

"There is something," I say wondering why I didn't think of it sooner. Probably because I've been taught my whole life to handle things on my own. "It's not guaranteed to work, but it's worth a try. We could go to my sister goddess, Charmina."

"You think the goddess of love will help us?" Luce asks.

"It's the only thing I can think of."

"But gods don't typically mix." Though his words are contrary, Marric has nothing but concern in his gaze.

"Charmina and I are friends." More importantly, she and my mother were friends. She may know things my mother was unable to teach me. The question is, will she share them with me?

"I haven't heard of such a thing before," Luce says.

"It's common in the heavens to be friends. It's down here where gods don't mix. We're each trying to retain our own worshipers—that way, we're more likely to have them join us in the afterlife. So we try to keep our temples separate."

"But worshipers go to more than one temple," Luce says. "It's only the buildings themselves that stay separate."

"And we would change that if we could."

"How do you decide which god someone is under after they die, then?" Marric asks.

"Whichever one they worshiped the most with their heart," I say. "That's the one they'll go to."

He persists. "What if there's a tie?"

"There's never been one before. There's always a god they love and serve the most."

"This stuff is all so weird." He bends down and picks up my chain.

I try not to take offense. After all, he wasn't a believer before I came around. He doesn't know much about us, like most worshipers do.

"We should get going," he says.

"Are you coming with us, Luce?" I ask.

"I don't know if I should. I'm supposed to be here, at the temple, in case worshipers come in to talk with you, though I won't be doing any of that until you get back to the heavens. But the people—I think they need me here. Then again, if something happens to you and we can't get you back to the heavens, all life may be forsaken."

I'm not sure it's as dire as all that. Then again, I do create things. Not everything has to go through me to be created once it's been made before, but the world would stagnate. Even if someone had a new idea, they'd never get it to work without me.

Current creations would slow, not stopping altogether but definitely harder to come by. This could be devastating for the world as the population decreased. Maybe it eventually give way all together. Who knows what the full consequences may be?

No wonder she's so torn.

"Marric can take care of me all right," I say, hoping he doesn't mind. "We can send word to you if I have need of you. Stay and take care of the people. Continue to serve me as my priestess."

She bows low. "Thank you, Izlana, goddess of creation. I will endeavor to serve you however I can be most helpful."

"Thank you."

"Do you need anything for the road?" she asks. "You can take the rest of the food."

"We don't need anything," I say. "In fact, I'd like to leave you with a gift. Marric and I will go into the room you first took us to, and you will find your gift there."

"I'm humbled by your generosity."

It doesn't seem nearly enough. I'm just doing what I can.

CHAPTER 26

HAVING FILLED the room with the table with as much food and krats as we can, we give Luce our goodbyes and leave. It's sad to go from this place. It will always hold a dear place in my heart.

"How far to a temple of love?" I ask Marric, trying to focus on something other than my sad feelings.

"The closest one was by the ruined temple of creation we visited. We can try for it and hope it hasn't also been destroyed. In the opposite direction, there's a temple about three days' journey from here."

I try not to groan. Three days? I'm so sick of walking. Too bad I can't conjure up horses. But I can make krats, which could buy us a couple. "Is there an inn or a stable around here where we could purchase some horses?"

"That would make things go quicker. I don't know why we didn't think of it before. There are stables in the closest town."

"Which direction is that in?"

"Same as the temple that's a three-day journey. Less with horses."

"Let's go to that temple. The other one may still be standing, but I don't want to chance wasting our time."

"Fair enough."

After making a bag of krats, we head for the closest town. It takes about an hour to get there. We stop on the outskirts and look around. It appears safe enough, like any normal town with cute little cottages. Wooden fences line the yards. It's a pretty scene, yet something feels off about it. I wish I knew what.

"We should go into town," Marric says.

"Yeah."

But neither of us moves.

"Do you feel like something's wrong?" I ask.

"I do, but I don't know what it is."

"Me either."

"Let's go," he says. "We'll keep an eye out for any trouble."

We stroll forward as if we're right where we belong, but really, I'm on edge. Every part of me is looking for danger, trying to spot what's wrong. The farther into town we get, the more off things feel.

"I know what's wrong," Marric says.

"What is it?"

"There are no people about."

He's right. There's no one, anywhere. Not that I have much experience with these things, but it seems like there should be at least some people. Everything is so quiet.

"Should we keep going?" I ask, uncertain what the right answer is.

"We'll stick to the plan." Though he moves a little closer to me.

The houses grow nearer together and more are made out of stone. After a small distance, they give way to the market.

"The stables are over here, by the inn," Marric says.

There's a sound of footsteps so we walk faster. I follow him toward the stable where there are some fenced-in horses and a barn, which I hope has more horses in it because the ones out are sad specimens.

"What have we here?" a male voice asks.

Marric whirls around, and I follow suit.

Several soldiers—not ones of Pennington's thankfully—stand there in matching uniforms of dark gray, swords strapped to their sides.

"We're here to buy horses," Marric responds. "Then we'll be on our way."

"Hold on," says a mustached man, who is in front of the group. "Don't be in such a hurry. We'd like to get to know you better first."

Though his words are nice enough, the gleam in his eye has me wanting to run.

Mustache takes a step closer. "Seems you're strangers around these parts."

"We are," Marric says.

"Then you don't know this town is now under my rule."

His rule? What about the gods' rule? What about Pennington? What is going on here?

"I didn't know that," Marric replies. "It's good to meet you, sir."

"The thing is," Mustache continues like Marric never said anything, "you're totting around a slave. Only slaves around these parts belong to me."

My unease claws its way into fear. I lean my head forward a little further, to better hide my face.

"We'll get our horses and be on our way, then." Marric grips the end of my chain more tightly, knuckles turning white.

"I can't let you do that," Mustache says. "You see, by crossing into my town, you agreed to my rules. I'm going to have to ask you to hand her over."

Marric moves in front of me and pulls out his sword. "I don't want to fight you, but I will if I have to. We're just getting horses, and we'll be on our way. She's coming with me."

Mustache pulls out his own sword, and his men do as well. "Guess we'll do this the hard way, then."

CHAPTER 27

As the first *clang* of metal against metal sounds, I stretch forth my sword. It moves as if it has a life of its own. It angles to the first soldier I want to attack, and I close my eyes so I don't see the carnage. It connects, and there's a cry of pain.

I pull my sword back and open my eyes. Marric has taken out half of the guard, though Mustache is still standing. He's moved from the front of the group to the back. As much as he talks, he's afraid to stand up to his words. With the swords Marric and I have, he should be.

I run toward Mustache, knowing my sword will do the work for me. He smirks and backs up. My feet thud against the ground as I spurt toward him. My neck is yanked back, jerking me off my feet. For a moment, I forgot about my collar.

I twist on the ground to find Marric engaged in a fierce fight. By the time I turn back, Mustache is gone. With a quick curse, I jump back to my feet and rush to help Marric. I surprise his attacker from behind, knocking him across the head with the hilt of my blade. He falls to the ground with a *thump*.

Marric and I exchange a glance.

"Do we still get the horses?" he asks me.

"We may as well try."

I step over a body as we move to the stable. I'm not sure if he's dead or unconscious, and I don't want to find out. The fallen had better be in the same position when we get back. That or gone. I don't want to have to fight them again.

When we open the door to the stable, only horses are in sight.

"Hello?" Marric calls out.

No response.

"Guess no one's here," he says.

"That, or they're hiding from us."

"I don't blame them."

We walk deeper into the stable. A horse nickers.

"We want to buy some horses," I call out. "I promise no trouble."

A woman appears. She's in her late thirties to early forties, with sad brown eyes. "There's always trouble lately."

"We promise to buy two horses and be on our way."

She eyes us like she doesn't believe us. "How can I be sure? "

"Because we truly mean you no harm. We're good people, just looking for a faster way to travel."

She grunts at Marric. "You got your slave doing all the talking?"

"Long story," he replies.

"Long stories I don't got time for," she says. "But if you have the money, I'll sell you two horses."

"We've got money." He grabs the bag of krats.

She reaches out for it.

"I want to see the horses first," he says.

"Fair enough." She motions to several stalls next to us. "Pick two you like."

After checking teeth and hooves, and seeing which ones look well fed, I'm drawn to a black one, while Marric points to a white one.

"We'll take these two," he says.

"Good choice."

"We'll be needing all their gear with them. There's enough here for everything." He jingles the money in the bag.

She nods and gets the horses saddled up. Honestly, I don't know what all she's doing. I've never ridden a horse before, but the thought is thrilling.

Once the horses are ready, she brings them over, reins in hand. "Money first, and then you can have them."

Marric hands the bag over at the same time as he takes the reins. "Pleasure doing business with you."

"Don't come back," she says.

Marric leads the horses outside, where the men are still on the ground. He gives me a few quick instructions, and then helps me to get up on the horse. The height is breathtaking, in mostly good ways. Everything looks different from up here. Skewed.

Marric gets on his own horse, which looks slightly awkward, while trying to hold my chain.

"Maybe we should have gotten one horse and ridden together," I say.

"We'll go faster this way."

We take off, Marric guiding me forward, my chain hanging between us. As we trot off, I look back at the bodies lying on the ground. Remorse fills me. I don't want to hurt anyone, even someone out to hurt me, but there's no way I can let them stand in the way of getting this collar off and returning to the heavens.

CHAPTER 28

I FALL OFF THE HORSE, but Marric catches me.

"Careful there," he says.

Though my dismounting wasn't graceful, I can't care. I hurt too much. "I never knew riding horses could be so dangerous."

"You'll feel better in a couple days. Are you steady now?"

I don't want him to let me go. It's nice in his arms. "I'm fine."

From the way he walks away from me, I know he's stiff and sore too. I can't imagine what it'll be like when we wake up tomorrow.

He leaves my chain on the ground and moves to the front of the horses.

"Do you need any help tying them up?" I ask.

"I got it."

Wishing I could still create my own things so I could help, I sit on a nearby log. Of course, if I still had my creative power, I wouldn't be on this trip with Marric. I'm not ready to leave him, so I suppose there is a bright side to things. Even if I did have my power, I'm not sure what I'd create. I'm used to making things for other people. Like flowers to bring beauty to the world and joy to the hearts of the people.

Once he finishes with the horses, he has me create food for us. A warming bowl of lamb stew for each of us, along with a hearty loaf of bread. After a day like today, it tastes amazing.

"I have a question for you. How can you create meat to eat, but not create an animal?" Marric asks.

"It's simple. This isn't real meat. It's what I make that's an approximation of what that meat would taste like, but made from other things that are known in the heavens." Though I can't quite duplicate the food in the heavens, much to my chagrin.

We're getting near the temple, and I want to keep going, but it's night, so we have to stop for some rest. We rode hard all day and made good time, but I wish we were even faster.

"There's something I've been wondering. What about people who don't believe in any god?" Marric asks. "Where do they go after death?"

With a heavy heart, I say, "There is no afterlife for them."

He's silent.

"It doesn't have to be that way for you," I say. "You know we're real now. The only thing you need to do is pick a god to worship. Follow your heart."

He looks right at me. "That won't be hard to do at all."

This makes me blush. I'm grateful for the dark; I don't want him to see it. I don't want him to know how he makes me react until I know how I feel and what to do about it. I hope when we reach Charmina she'll have answers for me that aren't just about getting this collar off.

"How does knowing that some people will not have an afterlife make you feel?" he asks.

The question startles me. "Honestly, I haven't thought of it before."

"Think about it now. How does it make you feel?" The earnestness in his gaze has me wanting to say the right answer, but I don't know what the correct answer is.

"Maybe a little sad. If I knew them, it might make a difference.

It's hard to imagine there's no life after this one." Even for gods. Where will I go after I die?

"A little sad?" He puts down his half-eaten bowl of stew and storms away.

Though I don't understand why he's upset, I put my bowl down, wishing I could follow him. But my chain doesn't go that far. I scuff the toe of my shoe in the dirt. How would I feel if Marric still didn't believe in me? If he wasn't going to receive an afterlife?

It doesn't seem fair. It's not his fault that he didn't believe in the gods. I lift my voice so he can hear me. "Maybe the gods should do more to present themselves to the world, instead of just hoping they'll get worshipers. Maybe we should be more forthright about our existence."

He moves halfway back to me. "You gods have temples everywhere. Don't you think that's enough?"

"We do, but most of us don't bother coming down from the heavens. We don't visit our people nearly enough. We make them go to our priests or priestesses, never giving them any personal contact. Maybe if there was more of that, more people would believe."

He sits back down beside me. "It'd be a good start, but I shouldn't be getting so upset. No matter what you do, there's always someone who won't believe."

"Are you speaking from personal experience?"

"Partly. I do believe now, but only because I saw you and the things you can do. It opened my eyes. Not everyone may feel the same way."

It's a lot to think about. The weight of a whole people. I've never thought about them before. It was always about me—how many followers I could get; how many would join me in the heavens; how much more glory than my fellow gods I might gain.

But now, things feel different.

"We should get to bed. We have a long way to go before we reach the temple of love," Marric says.

"Make me create a tent and two sleeping rolls, and I'll zonk right out." It feels as if my body's half asleep, though my mind is full.

As we prepare to sleep for the night, the thought of the people on this world continues to haunt me. How could I never think of them? How could I think so much of myself? Maybe it's time I look at being a goddess in a different light.

CHAPTER 29

BY THE TIME we reach the temple of love, I'm sore but not as achy as before. We leave our horses tied up in a nearby grove. Looking at the temple reminds me of how different gods can be.

It's in the middle of a lake, surrounded by water, except for a bridge we'll need to cross to get there. Behind the temple is a waterfall that flows into the lake. The temple is lit by the sun's evening light, which makes it glow a soft orange-pink. It's made up of several different buildings. One is in the center, which the bridge leads to. Two others stand to the side and one in the back, linked together by elaborate bridges.

The doorways come to a fine point at the top, and none have actual doors. Through the opening, I see the main building has an inner part that's surrounded by candles. On what looks like a giant flower pedestal is the giant statue of Charmina.

"It's breathtaking," Marric says.

"It's made for lovers to wander through."

He looks at my chain in his hands. "I wish we weren't going in like this."

I wish we weren't going at all, but I need the help. It feels like I should have all the answers. That I should know how to do this without any help. "If I have to go in, I'm glad I'm going in with you."

"Izlana?"

I turn to face him, ignoring everything—even the beauty of the temple and the need I have to get my powers back. Everything except him. "Yes?"

"I want you to know that—"

"Welcome to the temple of love. How can Charmina serve you this day?" a young woman in her twenties asks, and though her words are welcoming, her gaze is guarded, and her hand rests inside the folds of her cloak. She has ribbons of braids, and I see a mole above the right side of her lip.

As much as we need her, the last thing I want to do is acknowledge her. I want to go back and find out what Marric was going to say, but the moment is lost. "We need to speak with Charmina," I tell her.

This seems to ease her a little, but she doesn't take her hand out of her cloak, where I think she's hiding a weapon. "I'm afraid she only speaks to me, but I'd be happy to pass on a message for her. Have you fallen in love with each other? Slave and owner?"

Have I fallen in love? I resist glancing at Marric. "I'm afraid it's much more complicated than that."

I pull my hood down, so she can see my hair and face clearly.

She gives a little gasp. "Hurry in."

She takes off, and we follow after, though I'm not sure what good it will do, going into a building that has so many holes for a person to see inside.

It's as beautiful on the inside as it is on the outside. The high, pointed ceiling makes it feel bright and open. There's intricate scrollwork all around. What's most important is Charmina's statue. That's what I need.

"What are you doing here?" the priestess asks. "There is talk of people looking for a slave matching your description everywhere. It's not safe for you here. If one of my patrons spots you and is in need of the reward money, I don't think I'll be able to stop them."

"Reward money? How much?" Marric asks.

"Ten thousand krats."

Wow. If I ever wanted to know how much a goddess is worth, I guess now I do. "That is an incredible amount of money." Probably made by me.

"Which is why you must go."

"Where else is safe for me?" I ask.

"Back in the heavens, where you belong. Away from this strife and the rumors of war."

That doesn't sound good. "What war?"

"I don't know for certain. I only know there's news of much fighting."

Ramco. What trouble is he causing now? I can't focus on the problems until I can fix my own situation, though. "I need to speak with Charmina."

"You can try, but she hasn't answered my call in days. What's more, she's never spoken to anyone except me since I became priestess at this temple."

"Things are going to be different today." They have to be. If she doesn't answer, I have no other recourse.

CHAPTER 30

THE PRIESTESS of love steps to the side and motions to the statue. "Be my guest, but I cannot help you."

Of course she can't. Nothing is ever easy. "I need privacy, please."

Her eyes widen. "I can't leave you alone with the statue of Charmina."

As well she shouldn't, with any normal person. But I am no normal person. I straighten to my full height and use a commanding tone. "I will not harm her. Leave us."

She gives a slight bow to me—the first she's done. "As you wish." With that, she hurries out the side door to the right. She won't be far.

Marric leaves the end of my chain on the ground by the statue. "When you need me, call. I'll be here in an instant."

"Thank you." I mean more than those tiny two words, but I don't don't know how to it. I take his hand before he can leave. "I mean it. Truly."

He takes my hand in both of his. "I will always be here when you call."

His words make me feel like I've never felt before. He leaves, our hands falling apart as he does so. The loss is one I have to deal with. For now.

As soon as he's gone, I turn to the statue of Charmina. She's tall and voluptuous. Her lips are pouty, and she has high cheek bones. She's everything I'm not, but we're both gods, so it shouldn't be intimidating. Yet it is.

I clench my hands together, then loosen them, willing my tension to go out. I don't want her to see my weakness if I can help it. Once I feel somewhat calm, I say, "Charmina, goddess of love, hear me and answer my call. This is Izlana, goddess of creation."

If I were a priestess, I'd have to kneel, put my head to the ground, and perhaps wait hours for an answer, trying over and over again to get Charmina's attention. I hope I don't have to wait that long. Not only am I in a hurry to get answers, but I also don't want anyone to see me. If someone does, they could turn me in to Pennington.

I call out for Charmina again, but still nothing. I don't want to be reduced to begging. It sets a bad precedence I'm unwilling to set. Submitting to another god could have lasting effects, resulting in me giving over all my followers and losing myself. At least, that's a possibility. I don't know for certain, and I'm not about to find out.

"Charmina, it's Izlana. I need to speak with you." I hope the pleading doesn't sound in my voice. I can't give into it now, but the more time passes, the more desperate I feel.

No wonder my priestesses are so eager when I finally answer their call. Being too lazy to get up at the moment is no longer an excuse for me to ignore them. Should I ever get back to the heavens, that is.

But no. I can't think like that. I will get back. I just have to get this stupid collar off. And to do that, I need—"Charmina."

"Quiet, child," the statue says, coming to life. Though it's still made of stone, it looks much more real. There's a golden hue to her hair, and she has bright-blue eyes, the color of sapphires.

I clench my jaw at the reprimand, but otherwise keep my feelings contained.

"There are many who would like to know you are contacting me, both in the heavens and on that world. You must not give yourself away."

At least she has a good reason for yelling at me. And to be fair, I did yell first. "I need your help," I say.

"And I need yours."

What could she possibly need my help for? I'm just a fledgling goddess with little knowledge. "I can't do anything until I have my power back."

"Then you must hurry. There is a war brewing."

"I heard that," I say.

"The war on that world doesn't concern me. Humans always fight. It is the war coming to the heavens that could be the end of us all."

"A war coming to the heavens? How can this be?"

"It's why Ramco trapped you on the world. He knew you would oppose him. Ever since he got rid of you, he's done everything in his power to get rid of the rest of us. He wants nothing but chaos to rule the world and all our followers to belong to him. The very existence of gods is at stake."

My heart feels as if it's crashed far past the floor. Who knew my being so naïve with Ramco would lead to such catastrophic events? I have to stop him. Though I'm not only still on the world but also have no access to my power. "If you help me get this collar off, I will come to the heavens as soon as I can and help find a way to stop him."

"If only it were that simple, child."

I grit my teeth at being *child* again—it's not as if I'm not a goddess as well. I've earned my rightful spot in the heavens. But I can't anger her past helping me. Using the nicest tone I can conjure, I ask, "What do I need to do to get rid of these chains?"

"You will need someone who is of great magic to remove it by the magic of the world."

"How do I find one who can do this?"

"There is a wizard—Idolo the Wise. He is the most powerful living magic user. If anyone can help get your collar off, he can."

Finally, some answers. "Where can I find him?"

"A cave at the North Shore, though you'll only find him if he wants you to."

That's not foreboding. "I know I'll discover his whereabouts." After all, if a god can't, who can?

"Please hurry," Charmina says. "There's not much time. We need you to help defeat Ramco. He's become quite persuasive." With that, she turns back into a statue.

She doesn't understand I'm only seventeen. I may be a goddess, but I'm still new at my job. My mother should be here to guide me, but with her unexpected passing, there's no one to teach me unless Charmina's willing to do so. Probably why I got myself into this predicament to begin with. How can I possibly help defeat Ramco?

Doesn't matter. One problem at a time. First, I have to find Idolo the Wise.

CHAPTER 31

"Marric," I call out.

Within a moment, he's at my side and picking up my chain. "Does she have answers for you?"

"Yes," Charmina's priestess says. "Does she?"

I'm not about to tell her there's a war brewing in the heavens. I'm not even sure I should tell Marric. It's a serious thing that has never before happened. If it does, who knows what chaos can ensue? I have to get back there as soon as possible.

"She did," I say.

"And?" the priestess asks.

"We need to be going," is the only answer I give her. "Thank you for letting us use your temple." I pull my cloak back over my head.

She sniffs, pointing her nose in the air. How did she ever get to be a priestess of love? She's not very caring. That may be because of who I am.

"Be on your way, then," she says. "And don't come back here. There are too many people looking for you."

"We won't be back for help. That you can be assured of." I'd rather cut off my own finger than deal with someone so rude. Of course, if the fate of the world and heavens rested on coming back, I'd eat humble dust and do it.

I turn and head out, Marric behind me. The night has descended, stars twinkling in the sky. The air is cool but manageable. We make short work of the bridge, quickly coming to where we left the horses.

"Do you want to talk about it?" Marric asks.

I have a sudden urge to rest my head on his chest and cry. But I don't. "Ever heard of Idolo the Wise?"

His eyes widen. "Don't tell me we're going to him."

"Why? What have you heard?"

"He's crazy. Off-this-world crazy. He's said to be more powerful than any warlock in the last three hundred years, but it's made him mad."

"Things couldn't be any better, could they?" I let out a huff. "We have to go see him. Other than Pennington, who I'm not sure would know how to get rid of my chains even if he was willing to, Idolo is the only one who can take off my collar."

"This begs the question then," he says. "Who put it on you in the first place?"

"I don't know," I reply. "I didn't see who it was. Norhe was the first to pull me around, but I don't know if he was the one to put it on me or not."

"It better have not been Idolo." Marric puts his hand on his sword.

I wouldn't want to be someone who upset Marric, especially with the sword I created for him. He's a deadly opponent. "We'll have to deal with that when it comes. For now, to the North Shore."

"To the North Shore."

He helps me up onto the horse, and then surprises me by getting on behind me.

"We'll switch horses after a little while. I want you close, in case someone attacks. It sounds like they're getting closer to finding us."

An eruption of joy goes through me as he puts his arms around me to reach the reins. I say, "We'll have to hope they don't."

"But when they do, we'll be ready for them."

We gallop off, the spare horse following after. I lean back into Marric, enjoying the pressure of his chest against my back. I feel more secure than I have in days. Of course, I still have worries. Worries about my collar coming off. Worries about war on this world. Most importantly, worries about the war Ramco's trying to start in the heavens. I have to stop him.

EPISODE THREE

Episode Three

CHAPTER 32

THE JOURNEY to the North Shore is a long one, most of it still ahead of us. Marric is pushing us along well, though, so we're making good time. But that doesn't make it any easier. At least I'm getting used to sitting on a horse for days at a time.

I rest my head on Marric's chest, grateful we're riding together. Not just because it means I can doze as we ride, but because I like his nearness. I haven't told him, though. It's a troublesome thought. If I like him in that way, doesn't that mean he should become my mate?

I don't want him to be. I'm only seventeen; I want to explore the world and heavens, not get tied down. Not to mention that there are wars I have to help stop. I hope those are only rumors. Real wars aren't something I want to deal with.

"Are you ready to stop for the night?" Marric asks. "There's a nice clearing here."

I don't want to, if only because I want to stay snuggled up next to him, but we can't stay like this forever. "That sounds good."

He pulls the horse to a stop and slips down. I'm not nearly as graceful, even with his help. Despite his protests, I've learned to help him with our two horses. It's the least I can do, even if he thinks a goddess shouldn't do such chores. Maybe I shouldn't, but it feels weird to sit around and let him do all the work.

Once the horses are taken care of, Marric says, "What should we have for dinner?"

I grin. This has become a thing with us—who can come up with the best thing to eat. "How about—"

"Did you hear that?" he asks.

I shake my head but listen close. There's nothing. "Is this your way of saying you don't want to play tonight?"

"I really thought I heard something." He scans the area around us. He's got my nerves on edge now.

"Where did it come from?" I ask.

"I don't know. Maybe it was a squirrel." Still, he doesn't let his guard down. As he looks at me, I can tell his attention is elsewhere. Maybe he's trying to draw them out? If there is a *them* out there.

In case that's what's going on, I continue with our game, but my focus isn't on it. "Roast duck with plum sauce and steamed buns?"

"That sounds good. Let's go with that." But though he holds the end of my chain and can access my power while I can't, he doesn't say anything to have me create it.

This reminds me of how frustrating it is not to have control of my power. If I did, we'd already be eating. If there's someone coming at us, I'd rather have something in my stomach. After traveling all day with little to eat, a good dinner is well earned.

He seems to relax, gaze not darting all over the clearing. "Are you ready?"

"Yes." Like I'm the one delaying. At least he has a good reason for being distracted. I'd rather be safe than sorry.

But instead of having me create something, he pulls the hood of my cloak further down my head so it covers part of my face. He then leans in closer. My breathing becomes rapid, despite my trying to control it. Is he going to kiss me?

I've never been kissed before, but I want him to do it. It sounds so exciting. Like something I should try, but only with him. Have his lips press against my own. Not that this is how I expected it to happen. Not at all. But I'll take it if he's going to pick now.

He grows closer. And closer. I want to close my eyes, but before I can do so, he misses my lips and goes for my ear. Not a kiss, then. Disappointment fills me.

"There's someone watching us," he says.

This puts every nerve at attention. "How can you be sure?"

Instead of replying, he twirls around, sword at the ready. A man—a soldier, to be exact—is coming at us full force.

CHAPTER 33

THE ATTACKER TAKES A STEP BACK.

"What do you want?" Marric asks, sword at the ready.

"I've come for the girl," the man says. "Hand her over, and there'll be no problem."

"Not happening." Marric grips the end of my chain more tightly.

A second soldier steps out, and then a third. We've faced worse odds before, but it still doesn't bode well. I'm about to pull my sword out when someone grabs me from behind and yanks me away from Marric.

Marric doesn't let go of the chain, but jerks backward, falling to the ground. He scrambles to his feet as I continue backward. I struggle against my abductor, but to no avail.

A moment later, Marric has a sword pointed my attacker's way, and everything stills.

"You know I've won," a male voice sounds close behind me. "Let us go, and we won't cause more trouble."

"I can't do that," Marric responds.

Suddenly, there's not just arms touching me, but also a blade at my throat above my collar. "If you care about her at all, you'll let us go," the man says.

I clench my teeth to keep from calling out. I can't die. Not now. There's no one else to be Izlana—all creation would end. I put my hand on the hilt of my sword, ready to do whatever I need to fight.

"You won't hurt her," Marric says. "You need her, or you wouldn't have come all this way for her. Who sent you?"

"You're right. I won't hurt her. But that won't stop me from hurting you."

The blade at my throat is gone. It twirls through the air until it strikes Marric in the left shoulder. I pull my sword out and plunge it behind me, into my would-be abductor. I don't wait to see the results. I don't want to see them. Instead, I rush to Marric's side.

He already has other attackers on him. Blades flash and clang together. My feet are firm on the solid ground. I move my sword, slicing into everyone who isn't Marric. His sword does the same, avoiding me.

There are more attackers than I thought, the numbers blurring together. My blade moves on, despite my weakening arm. Marric doesn't seem to be faring as well. His blade moves well enough, but he's gasping for air beside me.

Not for the first time, I'm thankful I created weapons that would hew through their opponents with ease. Without them, we'd surely be captured already.

I cut and slice and parry all the while. The soldiers are unfazed at first, but they grow more leery of attacking. Soon, they're backing away. I give chase until they turn tail and run, fast and far. My chain yanks me back, Marric's not following. I don't think we'll be seeing them again for a while.

"They're gone," I say between heaving breaths.

Marric nods, face pale. Then he falls to the ground.

CHAPTER 34

"Marric." I hurry to him, and put a hand to his wound, which is seeping blood.

"Fine. Just… Dizzy."

"What do I do?"

"Hard to say. Without looking. At. Wound. Stitch it. Maybe."

Panic blooms, threatening to overtake my common sense, but I force it down. "I don't have a needle and thread. I need you to create one." Not that I want to sew him back together; I'm not positive I'd do it right. But I'd be doing something.

He blinks heavily a few times.

"Marric, don't you dare pass out on me. You have to make me create something first."

Without opening his eyes, he says, "Izlana. Goddess of creation. Make. Me…"

"Make you what?" I want to shake him.

"A needle. Thread."

With that, my power rises up within me. I hasten to make a sharp needle and strong thread. I wish I knew more about what I'm doing. It'll have to be enough.

The thread and needle rest in my right palm. My hands shake, as I go to thread the needle. This will never do. I'll have to be steadier than this.

No matter what I tell myself, though, they won't stop shaking. I'll have to deal with it the best I can.

Once the needle is threaded, I move to the wound. It's not long, but it's deep. I feel like there's something I should do before I stitch it together, but I don't know what. "Marric, what do I do?"

He doesn't respond.

I curse heartily under my breath. Stitching it will have to be. At least the blood flow has almost crawled to a stop. I put the needle in and out, pretending it's through a piece of fabric. It's not the best job ever, but it's something. I'm much better at creating an already made pattern than sewing it on to something

Marric moans a few times but doesn't regain conciseness while I work, for which I'm grateful. I make a slow job of it, with uneven stitches, but the wound is closed when I'm done. It has to help. I don't have anything to cut the excess thread with, so I use my sword, careful not to hurt him further.

I don't know what else to do. We should leave this clearing. Whoever it was that came after us knows we're here. It's not a good place to stay. But I can't move him. I might be able to drag him a little ways, but to get far, I'd need to get him on one of the horses. Plus, he'd somehow need to be holding the chain the whole time. There's no way I could lift him. Still, I have to try.

I bring the horses over so one of them is next to Marric. Then I realize my next problem. I was going to grab him from under the arms, but that's next to his stitches. I don't trust that I should carry him like that and risk pulling his wound.

Taking his good arm, I heave him upward. We make it to a standing position, but my body is shaking. I can't take him much farther. I try to push him up and over the horse, but he isn't budging. This isn't going to work.

I put him back on the ground as gently as I can, and I tie the horses back up.

It's too bad the attackers didn't wait until after we'd created everything for the night. Then I would have something soft to lay his head on and a blanket to cover him up with. Not to mention, something for me to eat. He probably needs something as well, but I wouldn't know how to give it to him, even if we had it. We should have kept what I've been creating, instead of leaving it behind so the horses didn't have to carry it.

Determined to at the very least keep Marric safe, I sit next to him, sword in hand. It's going to be a long night.

CHAPTER 35

"Izlana?" Marric calls to me from far away. "Izlana?" Closer this time.

I open my eyes to realize I've curled up next to Marric, my head on his good shoulder, and fallen asleep. So much for standing guard.

Though it feels nice and cozy here with him, I sit up. "How are you feeling?"

"Like someone tried to rip off my shoulder."

"Unfortunately, they did," I reply. "Are you feeling well enough to create something? We could use some food and water."

"Yup." He creates a simple meal of oatmeal and fruit, along with some water.

"Who do you think those attackers were from?" I ask.

"If I had to guess, I'd say Pennington. Right uniforms, and they wanted to take you alive. Seems to me they wanted you more than they would a regular servant."

"Pennington. He's still out there, looking for me."

"Probably will be as long as he's alive."

"Wait until I have my power back, and then he'll never have

control of me again." I finish my breakfast. "I'm sorry you got hurt because of me."

He waves with his good arm. "Don't worry about it. You weren't the one who threw a dagger at me."

"If you weren't traveling with me, it wouldn't have happened. You should be home with your family."

"Even if I weren't with you, I wouldn't be with my family. I'd be off somewhere, earning money for my siblings. This is where I need to be."

His words warm me. Feeling brave, I ask, "Do you say that because you want to be with me, or because the world might end in chaos if you don't save me?"

He looks at me—really looks deep into my eyes for the first time since I woke up. Though there's pain riddled in his gaze, that's not all. There's something else there. Something soft and kind.

"I'm with you for both reasons."

I'll take that kiss now. But he's not in any condition for that.

"That's good to know." I gather stuff up, trying to leave as little of a mess behind us as possible.

He stands and goes behind some trees to use the necessity while I wait for him at chain's length, and then he does the same for me.

"Do you think you can get on the horse?" I ask him.

"It'll be hard, but I can do it. Would you give me a boost?"

"Not sure how good of one it will be, but I will try."

Together, we work to get him up and on the horse. Once we manage, I give a little cheer. "Good job."

His face is pale again. "Can you get up behind me? I think it'd be best if we rode together."

The way up looks much longer without him helping me.

He must see my hesitation, because he says, "There's a stump over there you can use. I should have spotted it sooner and used it myself."

I glance to where he's pointing. Sure enough, there's a stump, tall enough I should be able to get up. He leads the horse over, keeping a tight hold of my chain while I walk. Though I trust him, it'll be so nice when I'm not tethered to a certain place all the time.

It takes a few tries, but I manage to get on the horse in behind of him. With his help, I guide the horse.

"We probably shouldn't stop again for a while," he says. "We shouldn't have stayed the night."

"I was worried about that but didn't know what to do. Are you going to be all right if we don't stop for a while?" His wound concerns me.

"It won't make much difference whether we stop or go on. I may fall asleep on your shoulder, though."

"If it's not too uncomfortable for you, have at it," I respond, happy he feels comfortable enough to fall asleep with me at the reigns. "Make sure I'm going in the right direction first."

He chuckles, and then winces. "This injury is going to take some getting used to."

A lot of things will take getting used to. Like sitting so close to him. Though we've been doing that for a while now, it still feels new and wonderful. Maybe I don't want to get used to it. I just want to be happy with him.

CHAPTER 36

WE JOURNEY FOR A LONG TIME, clear into the night, before he says we can stop. After I take care of the horses and create dinner and some blankets on Marric's request, we settle in for the night.

I wake as well rested as I've felt since we've been on this journey. It's a nice change of pace. Until I realize how high the sun is in the sky. Marric usually wakes me. Why didn't he do so sooner?

I turn toward him. He's asleep. Strange. And his forehead is covered in sweat.

"Marric," I say softly, trying to wake him. It takes me calling his name three more times before he replies.

"Mhmm. Five more minutes."

"We can't wait five more minutes. It's already late in the day."

He opens his eyes, but his gaze looks unfocused. "That's not good." He sits up and sucks in a breath.

"Are you all right?"

"It's this blasted shoulder. I don't think I'll ever be right again."

Though I'm sure that's an exaggeration, I can't help but feel concerned. "Maybe we should take a look at it. You're not quite yourself."

He nods and slips his shirt from his shoulder.

The wound looks terrible. Red and pus are streaking from it. "I think there's a problem," I say.

He glances down at his shoulder and curses. "I'm going to need to you create some things for me. Even then, this is going to be slippery."

"What's wrong with it?" I ask, worry bleeding through me.

"It's infected." He curses again. "Are you all right if I ask for a few things?"

"Of course." Though I appreciate his asking. He could have me create whatever he needs whenever he needs it.

"Izlana, goddess of creation"—his voice is shaky—"make me some alcohol and dark honey."

I create what he asks for as quickly as possible. "What are these for?" I hold out the jar of honey and bottle of alcohol.

"They'll help fight the infection. I hope I'm doing this right. I've never had to treat one myself." He squeezes his eyes shut. "Pour the alcohol on the wound."

Sounds weird to me, but if that's what he wants, I have no problem doing it. I set the honey down, uncork the alcohol, and pour it down his shoulder.

He hollers, jerking away from it.

I pull the bottle back. There's about half of it left.

Marric is takes in a hissing breath.

"Sorry," I say.

He shakes his head. "No. It's needed. Just stings."

"I don't want to hurt you more."

"If we don't do this, I may die."

I point to his shoulder, disbelieving. "This might kill you?"

"Sure will."

My chest feels like I was the one stabbed. Despite his previous reaction, I go to pour more alcohol on his wound.

"Wait, wait, wait," he says. "Let me have you create some clean cloths we can use to soak it. That might be better than pouring it. Though it's probably going to hurt worse."

As much as I don't want to hurt him, I don't want him to die even more. We make quick work of creating cloths, and I pour the alcohol on one of them.

"Are you ready?" I ask.

He shakes his head. "Yes."

That's not confusing. Either way, I press the dampened cloth to his wound. He groans, making me wish it was me hurting and not him.

"What do I do now?" I ask.

"Put some of that honey on the wound and cover it with a cloth. We'll tie it on and keep it there. I'll eat some honey too, for good measure. I'm not sure which way works."

"Aren't you worried about your wound getting sticky?"

"I'm more worried about the infection getting worse."

I do as he directed while he eats some of the honey.

He says, "If I pass out, you need to keep doing this for me. Try and keep it as clean as possible."

I nod, though I'm filled with unrelenting fear. "Don't pass out."

He gives a small smile. "I'll try not to. But for now, we have to keep going. We should be farther away than we are."

We find another stump to help us get on the horse, and we're on our way. The whole time, I'm worried about Marric. What will I do if he doesn't make it? The thought of him dying makes my stomach churn. I need him. I care for him. The worst can't happen.

CHAPTER 37

THE NEXT DAY, his wound looks a little better, if still red and yucky. I can't help but hold out hope this is a good thing. After I treat it the same way I did before, we hit the road.

"How many more days until we reach the North Shore?" I ask, wondering if it wouldn't be better for Marric if he were in a nice, warm bed instead of traveling with me.

"Should be about three, but at this pace, it may be four or five."

A sprinkle of rain hits my cheek, then. I glance up to the sky. "I think it's starting to rain."

"Just what we need." He rests his back against me.

I settle into supporting him, careful not to bump his bad side. At least my front and his back will stay somewhat dry, if the worst should come. One hopes it's only a little sprinkle and nothing worse, though.

"How many siblings do you have?" I ask. "If you don't mind talking about them."

"I'd like to talk about them. I have three little sisters, the oldest of which is the one taking care of everybody right now. And four little brothers. The youngest boy is five."

The rain comes on now. "I'm sure you miss them," I say.

"I do, but it's also nice to have a break from them. We're really close, though. Usually, even when I'm working, we keep in touch regularly. We haven't been able to do that since I worked for Pennington. I hope they're doing all right without my monthly income, and that they're not affected by any of this talk-of-war business."

"It can't be as bad as Charmina said. There's never been so much as a hint of war in the heavens. I can't imagine one starting now, which means she could also be wrong about the rumors of wars down here."

"I'd believe that if we hadn't heard rumors of wars ourselves."

I sigh. "I guess I want to believe things could be better than they are. I don't want to be responsible for so many things."

"Don't worry too much over it now. We'll worry about getting your collar off first, and then we'll worry about these reports."

The rain pours down, soaking me through. "This can't be good for your wound," I say.

"It can't be healthy for either of us. Maybe we should find some shelter, only I'm troubled about those soldiers catching up to us."

They can't catch up to us if Marric's dead. Just me. Not only will I be alone, unable to move because I can't lift my own chain, but I'll be without Marric. That isn't an option. "Let's find a place to stop."

He points to some thick trees up ahead. "We can try there. The rain will probably still get us, but not as bad."

I guide us to the area he points to. It's getting easier and easier to control the horse. I was right to be eager to ride her the first time —but it's not as fun to do in the rain. We get close to the trees, and I half-slide, half-jump off the horse before turning to help Marric.

Marric and I tie both horses close by, and then we huddle underneath the thick foliage. It's raining so hard now it's difficult to talk.

"We should look at your wound while we're stopped," I yell.

He grimaces. I think it's because every time I look at it, I pour more alcohol on it, though it seems to be hurting him less. Infection is not something I want to take a chance with. He's too important for that.

"Let's wait until the rain clears," he yells back. He surprises me by putting his arms around me. "We need to keep warm."

Well, if it's for the sake of staying warm... I snuggle closer. Though we're both wet, it feels good to have my skin next to his. Not only is he warm, but he feels so good. Being cuddled up with him is oh-so-right. I wish it would go on raining forever.

As soon as I think that, the rain lessens. Of course it does. I shouldn't think such things about being closer to him because the opposite always happens.

Despite the rain letting up, he doesn't let go. "Maybe we should be going," he says.

"Maybe so."

But neither of us moves. I don't want to. Except there are bigger things than us going on. I turn in his arms so we face each other. Looking at him this close takes my breath away. All other thoughts leave. It's him and me.

His eyes are that perfect hazel that has me wanting to stare into them forever. His thumb brushes my elbow, and I shiver.

"Are you cold?" he asks, the rain a pattering now.

"Not at all." I've never been so far from cold in my entire life.

He lifts his hand from my elbow to my hair, which I'm sure is wet and clumpy, but it doesn't stop him. He runs his fingers through it, bringing my head closer to his. His breath is warm against my skin. Maybe I am a little cold after all, but he makes me feel alive and vibrant.

One of our horses neighs. The smell of rain fills the air with its fresh clean scent, but underlying that is the scent of him. Masculine and woodsy.

I wish the god of nature or whoever is making it at the moment would keep the rain coming for a long, long time.

Marric tilts his head toward mine. I lift mine and lean in closer. This time, he's going to kiss me. He's not going to whisper in my ear. His lips will touch mine, and it will be the most wonderful thing I've ever felt. I wonder what it will feel like. What will happen when our lips meet?

"Well, look what I've stumbled on," a man says.

I jerk my head up to find Mustache standing not ten feet from me.

CHAPTER 38

MUSTACHE IS SURROUNDED by a good dozen men. What is he doing here? This is bad.

"Sorry to interrupt such a tender moment." He smirks. "Or not so sorry. This time you won't get away."

Marric and I whirl around at the same time, pulling out our swords.

Mustache laughs. "Your weapons are useless. See, I've got arrows trained on both your hearts."

I glance around, and sure enough, he's telling the truth. There are four men with bows and arrows pointing straight at us. Our weapons are useless when they can't be used at a distance. Is there anything I could create to stop this from happening? I don't know. I wasn't trained to fight.

"What do you want from us?" My pulse is racing.

"There's no us, just you," he replies, walking a few steps closer. "You see, after you two got away from me before, I began to hear talk that Pennington was looking for a girl with white hair and emerald eyes. A girl that was no girl at all, but a goddess whose power could be wielded to create anything a person desires. I'm thinking that girl is you."

I laugh, trying to downplay my importance. "I think you've been listening to too many rumors. A girl like that can't exist."

"She's right," Marric says. "Someone like that doesn't exist."

He paces a few feet, eying me as he goes and ignoring Marric. When he returns to his original place, he says, "Forgive me for being rude. I am Saldor, and I will soon rule this world."

I attempt to keep the fury from my face. No man owns this world. "Not if Pennington has anything to say about it."

He waves like he's brushing off the notion. "A minor annoyance is all. He'll soon be taken care of."

What can he mean by that? "He has more men than you."

"Ah, but, I found his secret weapon—the thing that brought him into power."

"You're fooling yourself." But I'm worried about what his plan entails. It can't be good if it's going the direction I think it is. Me.

"We'll see." He snaps his fingers. "Kill the boy."

"Wait," I cry. "Don't."

He holds up his hand to stop his men. "Give me a reason why I shouldn't."

The only reason I can think of gives me away, but it's worth it if it saves Marric's life. Though it's the last thing I want to do.

"I'm waiting," Saldor says.

"Because if I am who you think I am," I say, "then you need him to carry my chain." I hope that's enough to save Marric. If not, I'll have to tell them he's the only one who can use my powers for creation. There will be a problem if they try to hold the chain. If someone else has magic, they'll be able to take the chain away just fine, and I'll have no other recourse.

Saldor considers what I said. "Boy," he says to Marric, "put the chain on the ground and take five steps away from it."

Marric looks to me. I nod.

"This isn't a good idea." But he slowly puts the chain on the ground and backs away.

"Don't try anything funny." Saldor saunters forward, flicking his gaze back and forth between me and Marric. He squats down beside the end of my chain, puts his hand on it, and tries to pick it up. Nothing.

He tries again with the same results.

"Loplo," he says. "Try to pick this up."

A soldier steps forward and moves to pick up the chain. It remains on the ground. One-by-one, the soldiers give it a try. Even the people aiming arrows at our hearts take a turn, though carefully, so we can't get away.

When the last soldier fails, I try not to let my relief show. None of them have magic. "I told you. Marric is the only one who can carry my chain."

Saldor eyes Marric with new appreciation. "Save the boy. He's coming with us."

"And what makes you think I'll do what you want?" Marric asks.

"Because I have something you care about," Saldor says. "This girl. Now get her chain, and let's get out of here. Loplo, grab their horses. Penhe, their swords."

Not our swords. If they try to use them, they'll realize the blades have the power to work on their own. I should have made them only work for Marric and me. But a man I'm assuming is Penhe takes them from us, and there's nothing I can do.

Marric takes my chain, though he doesn't look happy about it. The soldiers surround us in a tight circle, and Saldor leads us south. The way we came, not the way we need to go. We're his prisoners. At least we are together, but it's a small consolation when the fate of the world and the heavens depends on me.

CHAPTER 39

WE TRAVEL for two days before we come to a camp. The rumors are true. They're preparing for a war. There are tents all around and soldiers in even more places. Most are training, but some are eating or simply staring at us. It smells of body odor and metal. The sun is out, shining bright, making the smell worse.

I'm grateful for my cloak keeping the sun off my skin, but the only other thing I have to be grateful for is that Marric is still with me. I'll forever be thankful that he was able to come with me, but that doesn't stop me from feeling guilty he's in this situation too. How are we going to escape with so many people around?

Saldor leads us to the middle of the camp, making our escape even less likely. "Now," he says, "make me weapons for my army."

So, he doesn't know. "I can't."

He scowls. "You will."

Marric takes a step closer to me. As thankful as I am for his protection, it really isn't much in his current state.

"She's not lying," Marric says. "She can't create anything. The collar keeps her from doing that, which is what we were on our way to fix before you so rudely interrupted us."

Saldor slugs Marric. My chain pulls as Marric goes stumbling backward. I hurry to his side. His hand is to his face where he was hit, and he's glowering at Saldor. "It's not a lie," Marric says. "You should have learned more about what exactly you were going to capture."

"I nabbed a goddess, and I want that goddess to make me weapons." Saldor focuses his gaze on me. It's sharp and unforgiving.

Do I give in and tell him Marric can create things in my stead, or do I continue telling him the half-truth that I can't create anything? I don't know what the right answer is. I don't want to put Marric in more danger, but neither do I want to give this madman more power than he already has.

"It's true that I can't," I say. "You have to believe me."

"I don't have to do anything." Saldor pulls a dagger from his belt and brings it to Marric's throat. "But if you want him to live, you'll do what I ask."

Fear grips me. "You can't kill him; you need him to carry my chain." Though with a camp this big, there's bound to be someone else who has magic. As long as Saldor doesn't figure that out, Marric's life should be safe.

"You're right." Saldor moves the dagger from Marric's neck to his wrist. "But I can maim him all I want. All he needs is one hand and a beating heart. We can carry him around, if need be."

I'm sick to my stomach. Would he go so far? I can't imagine one human doing that to another. It's a horrid thought I can't bear.

"She can't do anything," Marric calls out.

A thin line of red appears under the dagger's blade.

"Wait," I cry. "Wait, please. I'll give you what you want. I swear it. Just don't hurt him."

"Don't give him anything," Marric says. "I don't need two hands."

Sweet, loveable fool. Yes, he does.

"Tell me now," Saldor says, "or I finish the job."

My gaze locks on to Marric's wrist. "Take your blade away, and I'll tell you how you can get what you need."

CHAPTER 40

"How do I get swords for all my men?" Saldor demands.

I don't want to give him anything, but since I want Marric to keep his hand, I have an idea of how I can trick Saldor. It's doubtful it will last long, though, so we'll have to find a way out of here soon.

"It's true I can't create anything myself while this collar is on," I say. "But Marric has the power to make me create things."

"Is this true?" Saldor asks Marric.

Marric looks to me.

"It's all right," I say. "Tell him."

Marric's lips thin, but he says, "Yes. It's true."

Saldor's eyes light up. "Then create me my swords."

"How many?" Marric's voice is a grumpy sort of resigned.

Saldor's is exactly the opposite. "Seven hundred and fifty-three."

Marric shakes his head and whispers to me, "We can't do this."

"I can hear you," Saldor says.

Still, I whisper back, "I promise it'll be okay, Marric. We'll figure things out."

Whether he knows what I'm about to do or trusts me, he goes

ahead. "Izlana, goddess of creation, make me seven hundred and fifty-three blades."

My power springs to life and begins to mold the swords, only as I create them, I add my own special component. I make each blade so it can only nick or scratch the intended victim. None of these swords have the power to kill or maim.

Somehow, I manage to keep the smile from my face.

When the first batch of swords is done, Saldor gives a gleeful laugh. "Penhe, start stacking these swords and passing them out. Quickly. She's already making more."

I ignore the man that takes the swords from me as I finish creating another. I have a job to do. If I weren't a prisoner, I would take this time to relax. Creating things is what I'm meant to do, after all. But as the situation stands, I dart my gaze around every few seconds, taking in the growing crowd around me. And Marric.

Poor Marric is looking on with brows drawn and a frown on his face, but he trusts me enough to let me do this. It's the one thing I could think of, to keep him safe without giving Saldor more power than he already has. If anything, it'll take away some of his power.

The group is eager at first, happily taking their new swords as they are created. And their number grows until I'm surrounded by more people than I can count. Eventually, I give up trying to watch them all and take a seat on the ground. Pennington would have a nice stool brought in, but Saldor doesn't care about my comfort. I don't know if the difference between them is good or bad. I suppose we'll find out if Marric and I can escape before making any decisions about Pennington and Saldor.

As I create the five-hundredth sword, the crowd starts to wane. I'm not much of a spectacle by now. It gets to a point that they form a line and leave as soon as they take the blade from me. Some take two, to give one to their comrades.

The only people who don't lose interest the entire time are Saldor and Marric. They watch me with different expressions but the same intensity. I hope Marric forgives me for cooperating with Saldor once he realizes what I'm creating.

Saldor now knows that I can create and how I do so. His power will be as limitless as Pennington's was, unless he keeps allowing loopholes for me to go through. But Pennington figured out pretty quickly that he needed to word things carefully. Saldor will most likely be the same.

We have to get out of here. As I finish the last of the swords, I look around for a solution. Even if they put us at the outer part of the camp, there are still people keeping watch. It's just as well. I doubt I'm to be kept anywhere but in the middle of that camp.

I do see one thing that might help, though. A man drinking out of a mug. The problem is convincing Saldor he and his men need drinks, without making him suspicious. It'd be easy enough to add a little something to the brew.

I hand off the last sword.

Saldor takes it and runs his fingers down the middle of the blade. "It's a fine weapon." He turns to Marric. "I see you'll need your tongue. Pity I can't cut it out for misbehavior."

I'm going to be sick. If my plan fails, Marric is sure to be the one to pay for it, and now Saldor knows he can be used to gain my cooperation. Not that I can do anything at this point. It's all in Marric's hands and words.

"Penhe, take Marric to the prisoners' tent. Loplo, build a tent around our Izlana and give her some blankets." Saldor turns to go.

My chance is slipping away. Who knows what the morning will bring? It's now or never. "It's too bad you're not rewarding your men for finding such a prize."

He stops. Did I take it too far? Is he going to suspect?

When Saldor looks at me, it's with speculation in his eyes. I want to shrink under his stare, but I don't move; I stay right here, looking back.

"It's not a bad idea," he says. "We do need food. Marric, grab the end of her chain and order her to make enough food for me and my men."

This time Marric doesn't hesitate. Either my bringing up the idea or the fact that it's food doesn't scare him off.

"Are you all right with this?" he asks me.

Saldor laughs, though there's no humor in it. "She's not the boss around here. I am."

Ignoring him, I nod.

Marric says the proper words to have me create food for over seven hundred people. He doesn't say what. It's not a drink, but I can work with food too. If I was vindictive, I would only make gruel, but I want them to eat this, so I produce the most sumptuous meal I can. Veal and venison roasted together, surrounded by lots of vegetables. Breads of all kinds, from the heartiest wheat to the finest white. Fruit never seen around these parts, all of it made to taste better than anything they've ever had. And every piece of food laced with a sleep drug that will kick in several hours from now.

I only hope Marric doesn't eat.

CHAPTER 41

AFTER THE MEAL is cleared and Loplo builds a tent around me, I'm left alone to stew. I wish Marric were left with me; us being separated was not part of my plan. With my luck, he'll be locked up, and there'll be nothing we can do with the time I've created for us to escape.

I wish I could have told him my plan—let him know not to eat the food. If he did, it'd be just as bad as him being locked up, only I'd also feel guilty for being the one to knock him out.

Time passes all too slow. More things start to worry me, like what if everyone didn't eat? I put a delay on the drug, so they'd have time to finish before anyone would fall asleep and make the rest of them suspicious, but that doesn't guarantee they ate. If one person with a weapon stays awake, our chance might be lost.

I can't handle it. I go out and sit on the ground. My chain can't go much farther than this, so there's no escape unless Marric can help me.

The soldiers passing by look at me with great interest. I pull the cloak further over my head.

"What do we have here?" one of them asks.

"Move along," another male voice says.

I turn around to see there's a guard stationed to the side of my tent. He must be who spoke. I'd like to think he did it because he has my best interest at heart, but I'm sure it's because of orders.

Several more men pass our way and try to get a good look at me. I ignore them, and they're told to keep going.

I sit here for so long, my rear is going numb. After some time, I stand and realize no one has been by in a while. In fact, the whole camp seems to be quiet.

Good. My plan is working. I glance back at my guard. Maybe not. He's wide awake, watching me with keen blue eyes.

I pace in front of my tent. There has to be a way to make the seconds go by faster because some things a person can't wait for. But there's nothing for it. Time goes as slowly as ever. It's a wonder the guard finds nothing suspicious about the camp growing so quiet. Though night is coming on... Perhaps this is how they always are after dark. Maybe my plan failed.

There's the snapping sound. I whirl around to find Marric looking better than ever, despite the bruise on the side of his face. He's on the opposite side of the tent from my guard. I glance at my guard, who's still watching me but doesn't seem to have noticed Marric.

I continue pacing but keep my head up, looking around as I go. The only person moving about is Marric. Though it's getting harder to see in the dim light, I'm pretty sure my plan worked on everyone except my guard. Now we only need to sneak past one person, and not an entire army, even if that person is armed.

Marric walks right up to the tent when my guard spots him.

"Who are you and what are you doing here?" the guard demands. Good. He hasn't recognized Marric as a prisoner.

"I have orders to take her to Saldor," Marric says. I stop as close to him as I can.

The guard stands. "No one told me."

"That's why I was sent. You'd better let me take her before he gets angry."

The guard's hand is on his hilt. "I don't think so. Saldor said he'd come get her himself and not to let anyone else near her."

Marric doesn't have a sword, nor does he look like a soldier. It can't be much longer before the guard figures that out. What are we going to do? There has to be a way to give Marric enough time to grab my chain so he can have me create a weapon for him.

"Get away from her," the guard says, pulling out his sword. "Now."

Marric dives in the tent, toward the end of my chain.

The guard hurries after him. Right before the guard reaches my chain, where it lies on the ground, I give a great jerk, tripping him. He falls flat on his face, his sword tumbling away.

I race to pick up the sword before he can grab it, but my chain holds me back. The guard reaches the sword and calls out, "The prisoner is trying to escape."

The chain rattles, and I know Marric grabbed hold of it.

"Create two swords," I call out to him.

I don't hear anything, but next thing I know, there's a tug on my power, trying to create two swords. I create the same blades as I did before, making them so they're swift and always hit their target, but this time, they can only work like that in my hands or Marric's. The guard is coming at me by the time the first one is complete.

As I create the second one, I aim the first toward the guard, letting it do its thing. It cuts into him easily, his own sword useless. I pull back once he is injured, and I now hold a sword in each hand.

"You won't get away," he says as he bleeds on the ground. "This camp is too full of people for you to escape."

I ignore him and hand Marric the weapon as he comes out of the tent with my chain in hand.

"Are you all right?" Marric asks.

I want to plant a kiss on those good-looking lips of his. "I'm so happy to see you. I was worried you would either eat the drugged food or be locked somewhere you couldn't get out of."

"Nope. I was guarded on the other side of the camp when they all fell asleep. Brilliant plan, by the way."

"Thanks. Let's get out of this place."

CHAPTER 42

WE HEAD toward the place they have our horses tied up. There are a few other horses with them, but not enough for the whole camp. It's weird, seeing people asleep all over the place. Eerie.

"We should take these horses with us, at least a short way," I say.

"Wise thinking." He unties the extra horses, while I attend to ours. He says, "You shouldn't have created those swords for Saldor's men. Who knows what havoc they'll create with them? I could have done without my hand."

"Don't worry about it. They're the opposite of ours."

He turns toward me, a big grin on his face. "Brilliant. There's a reason you're a goddess."

"I only hope they don't realize I've tampered with their swords," I say. "At least, not until after we're long gone. I don't think anyone in the camp will fight with the intention of killing their own comrades, so we should be safe."

"I don't think that's something we have to worry about. We'll get their horses and be on our way before too long. They won't have a way to catch up to us."

Marric finds a couple of saddles. I help him on one of our horses, and then he reaches down to help me.

"How's your shoulder?" I ask, as we travel north.

"It's fine."

Sure it is. But there's nothing I can do about it. I can only try to get us where we're going as fast as possible.

The farther we travel, the more Marric leans on me. It's near dawn when he's inclining all the way on me.

"Hey. Are you all right?" I ask. "Do you need to stop and rest?"

"We can't," he mumbles. "They'll catch us. Let's switch horses. Give this guy a rest."

He seemed so much better before, what happened to make him worse? Did an infection set in again? Or maybe I'm making things out to be worse than they really are. It takes some doing to dismount from this horse and climb onto my black one. Marric seems weaker than ever, swaying on the horse while he waits for me to get on.

Once I'm settled behind him, I say, "Have me create a rope."

"What for?" He sounds so different from his usual self; it scares me.

"I'm going to tie us together, so you don't fall off the horse."

"That's probably wise." He has me create a rope, and I wrap it around us with his help and tie us together the best I can. I hope it's enough.

As soon as we're on our way, Marric puts his head on mine, slumping backward.

"Marric? Are you all right?"

No reply.

"Marric?" My panic is entering my voice, but I can't bring myself to care. "You have to wake up."

I reach behind me to feel his head. It's burning. His infection must be getting worse. I need to clean it. "Marric, we have to stop."

"No," he finally mutters back.

"We're almost back to where Saldor caught up with us. It has to be safe."

When he doesn't reply, I take matters into my own hands. I find a clearing up ahead and pull the horse to a stop. The rest of the horses follow suit.

"I'm going to untie us now," I say. "You have to get off the horse. Can you do that?"

"Mmm," is the only response I get.

It has to be enough. My fingers shake as I work to untie the knot I made. I should have insisted we stop before. I don't know what I was thinking. I should have put more effort into making sure he's well. Instead, I took us on a tiring journey, trying to get away from Saldor and his men.

Forget untying the rope. I pull out my sword and slice through it. Once done, it's a lot of work to get the rope unwound from around us. Marric barely helps.

"Do you want me to dismount first, or do you want to?" I ask him.

No reply. To make matters worse, he's leaning on me heavily.

"I'm going to get off the horse first," I say. "Then I'll help you. But you have to hold on until then. You hear me?"

"Mmm."

I don't know how well this is going to go, but I have to try. I throw my leg over the horse and stumble off. Marric sways heavily, to the point I worry he's going to fall.

"Stay with me." I put my hand on his leg, reaching up for his hand. "Give me your hand, and I'll help you down." I hope I don't take us to the dirt if I can't support him.

He gives me his hand and slides from the horse so quickly we both tumble. He lands on me, and I grunt, the air knocked out of me. He half-rolls off me, and I half-push him off. Guilt pricks me for doing so, but I can't help him if I can't move.

It doesn't feel like anything's broken, just bruised. I turn to him and rip his shirt so I can see his shoulder. It's worse than ever, leaking yellowish pus, red streaks coming off it in all directions.

"Marric, you have to make me create something to fix this. It's really bad."

He groans.

"You have to give me more than that. I don't know what to do."

"Get to Idolo."

"You think he can help us?"

"Magic."

"His magic can heal you?" I'm desperate for an answer.

"Maybe."

Maybe isn't enough, but it's all I've got. "What about Medina? Isn't there something you can have me make to help?"

"I don't know. What we made before."

I have him make me create more alcohol, a shirt, and honey. After a quick cleaning and putting his new shirt on, which is a real struggle, I help him back on the white horse. He falls three times, before we manage it.

I hop on the horse and tie us back together. I let the other horses go. Even his black one. I won't be stopping again until we reach Idolo. Marric has to make it until then.

CHAPTER 43

I'M EXHAUSTED BEYOND BELIEF. Marric hasn't answered me in hours, but I feel his pulse where I hold his wrist. I hope he's getting a restful sleep—one he'll come back from. The thought presses me on harder. My poor horse is about done in. Maybe it was a mistake to let the others go. It doesn't matter now. I don't have any other option.

We've reached the North Shore, only no one's here. I've been wandering for what feels like an hour, attempting to find something, but there's no one around.

"Marric, you have to help me. I don't know what to do."

Of course, he doesn't respond. I try not to panic, but dread is creeping up on me.

If I had my power, I'd make a compass that could point to Idolo the Wise, but without my power, I'm as useless as a human. I should have thought of it while he was still awake. Why didn't I think of it sooner? Because I'm a fool.

I head toward the last area to the east I haven't explored. I can tell by looking at it that it's nothing but flat land as far as the eye can see, but I have to try.

Despair fills me. I don't want Marric to die. What's worse is I can do nothing to stop it. I can't create anything. I can't find Idolo. I can't save Marric.

He feels so hot, slumped against my back. Hotter than a person should be. I'll head for the open sea and put Marric in it. If I can get him off this horse. There's no other way I can think of to cool him down. I don't even know if that will help; I only know I have to do something.

As I move to the last of the flat land, I call out, "Idolo the Wise, please. I need your help."

Of course, nothing happens. I call several more times, but there's nothing for it. Either Charmina lied and he was never here, or he left after she told me where he was. I don't know what to think. She needs this collar off of me as much as I do, if she's telling the truth about there being a war in the heavens.

I head to the ocean, giving in to my last resort. I have little alcohol and honey left—not that they seem to have helped in a while. Marric needs much more than I can give him.

"Izlana," a male voice calls out. "Goddess, I'm over here."

I turn to find a young man running toward me. He's got short blond hair and appears youthful from this distance. He must be no older than fifteen.

"Who are you?" What does a youth want with me? And how does he know my name?

"I'm Idolo. Quickly, follow me. We've got to work fast if we're to save your escort."

Idolo? My escort? None of this makes sense. But he sounds as if he's here to help. I have to follow him. He's the only chance we have.

I follow him back toward an area I already searched through. Flat, the same as everything else. Only when this Idolo stops, a cabin appears. Maybe he really is Idolo the Wise.

As soon as I stop next to him, he says, "Untie the rope. We have to get him in the house."

I do as he says, my fingers stiff from days of riding and trying to keep Marric with me. The knot finally comes undone, and though Idolo is small compared to Marric, he helps catch Marric as he falls off the horse.

I slide down after Marric, stumbling a little. I don't bother tying up the horse. I hurry to help Idolo carry Marric inside.

Marric is limp except for his hand, which still holds tight to my chain. His muscled body makes him heavy. His feet drag behind us, and his shoulder probably hurts the way we're carrying him, with one of us on each side of his torso, our arms around him. But it's the best we can do.

Idolo's front door is open. We drag Marric through it, doing a kind of sideways twist. There's a couch in the front room, where Idolo says we should lay Marric. I'm grateful it's right there because my muscles ache and I'm sweating. It's nothing compared to how my heart feels, though.

"What can I do?" I ask Idolo.

"Where's his wound?"

"In his shoulder."

"Take off his shirt." He disappears into a back room.

I get to work, trying to get Marric's shirt off of him with shaking hands. I resort to cutting it with my blade and ripping it the rest of the way open. I avoid glancing at his wound. It smells foully. How is he going to survive from this? I don't know.

CHAPTER 44

IDOLO COMES RACING in the room, arms full of what look like potions. I hurry out of the way but close enough that I can see what's going on.

"Tell me what I need to do," I say.

"Hold that." Idolo hands me a jar of pink liquid. "And that. And that." He hands me two more jars, one with a blue liquid and the other with a sick-looking brown one. "I need to pull out the infection with magic. It's the only thing that can save him. His wound is much worse than I thought it would be. I have no idea if he'll make it."

Tears form in my eyes, and I rapidly blink the salty water away.

Idolo puts his hands on Marric's shoulder and mumbles something under his breath. The longer this continues, the more stressed I become. I bite my lip to keep from saying something. I don't want him to lose his focus, but I'm aching to know what's going on.

Finally, Idolo turns to me, face pale. "Give me the brown potion."

I hand it to him, clinging to the other two. Marric looks a little better now. His face isn't so white, and he doesn't seem to be sweating as much. His wound no longer has pus in it, but angry red lines go through it still. We're not out of the woods yet.

Idolo pours the brown liquid over Marric's shoulder and wound. He rubs it in, not as gentle as I would expect him to be with a wound like this.

This time, he holds his hand out without turning. "The pink one."

I hand it to him, and he does the same thing with it before racing out of the room. Marric is panting. I kneel down by his legs, take his hand, and give it a squeeze. He has to survive this. He just has to.

Idolo comes back in the room with a wet towel. I start to get up, to get out of his way, but he goes around me.

"Stay there," he says. "He can use as much of your support as he can get."

Idolo works fast, cleaning the potions from the wound. Once they're all clear, he asks me for the blue potion. I give it to him, and he uncorks it and ever so slowly pours out the tiniest drop onto Marric's shoulder.

"This one is potent. It can kill a man, but if we don't use it, he'll die for sure," Idolo says.

"What do we do now?" I ask.

"We wait." He covers the wound with a bandage and places a blanket over Marric.

I don't move from my spot next to Marric. I keep holding his hand, wishing there was more I could do.

Sometime later, Idolo brings a bowl of stew. "For you," he says.

I don't take my gaze off Marric. "I'm not hungry."

"You have to eat, to keep your strength up. You still have a long journey ahead of you."

Reluctantly, I take the bowl and eat. The food is probably fine, but it tastes bland. It's hearty, though, with lots of meat and vegetables. It's been a long time since I ate. My poor stomach aches for food. Idolo brings me a second bowl and a third.

On my fourth bowl, I slow. "Is he going to be all right?" I ask Idolo.

"It's too soon to say. He would be dead for sure had you not brought him to me as quickly as you did."

That reminds me "How did you realize we were coming? How did you know Marric was injured?"

He smiles, and his eyes take on an experienced look that belies his age. "I know a great many things."

"How?" I demand. "I have a right to know."

He simply says, "Magic."

That's unhelpful, to say the least, but then, does it really matter? Do I have to understand everything? Most mortals think I should, but far from it. I have a lot left to learn, and there are more important things I need from Idolo right at this moment.

"Do you know how to get me out of this device?" I ask pointing to my neck.

"I do. Only Marric or I can accomplish such a task. Well, and Pennington, but he won't."

No, he sure won't. But Marric? I knew he was strong, but I didn't know he was that strong. "How can it be done?"

Before Idolo can respond, Marric turns to the side and heaves. When he's done being sick, he sits up and blinks. "Where am I?"

Idolo's done it. Marric is alive.

CHAPTER 45

IDOLO and I help clean up Marric and give him a shirt to put on. He sits up, looking as good as I've ever seen him. My heart is full at the sight of him. I never want to take my gaze off him again.

"What happened?" Marric asks.

"What do you remember?" I ask.

"Riding the horse away from Saldor's camp. I think you cleaned my wound," he says, looking at me.

"That's right, I did. And then I brought you here, where Idolo healed you."

Marric glances around the room. "Where is he, so I can thank him?"

"I'm right here," Idolo says.

Marric's eyes grow wide. "You're Idolo the Wise?"

"I am," Idolo says.

"Thank you for my life. I owe you a great debt."

"And you will pay that debt," Idolo says. "You are not yet finished escorting Izlana through this world and into the next. You must complete that task, and your debt to me will be repaid."

"I don't understand," Marric says, looking at me. "I need to help her in order to repay my debt to you?"

Idolo nods. "It's the only thing you can do to repay it."

"What I don't understand," I say, "is how he's going to get me to the heavens."

"It will come to you when it is time, but right now, that's one thing we don't have. Take your swords, both of you. Pennington will be here shortly."

"Pennington?" Fear makes my chest ache.

"You have to tell us how to get the collar off." Marric grabs hold of his blade.

I take a hold of my own sword, my grip tighter than it should be.

"You will know what to do," Idolo says.

"Why don't you tell us?" I ask.

Before Idolo can respond, the door bangs open, and Pennington storms in. "Give me the girl," he demands, as several of his men pour in around him.

"You can't have her." Idolo surprises me by standing in front of me, a dagger drawn.

I should have had Marric help me create a long sword for Idolo, but the dagger will have to be enough. Before I can do anything, Pennington runs Idolo through.

CHAPTER 46

RAGE CONSUMES ME. Idolo is not only the only one who can tell me how to get this collar off, but he also saved Marric's life. Not to mention he's young. He still has his entire life ahead of him.

I let my blade do the talking, fueling it with my fury. I step over Idolo's body, careful not to look at him while there's still a fight going on. Grateful my sword knows what it's doing, I let it.

Men fall at my feet as quick as they move to shield Pennington. Guilt stabs at me over their death or injuries—they're just protecting him, after all. But I can't allow myself to be taken hostage once again. And I certainly can't let them harm Marric or Idolo further.

Soon, Marric is at my side. Together we fight, fierce and strong, though I know it's not our skill getting us by. Our swords pierce and jab and attack like nothing else. Pennington is backing away.

One man comes at me with a howl. His blade moves so fast, I don't know how I'll keep up with it, but my blade keeps going like it's nothing, ducking around his and cutting him with ease.

The cowards are running from us. I move to chase Pennington, who's getting away, but Marric calls me back. "Idolo needs us."

I restrain myself. After making certain neither Pennington nor any of his men are coming back, I turn back to Idolo and Marric.

I try not to think of the bodies I'm stepping around. Marric is already on the floor where Idolo lies. I kneel down beside him. Idolo's eyes flutter. His wound looks like he's not going to make it through the next minute.

"Marric," he says in a strained voice, "you must use your magic to unlock Izlana's collar."

"But I don't know how."

"Let the… power of the earth… guide you." With that, the light goes out of Idolo's eyes.

CHAPTER 47

Marric and I go through the bodies of the slain men, looking for survivors. We find three with varying degrees of injuries and do what we can to help them. Marric has me create what's needed to take care of them the best we know how.

"Bury your dead," I tell them. "Then be on your way. Don't let me find you on Pennington's side again, or you'll end up like these men."

"Yes, ma'am," they all say, like good soldiers.

Hopefully they can go home to their families or whatever awaits them.

With a little of Marric's help, we dig a grave for Idolo. Marric's still not fully recovered, but he does what he can, while I do the brunt of the work. My hands ache, but it's nothing compared to how my heart twists.

We find a nice spot behind the back of his house, where there's a little garden. We do what we can for him, trying to make the area nice before leaving. It's not much, but it's something.

"I wonder if he had any family," I say.

"With as young as he was, his parents could still be around,"

Marric replies. "But I get the feeling he knew he was going to die. Maybe he already sent on word to them."

"I get that feeling too." Sadness creeps over me. I barely knew him, but he gave his life for me.

We walk around to the front of the house.

"Should we try to open the collar again?" I ask. Neither of us has brought it up since Idolo's passing, but I can't wait any longer to get it off.

Marric doesn't look at me. "I don't know if I can."

"Idolo believed you could."

"But I don't have that much magic. What I do have, I've barely used."

I take his hand, trying not to be self-conscious about it. "I understand you're scared. It's hard, but this is something only you and Pennington can do now, and we both know Pennington never will. I believe in you. You can do this."

He closes his eyes and squeezes my hand. I remain quiet, letting him think things through. It takes far longer than I'd like. It's hard to stand here, saying and doing nothing, when there's so much that needs to be done. But I have to let him figure this out for himself.

When he opens his eyes, there's a new resolve in them. "There is a lot of magic in me. I can feel it. I'll try not to be afraid."

"Thank you," I say, realizing how much this is costing him. After his father's torture using magic, it's got to be one of the hardest things in the world to do.

He leaves the end of my chain on the ground and brings both hands up, each on one side of my collar. He takes a deep breath. "Here we go."

I study his face. He's concentrating harder than I've ever seen him before, though I wish I could see those hazel eyes of his. I hold still, trying not to distract him any more than my being here does.

As time passes, I wonder what it is he's doing. I assume he's reaching inside for his magic, trying to figure out how to harness it. I don't know what I'll do if it doesn't work. I can't handle wearing this collar the rest of my life.

How would I be able to serve the people? Marric would have to go with me everywhere, asking me to fulfill every little request. It's been hard enough doing it this long, I can't imagine having to do it all the time. My followers need me. The human race needs me. I can't fail them.

"Izlana, goddess of creation, this collar will be locked no more." When Marric speaks, it startles me, but I don't move.

There's a faint *click*. He opens his eyes and smiles while he slips the collar off my neck.

"You did it," I say in a hushed voice.

"I didn't know I had it in me."

"But you did." The air stings on my neck, but it feels oh-so-good.

"You're free," he says.

And it's true. I am. I can create anything I want to, and not a soul can stop me.

EPISODE FOUR

Episode Four

CHAPTER 48

I MAKE A NEW CLOAK, just because I can. Granted, my old one was filthy and tattered, but I don't *need* a new one. I want it. Especially since I have my powers of creation back. I untie my old one, let it fall to the ground, and swing the new one around me before tying it right.

"What are we going to do about this collar?" Marric asks, picking it up the collar that was around my neck and is now open.

"I don't know. It seems like a dangerous thing to leave lying about," I respond, pulling my hood over my hair.

"It'd be a pain to take with us." He heaves it upward, the chain it's linked to following after it.

"Can you destroy it?"

He studies it. "I can try."

"It would be worthwhile. I don't think we want to hide it. Someone might find it. Not that they'd know it could harness a god, but I don't want to take that chance."

He nods. "It might take me a minute."

I'm eager to be on my way. To find an entrance to the heavens and stop wars both there and on this world, but this must be done.

I create a soft rocking chair and sit in it to look at the world around me.

Idolo's house is before us, surround by flat lands, except to the north, where there's nothing but sea. It's not my preferred landscape, but it's nice in its own way. It took several days' journey to get here. It could be twice as long to find a gate to the heavens.

I don't want to stay on this world any longer than I have to; it's not treated me well. But I don't even know where a gate to the heavens might be. When Ramco brought me over, I wasn't paying attention. I thought he'd stay with me. And then, when I was captured, I was so distraught over being collared I didn't take in the path we followed.

Lesson learned. Doesn't matter how distraught I am; I have to pay attention to my surroundings. Now I'm going to have to pay for it. Unless I can create a compass that tells me how to get there. It would have worked for Idolo, but I don't know if it would work for the heavens.

While Marric continues working on the collar, I focus my power on making a compass. It doesn't take long for one to appear in my hands, but the arrow swirls around, pointing first one way and then another. It continues moving around no matter if I stay still or try to follow it. I sigh. A compass isn't going to work.

Maybe Charmina will tell me how to get home. The goddess of love was helpful last time I spoke with her. She may be willing to help again if she's as eager to have me back home as she says she is.

I'm not going back to the temple we went to, though. That priestess was onerous, to say the least.

There's a sloshing sound, and Marric is standing before a puddle of iron.

"You did it." I'm most impressed with his power. I knew he would be strong since he could get the collar off me, but to see him reduce it to a puddle makes me all the more in awe of him. Never thought I'd be in awe of a mortal.

He shrugs. "Magic is getting easier to do. Not that I want it to."

I go to him and put a hand on his shoulder. "You're brave for taking control of it."

He takes my hand in his. "Brave or stupid. One of the two."

"Definitely the first, even if it doesn't feel that way."

He sighs. "Where to? Seems like we worked so long to get the collar off you that I don't know what to do next."

Same here. But there's one thing we have to do. "You should go home to your family. They need you."

"No. I promised Idolo I'd escort you from this world into the next."

"Well then, we'll have to take a detour to see your family."

For a brief moment, his eyes brighten. Before I can fully comprehend how much this would make him happy, the look is gone. "We can't do that. Not with wars going on in both the heavens and this world."

"They aren't wars yet. We still have a little time," I say. "Besides, this is what I'd really like to do."

"If you're sure?"

"I am. Before we go, what can I create to make this journey easier for you?"

CHAPTER 49

I CREATE A MEAL FOR US. Other than sustenance, there's not much we need besides rest, but I'm too anxious to be away from this place to relax. Pennington knows we're here—though now I have my power back, I'm not scared of him. Let him face my wrath.

We share the horse, with me riding in back, arms around Marric.

"How far is it to your home?" I ask.

"If they're still in the same place, it's a three-day journey." His voice is almost giddy.

That's longer than I hoped it would be. Maybe I shouldn't have offered to visit his family, but I can't take it back when he's so excited to see them. "Do you think they'll be somewhere else?" I ask.

His chest moves against my arms, as he sighs. "I hope not, but they haven't heard from me in too long. If they needed a job to pay their bills, they may have moved."

"We'll hope for the best, then," I say, relishing the feel of him in my arms. "If they aren't there, someone is bound to know where they went."

"We can't spend much time looking for them, though."

He's right. The three-day journey is a lot to take out of my time while trying to get back to the heavens, but I can't leave his family to the unknown any longer. He's done so much for me, and it's the least I can do for him.

We ride until nightfall and then make camp. It's much easier when I have my power, instead of needing Marric to ask for every little thing. It's freeing.

We continue our travel like that for two days. On the third day, Marric is tense on the horse.

"Are you all right?" I ask.

"I'm fi— Actually, I'm stressed about today."

"Do you want to talk about it?"

"It's just that I don't know what to do if they aren't there. And if they are, what condition will they be in? I can't imagine they'll be too happy to see me after I abandoned them."

I give him a gentle squeeze. "It'll be all right. I'll be with you."

"Thank you."

We've passed more people on the road today than any of the previous days. The road's getting downright crowded. People are flocking to the city. Men. Women. Children. They're all here—all headed the same way as us.

Most of them of them look weary, their clothes threadbare and tattered and exhaustion lining their faces. Children are the worst. They don't try to run and play, like I'd expect, but stay close to any adults they're with.

If I weren't trying to keep my status hidden, I'd create them toys and treats. As is, I have to hurt, watching them and knowing I shouldn't do anything for them.

When we get to the city walls, soldiers stand on both sides of the gate. They scan the crowd, but I don't know what they're looking for. I keep my hood pulled low over my eyes and hug Marric tight. If they're looking for me, they're going to be in for a surprise if they try to stop us.

But they don't. We get through the gate just fine.

"I'm getting down to lead the horse," Marric tells me. "There are too many people here. You stay on, though. I don't want to lose you in this crowd."

He slips off the horse, taking the reins. I keep my gaze focused on him instead of the city around us in case something happens. I can't lose track of him.

He leads us through the cramped streets like he knows where he's going. I wonder how long he lived with his family here before becoming a servant in Pennington's household. And why did he travel so far to become a servant?

"Refugees to the right," a soldier calls out.

Refugees? Is that what all these people are? What are they running from and why?

When Marric tries to go to the left, a soldier stops him. "Where do you think you're going?"

"My family lives this way."

"How do I know that for certain?" The soldier asks.

"You could run and get my family. They could vouch for me." Marric continues to give directions to where his lives, directions that don't make much sense to me, but the soldier is nodding.

"Very well. I'll let you go, but don't cause any problems."

The soldier lets the horse pass, and we're in a street with barely any people. It's strange after being so crammed.

"Let me walk beside you," I tell Marric.

He stops the horse and lets me off. Together we walk down the street. I have the strongest urge to take his hand, but I don't know if I should.

The houses become more and more rundown as we go, until they're just shacks. The odd thing is, there's no one about. Not a soul. After the crowds we encountered entering the city, it's eerie and leaves me feeling like we don't belong. Like we should turn back the way we came. As a goddess, I'm not accustomed to such places. But for Marric's sake, I keep trudging forward.

The road kicks up dirt as we go. I feel like I could use a good hot bath and a warm meal. I could create these things if it weren't for our current circumstances, but maybe Marric's family will need my power for creation more than I want it. The city around us says as much, but who knows what we'll discover when we find them?

Marric comes to a stop outside a house that's got a clean exterior but is as run down as the others. A broken window. Sagging roof. Door barely hanging onto its hinges. It's a sad sight, but if it's home, it must be welcoming to him.

I clasp my hands together. What will his family think of me? Will they be disgusted with me for taking him away this long? Will they hate me because I'm not like them? There are too many unknowns and not enough answers. I hope all goes smoothly.

CHAPTER 50

MARRIC GLANCES AT ME. He seems as nervous as I feel, if not more. "I'm going to leave the horse out here, but it may get taken."

I shrug. It's the least of our worries. "We can always buy another."

But to make him feel better, I create a rope and hand it to Marric to tie the horse up. With a deep breath, he knocks on the door. There's a scurry of movement inside, but then all falls quiet. He knocks again. Silence.

Finally, a female voice comes. "Who's there?"

"It's me. Marric."

The door bursts open so fast, I'm afraid it'll fall off its hinges. A beautiful girl about my age comes hurtling out and into Marric's arms. He staggers before holding her tight. She's got brown hair and the same hazel eyes as him. Eyes that find mine and widen.

But she doesn't say anything. She holds on tight to her brother. At least I assume this is his sister, the girl he talked about. She certainly looks like she could be.

"It's all right," Marric says. "I'm home now."

He doesn't say anything about how we have to go soon. How

we've got important work that must be done for all of humanity. He whispers sweet reassurances.

"What am I thinking?" she finally asks. Her voice is a sweet melody. "Come in." She looks me over with a speculative eye as she urges her brother in.

MARRIC REACHES a hand out toward me. "Brusha, this is my friend. She's going to be staying with us while I'm here."

I take his hand, grateful for something to hold on to. Even more grateful that it's him.

She ushers us in and shuts the door behind us. Inside, several pairs of eyes stare at us in the gloom. Once they realize who Marric is, they rush him, hugging him and forcing him to let go of my hand.

While he's dealing with his younger siblings, Brusha turns to me. "I didn't catch your name."

If I told her, she wouldn't believe me. "You can call me Izzy."

Marric catches my eye, but then is turned back to his crowd of siblings.

"Welcome, Izzy. I'm sorry we don't have more to offer you," Brusha says.

"I have everything I need. Thank you."

She nods before focusing on her brother. After the kids have finished hugging him, they settle down and sit on the floor. That's when I realize there's no furniture in the place, only a bundle of blankets over in one corner and a chest in the other.

No table. No chairs. No beds. Just one tiny room with a door in the front and a door in the back and one broken window for light. These are the conditions they're living in. No wonder Marric has been so worried about them. They look as if they need a good meal. I'm ready to create one for them right here and now, but I don't know if I should do it in front of them yet.

"It's so good to see you all," Marric says. "I've missed you."

Brusha's expression goes from one of love to a stern, straight-lipped one. "Where have you been? Why haven't you written? I knew you shouldn't have gone to a different town. Have you been with this girl instead of making a living for us?"

The words hurt, though they aren't directed at me. I have distracted Marric from his family, even if I sorely needed him. Without him, I'd still be under Pennington's control, and who knows what the world would be like? Marric was needed where he was. I just feel bad it's hard for them to understand.

"I'll answer what I can," he replies. "But first, I want to look at you. You can't imagine how much I've missed you."

She seems to soften at this, her lips no longer a thin line. "We've missed you too."

"I'm sorry I haven't been able to write or send money."

"It's all right," Brusha says, looking down. "I was able to find work helping Silca, down at the market."

"Who watches the children?" Marric's voice is almost stern.

I haven't seen this side of him before, loving and caring over his family. It's a side I like, though he shouldn't have the entire weight of his family on his shoulders.

"I watched them," a girl about thirteen says. "I would have gone to work too, but Brusha insisted I was needed here more."

"As well you were," Marric says. "You've done good, Brusha."

"Not as well as I would have liked, but we did what we had to," she says. "What about you? Where've you been? We were so worried that something happened to you."

"Nothing so bad." Marric glances at me.

"Did you go and get yourself married?" Brusha sounds cross.

I blush.

"Nothing like that," Marric says, and though it's true, my heart gives a little pang. "I have been helping her, though."

"You've been helping her instead of your own family?" Brusha turns to me. "No offense."

"None taken," I say. "I can't imagine how hard it's been on you."

"She was locked up. What should I have done? Left her there?"

This seems to soften Brusha. "No. Of course not. It's just that... well, don't you see who's missing?"

I do a quick count of everyone in the room except me and Marric. There are only six people. Marric said he had seven siblings. A foreboding squeezes my chest.

"Where's Neham?" Marric asks in a low voice.

"He's been conscripted."

CHAPTER 51

I GASP.

Marric's shoulders slump. "How did this happen? Who conscripted him? We're not even at war."

"Where have you been?" Brusha asks. "We're on the brink of war. Both General Saldor and Lord Pennington are trying to take over this land. They've been taking our men and boys, coming through with other soldiers demanding they be served or they'll hurt the men's family."

Anger boils in me. "Not if I have anything to say about it."

She looks at me with crinkled eyebrows. "What can you do?"

I shrug. Maybe I can trust them, but I don't want to tell them unless we have to.

"We've been trying to stop Pennington and Saldor," Marric says for me.

"You?" Brusha asks. "What could you two possibly do against the strongest men in the world?"

"Fight. It's what we should all be doing," Marric says with conviction. "Which army conscripted Neham?"

"Saldor's men."

Marric gives me a sharp look. He's probably thinking the same thing as me. Neham could have been in the very camp we were held in. Not everyone came to get their swords when I made them. I'm more grateful than ever that I made those weapons not dangerous. Though maybe that's a problem for Neham. Maybe he won't be able to defend himself. What have I done?

I may have just killed Marric's little brother.

Marric will never forgive me. I'll never forgive myself.

"When did they take him?" Marric asks.

"About a month ago," Brusha says.

"There has to be something we can do," I say.

"There isn't," Brusha says. "Not unless you want to die. Saldor is killing all who oppose him."

"So we've noticed. We'll find a way to save him." I put my hand on Marric's back.

Marric says, "He's so young. I can't imagine him having to deal with a war."

I can't either. "Where is Saldor now? Do you know?"

She shakes her head. "He didn't come for Neham himself; he sent other soldiers. Pennington has been doing the same. It's why the streets are so empty. Everyone is hiding unless they're refugees, and they have no other choice but to be out in the open. Even the market is only open one day a week instead of six."

That explains what we saw when we came in. "We can't stay. We have to go find your brother."

Brusha looks at me with newly found respect.

"How can we go against an entire army?" Marric asks.

"We'll find a way, but the longer we wait, the more likely..." Something bad will happen to Neham. I don't dare say it aloud in front of the children.

"I know," Marric says. "But we have to get you back home."

"Where is home for you, Izzy?" Brusha asks.

"I don't know. We need to find out."

She gives me a quizzical glance. "How can you not know?"

I shrug. It's too complicated to explain without giving away who I am. "Do you know where the refugees are coming from?"

Brusha says, "All over the countryside. People who had farms. The town Saldor originated from. All over. People know it's safe here. Or at least, it was."

"Do you have food?" Marric asks Brusha, bringing us to a topic that feels more important.

She lowers her head, and her response is a quiet *no*.

That explains why the children are so thin.

"We'll go get some for you." Marric give me a meaningful look. "But then we'll have to go again. I need to get Izzy home, and then we'll go save Neham."

I want to argue with him, but there'll be plenty of time for that.

"When will we see you again?" Brusha says.

"We'll be back with food soon."

"The market isn't open today," she says.

"We'll find some. Don't you worry. And it won't take long."

"And after you come back, how long will you be gone this time, searching for Neham?"

"As long as it takes."

I put on my fiercest expression. We will be getting him back.

CHAPTER 52

WE HURRY out of the house through the back door. There's no one out there. It's as good a place as any to create things. Though the houses around us have windows, most of them are covered with fabric. I'll have to chance it out here.

Marric stands in front of me, silent. I create sacks of food—some fresh, like apples and bread. I make dried meat and dried fruit. I didn't see a way for them to cook, so I don't add things like flour to the list.

I also make a small bag of krats.

"Thank you," Marric says. "You didn't have to do all this."

"I wish I could do more."

His gaze brushes over my lips, and I have the urge to lean into him. But now's not the time. Not with his brother conscripted and me trying to find the heavens. I'll be leaving soon. I can't complicate matters.

Marric takes the bigger bag of food from me. It should be enough to last them a while if they're careful. And there's plenty of money to buy more.

I follow him back inside.

Brusha looks up, startled. "You weren't kidding about not being gone long."

Marric goes to the trunk in the corner and stashes the food in it.

"How did you have money for all of this?" Brusha asks.

"Don't worry about that." I hand her the bag of krats. "Don't spend a lot at one time, or you'll draw attention to yourself."

Her eyes grow big as she peeks in the bag. "Where did you get this?"

"I have my ways," I reply.

"I can't accept it." She holds out the bag.

"I won't take it back," I say. "I have no use for it."

"Please take it," Marric says. "It's the least we can do. Sorry I can't stay. Please keep the children safe until I come back."

"I'll do what I can," she says. "We're careful, and none of the other boys are old enough to join an army, so we'll be fine. I'm more worried about you."

"I'll be all right. I have Izzy to protect me."

Brusha looks at me like she doesn't believe I'm much of a threat to anyone. I don't blame her. I can't appear like much. But I put my hand on the hilt of my sword, as if to say I'm a tough warrior.

"Where's the closest temple?" I ask.

"Ramco's is the closest, just outside the city," Brusha says.

"That won't do," I reply. "What's the next closest?"

"Azer, god of wisdom, has one about five miles west from here."

"That's better. We'll go there."

"You're going to worship?" she asks. "In hopes the gods will give you strength to find my brother and make it to your home?"

"Something like that."

"We should go," Marric says.

"At least stay and eat with us," Brusha says.

He shakes his head. "I would love to, but the sooner we get going, the sooner I can find Neham."

One by one, he takes the children in his arms and whispers in their ears. When he gets to Brusha, unshed tears shine in his eyes. I can't imagine what this must be like for him—finding his family in such a state, only to have to turn around and leave. At least we could provide food for them. I'm grateful we came, if only for that.

"I will return, little sister," he tells her.

"You'd better."

"I will, with Neham in tow."

"What about Izzy?" she asks, turning toward me. "Will we see you again?"

I almost tell her to go worship at a temple of creation and I'll be sure to visit, but I can't promise that. Maybe I can leave word with Marric to tell her so, after I'm gone and safe.

"I don't know," I say. "It seems unlikely."

Brusha looks from me to Marric and back again. "But I thought..." She shakes her head. "Never mind. It was good to meet you. Thank you for all you've done for my family."

"I only wish it was more."

With that, we're out the door. Luckily, our horse still awaits us. I don't climb on, though. I walk next to Marric as we make our way. I can't help but feel like we're leaving good people behind and going to find worse people on our trip. Saldor will get what's coming to him, though. I'll make certain of that.

CHAPTER 53

IT'S HARDER LEAVING the city than it was getting in. We're going against the crowd of people, all of whom must think we're crazy for wanting out of the relative safety the walls provide. If Saldor and Pennington are taking away their men and boys to fight in a war, it can't be as safe as they imagine.

Once we're out of the city, I ask Marric, "Do you know where the temple of wisdom is?"

"I do. Should we go there first or try to find Saldor's army?"

"It's a tough call. We know where the temple is but not where Saldor is. Another problem—we don't know how to get your brother out of the camp once we find Saldor's army."

"That's true. I'm just anxious to get him away from the fighting."

"He shouldn't have to be there. With any luck, there's more marching and training than fighting going on right now."

He nods, but I know his heart isn't into it. "Let's ride. We'll be at the temple of wisdom in a couple hours that way."

He climbs on the horse before helping me on too. We ride together, and though it's nice to be with him, I'm filled with tension. How are we going to rescue his brother? We know most of their weapons are useless, except for the two swords they took from us that will always hurt their enemies. Those two swords alone are cause for concern. Plus, Saldor knows who we are, so it's not like we can pretend to want to join his army.

We'll have to sneak in, but there's no telling if we'll find the right camp.

"Where do you think we can find Saldor's army?" I ask Marric.

"I don't know. It's funny that we were just running from him and now we want to find him."

"Yeah." I shift my position. "They may be where we left them. If they're not, we can always listen for rumors. It shouldn't be too hard to find an entire army."

"*We*, huh?"

"Yes, *we*."

"I thought that you'd have us go to the heavens, for me to drop you off, before I went on the search for my brother."

I don't have a quick response to that. What I want to do is help him, but I'm not sure I'm supposed to. The world and heavens could depend on this decision. It's not something to be taken lightly.

"Maybe we should see what happens at Azer's temple," I say.

"Do you know Azer?"

"I know all the gods."

"It's still weird to think you know them. That you're one of them." He puts a hand on one of mine, where they're wrapped around his waist. "I can't believe I'm touching a goddess," he says.

I rest my head on his back and give a little sigh. "I have to tell you something."

"That sounds serious." He doesn't let go.

"It's that,"—I take a deep breath—"I think I have feelings for you."

He stiffens.

Did I say the wrong thing? I shouldn't have admitted my feelings for him. The way he's acted, I hoped he felt the same way, but clearly, there's something else going on here. Maybe I misread his friendship for more.

I go to move my hand from underneath his, but he grabs it. "Sorry. I didn't mean to react like that. It's just hard to believe." He slides down and helps me off, keeping his hands at my waist long after he needs to. Looking into my eyes, he says, "I have feelings for you, too."

A surge of joy rushes through me. His gaze dips to my lips. I want a kiss so much, but the way things are going to be, I shouldn't complicate matters more. In fact, I shouldn't have said anything. No matter how happy what he said makes me, it's not the right thing.

"We should get going," I say.

"Right."

We climb back on the horse, this time with me in the front. He wraps his arms around me while holding the reigns. I feel safe and protected, like nothing can ever hurt me, but it's not true.

Still, I enjoy the moment for what it is. I like him too much not to.

The sun starts to sink in the sky. If we don't get there soon, we'll have to stop for the night.

"Are we going to make it there?" I ask.

"We should be able to see it already. I don't know why we can't."

A sense of foreboding pricks me. "We should move faster."

He urges the horse on. It's not much longer before we see the ruins of what must have once been a great temple to the god Azer.

CHAPTER 54

WE WALK through the ruins of the temple while our horse waits outside.

"How can someone have destroyed another temple?" I ask. "Don't they have any sense of what's sacred?"

"Apparently not." Marric picks up a chunk of what looks like white marble. "This place has been obliterated. Magic must have been a part of it with how big this explosion seems."

We look at each other, and at the same time say, "Pennington."

"Why would he be destroying temples, though?" I ask.

"It's a good question," a male voice says.

I turn around to see a man of about forty wading through the rubble toward us. "Who are you?" I ask.

"I'm Tylew, the priest of this temple. Or I was. What are you two doing in the ruins?"

"I was hoping to find some answers," I say. "But I can see that's not going to be the case." What am I going to do? Will I find a temple where I can talk to a god, without it being ruined?

As Tylew walks closer, he gets a better look at me and bows. "Izlana, goddess of creation, forgive me. I did not recognize you."

"It's fine. I'm in hiding, anyway."

"Yes, I've heard men are looking for you. Only you're no longer wearing the collar they spoke of."

I grin. "Nope. I'm free to do as I will, and no one will have power over me. This is Marric," I say as Tylew joins us.

Tylew nods. "Pleasure to meet you, though I wish it were under better circumstances."

"Do you have a way to contact Azer?" I ask.

"Alas, the statue of the god of wisdom was broken when Pennington destroyed the temple. There's no way to contact him. I've only been staying around to help patrons who come this way seeking guidance. Unfortunately, with the temple ruined, there have been less and less of them."

Curse Pennington. I'd bet anything he's not destroying Ramco's temples, though.

"How long ago was your temple destroyed?" Marric asks Tylew.

"About a week."

I bite my lip. I'm not sure I should give away the fact that I don't know how to reenter the heavens, but if I don't ask, how will I find out if he knows? That settles it. "Do you know of any entrances to the heavens?"

His brows raise. "You do not?"

"I'm looking for one." I evade an answer, though in doing so I give it away.

"I do not know. Azer never had need of me to use one to guide a human to. He already has a mate, and I could speak with him through the statue."

I remember Azer's mate—a woman about his age, kind and gentle. Not that I had much interaction with her. The mates of gods tend to stick together, rather than interacting with other gods, except for rare occasions like a feast. That won't be happening now. Not with Ramco trying to start a war in the heavens.

"I'm sorry I can't be more help to you," Tylew says.

"Thank you, anyway," I reply. "Best of luck to you."

"And to you."

Marric and I make our way out of the ruins. When we're out of earshot of Tylew, Marric says, "Do you think he was telling the truth?"

"I believe so. There wouldn't be reason for him to know where an entrance is. I need to speak with another god to find out."

"How are we going to contact one?"

"We'll have to keep looking."

He sighs.

"Not before we find your brother, though," I say.

"We can't do that. You have to get back."

"I do, but there are temples on the way to the last place we saw Saldor's camp. Aren't there?"

"There are two."

"Which two?" I ask.

"A temple of pain and a temple of beauty. Will either of those work?"

"Maybe. We should try them both, though I don't trust either."

"The temple of pain is closest."

"To the temple of pain we go." Even if I don't trust them, we will get answers.

CHAPTER 55

LATE THE NEXT DAY, we stand before the temple of pain. It's obsidian, with sharp points and edges everywhere. The entrance is the worst of all. Two sharp spikes come out from each side of the doorway. Only a child would be small enough to pass through without getting jabbed.

"I think you should let me talk to the priest," Marric says. "If everything looks right, I'll come back for you. Otherwise we should go on."

"No. If anyone is going in alone, it's me. You forget I have the power of creation."

"And you forget I have magic."

"Very well. But there's no sense in both of us getting damaged by those spikes."

"There's no entry without it," a gruff male voice says.

Out of the shadows, just behind the doorway, a man appears. He's wearing short sleeves that expose his scratched arms. I shiver.

"You must be the priest," Marric says.

"Keen observation."

"Can we speak with Tybalt?" I ask.

"If you want to speak with the god of pain, you must deal with pain," the priest says.

"I don't have a good feeling about this," Marric whispers to me.

"Me neither," I respond. In fact, my heart is telling me we should never have come here.

"We will speak with him another time," I say.

The priest steps forward, coming dangerously close to the spikes. "Don't be so shy. The god of pain loves visitors."

Retreating toward the horse while readying myself to fight, I say, "No, thank you."

I bump into something—or rather, someone. I turn to find a man with cuts similar to the priest's on his arms.

"We insist you stay," he says.

Marric pulls out his sword. "It's time for us to be going."

The man grabs me and wraps his beefy hands around my neck. "No. It's time for you to stay. We've been in need of someone to cause pain to."

As my air decreases, my panic increases. He squeezes my throat more tightly, and my neck hurts on top of my being unable to breathe. I try to kick him, but he laughs as my foot connects with his leg. The space around me grows black, surroundings fading in and out of view.

Marric barrels forward. Beefy Hands lets go, and I drop to the ground, gasping for breath. There's a grunt, and then Beefy Hands is on the ground beside me, unconscious.

Marric's at my side. "Are you all right?"

I cough and nod, still gasping for delicious air.

"We should go," he says. "I only knocked him out."

He helps me stand, and we hurry toward the horse.

"Don't move a muscle," the priest says.

I turn to find him pressing a sword into Marric's back. Marric can't fend him off from the back, and I can't get to the priest without him running Marric through.

"What do you want from us?" I ask to buy some time to figure a way out of this.

"Simple. We need more pain. Tybalt demands it of us, and we are happy to deliver."

I never understood why Tybalt has followers. Meeting some doesn't make things any clearer.

But that doesn't solve my problem of getting out of this mess.

I want to tell the priest Tybalt is a fool, but instead I ask, "What will happen to us if we go with you?"

"You'll live, which is more than I can say if you don't come with me. Now."

Marric is mouthing *no* to me, but what choice do I have? I can't let the priest run Marric through. I take a step forward. "You have to promise we'll be let go when you're finished with us."

The priest laughs, a maniacal sound that sends a shiver down my spine. "The only promise I'll make is pain. What comes after that is up to you."

That's not at all comforting. "What if I tell you I'm the goddess Izlana?"

"Then my god will be even more pleased with the pain I bring."

He has to be wrong. Tybalt will help me, not want my torment. I take another step forward. If this is going to work, I have to move fast. Faster than the priest can.

"Don't listen to him," Marric says. "Go on without me."

"Never." I pull out my sword and knock the priest's blade away from Marric.

As soon as he's free, Marric spins, bringing his own blade up. With both of us facing him, I'd expect the priest to cower, but he puffs up his chest. "Run me through. My pain will only make Tybalt stronger."

"This man is crazy," I say.

"Agreed." Marric steps forward and knocks the priest on the side of the head. When that doesn't knock him out, Marric uses some type of magic, rendering him unconscious.

Still, I don't put my sword away. "They aren't going to be happy when they wake up."

"Then I suggest we get out of here. Unless you want to try to talk to Tybalt while they're out?"

It's the last thing I want to do. But I create a rope and hand it to Marric. "Tie them up. I'll be back."

With that, I head for the black and sharp temple.

CHAPTER 56

THE SPIKES DRAW blood on both of my arms, so I have two lines of red on each bicep. I suck in air and do what I can to ignore the pain.

The inside of the temple isn't much different than the outside. It has spines of sharp stacks running throughout its walls. In the middle of the room is a statue surrounded by more giant needle-like spikes. The statue itself is made of obsidian like the temple.

"Tybalt," I call out, "I need to speak with you."

There's no answer.

Typical. I'm not begging him. Not the god of pain. Granted, I wouldn't beg any of the gods, but especially not him.

I call out several more times and wait for a reply. Still nothing. I look at the spikes more closely and notice the tip of the one right in front of the statue is covered in blood. I have a feeling I'm supposed to cut myself on it to bring the attention of the god of pain.

Not happening. I'm not mutilating myself to speak with him.

I'll have to try Dracia, the goddess of beauty. She has to be more reasonable than him.

I turn and head back toward the spikes that will cut me on the way out. I should have known better than to try to contact him. This was a stupid idea.

"Izlana, it's good to see you, even if you refuse to give into my customs." The voice comes from behind me.

I whirl around and see the statue has come to life. His red eyes are the only thing that's changed. Otherwise, he still looks like stone.

"Tybalt, thank you for coming to speak with me."

"Your mother was kind to me. It's the only reason I'm here."

Thank goodness for that. I don't know what I'd have done without mother's kindness. "I need to know something," I say.

"We all need to know many things, child. It's the nature of things."

"Where can I find an entrance to return to the heavens?"

He smirks, his obsidian lips curling upward. "You want to return to the chaos that has ensued since your departure?"

"I do."

"Too bad I like chaos. It brings a new charm to the heavens."

That doesn't bode well. "Please. You have to help me get back."

"I don't think so. Now, if you want to know how to worsen the pain of the people on the world, I'd be happy to help with that."

"You're sick."

"Tsk, tsk. You shouldn't go saying such things to the only god with your only hope."

I lift my chin. "I'll say whatever I want. It's obvious you don't care about the good of the people and the heavens."

"You didn't think I would care about such trifles, did you?"

I turn and head out. The only problem is those spikes. I'd like to find a way around them, especially with Tybalt watching me. But there's no escaping them, and I'm not about to stay in this place a moment longer than I have to.

I rush through, getting the pain over with as quickly as I can. I feel the blood dripping down both of my arms, and a laugh follows me out.

Marric meets me on the other side. "You're bleeding."

"You didn't expect me to come unscathed, did you?"

"I guess I thought, being a goddess, you'd find a way around the spikes."

"If only I could." I create some bandages, which Marric helps me put on. His ministrations are gentle and have me wishing there was more time to linger over my injuries.

The priest and Beefy Hands are still out for the count, tied together on the ground.

"Will they be able to get out themselves when they wake?" I ask.

"Honestly, I don't care. They're creepy, and I hate to think that someone else will wander upon them and be forced into their temple. But if they can figure out how to stand, they should be able to get to the entrance of the temple and use the spikes to cut the rope."

"Fair enough." It's more than they would give us.

Marric boosts me up on the horse before climbing behind me. As we start back on our journey, he asks, "Did you get any answers?"

I sigh, leaning back into him. "No. Nothing. Tybalt is as crazy as his priest. I should have remembered that before we wasted our time getting here."

"Don't worry about it. We had to try."

"I guess so."

"On to the temple of beauty?"

"Dracia should be more helpful." Though this incarnation of her is not just vain, but also a little foolhardy. We'll see if she has answers.

CHAPTER 57

WE RIDE as fast as we dare toward the temple of beauty. I don't have much hope for answers at this point, but we have to try. The problem is that every moment we spend on my quest is another moment we should be looking for Neham. It's a mix of what I have to do and what I feel like I want to do.

"We're not far now." Marric interrupts my thoughts. "Maybe a day out."

I relax against him, letting the contact soothe me. I want to be strong, to prove I am the goddess he knows I am, but it doesn't stop my emotions. It would be easy to avoid telling him, but something in me wants him to know how I feel. "I'm nervous about what's going to happen there."

"It's all right to be nervous. After everything you've been through, it's only natural."

"Thanks for saying so. It's still hard to think it's okay, though." More than hard, actually. It's downright onerous. "It's hard to imagine what we'll find there. If Dracia will even answer my call, and then, if she'll give me the answer I'm looking for."

"She can't be worse than Tybalt."

I give a dry laugh. "Nothing can be as bad as him."

"Don't jinx us now."

I sigh. "You're right." There's a far off crack. "Do you hear that?"

Marric brings the horse to a stop. We both listen. I don't hear the sounds of nature I'd expect. There's not anything. Maybe I misheard. Maybe it was our noises. Still, it's strange that there's not even the chirp of birds.

"I must be hearing things," I say.

"Perhaps."

Despite this, he keeps the horse motionless. I give up listening and lean back into him, just enjoying the feel of his arms around me.

Eventually, he spurs the horse on. We're both quiet as we go, with the sun on our faces and the wind tickling us with its breeze.

It's a fine day to be riding. If only we could be like this all the time. Just me and Marric. Get rid of all our cares. There's too much weight on us, it seems. I'm only seventeen, after all, and Marric's not much older. Why do the world and the heavens have to ask so much of us?

I push the thoughts aside. Marric is comfortable, warm, and welcoming. Just right. I wouldn't have him any other way. He's perfect for me. I wish we could be together. That I weren't a goddess. That I were a human like him, and we could marry.

But it can never be. I am a goddess, and he is a human. I could take him for my mate, but I wish for something more than that. Something deeper and real. A partnership. A chance to get to know one another better. To be part of each other's lives, worries, and joys.

Everything.

A mate is nothing like that. Not in my world.

Marric brings the horse to a stop. "I heard something this time."

I strain my ears to hear anything.

"It sounds like a lot of people, though it's faint," he says.

"I think I hear them murmur," I say. "Maybe they're over the hill to our side?"

"Should we investigate?" he asks. "There shouldn't be a town out here. Could it be Saldor's army?"

"Perhaps it's more refugees? Let's find out."

Marric slips off the horse and helps me down. When I'm on the ground, he takes my hand.

"Do you think the horse will be all right here, while we look?" I ask.

"He'll be fine."

We walk hand in hand toward the hill. The closer we get, the louder it is. Voices carry through the air, though I don't know what they're saying. Clanging sounds reach us, and I wonder what they could be.

When we get to the hill, Marric crouches down. I follow suit.

"In case they're not friendly," he says.

It's smart. There's no saying if they're refugees, though I think that's what they are. We creep closer and closer to the edge of the hill—or what I thought was a hill. It's more like a cliff, and the people are on the valley on the other side.

When the first people come into view, I think nothing of the groups we see, but the farther we go and the more people we see, clustered together and tents all around, the more something feels off. Something I can't quite place.

Marric gasps and backs up, taking me with him.

"What is it?" I ask.

He doesn't answer until we're well away, far enough that we can stand without anyone seeing us.

"We've found Saldor's camp," he says.

CHAPTER 58

"What's Saldor doing over here?" I ask.

"I don't know, but..."

I pull out all of my fierceness. "But your brother could be down there, and we need to go get him if he is."

Marric looks at me. Really looks, his gaze intent. "It will mean getting to the temple of beauty later than you expected."

"Your brother just fell into our laps. We can't let this opportunity pass us by."

"Are you sure? There's a lot riding on you getting back to the heavens."

More than I want to think about. "Yes, but there's a lot riding for you on getting your brother back. This is something we should do."

"Very well." He looks to where the camp is, though we can't see it from this vantage point. "How are we going to get him out of there?"

"I don't know. There were a lot of people down there."

"More than our swords can take on?"

"Definitely," I say. "Especially since they have two of our

swords as well. I don't know if they've realized what they have yet, but if they use them, we'll be in trouble."

"The rest of their swords will be next to useless against us."

"Unless they discovered I made them that way and traded them out."

"Where would they have traded them out?"

"Good point." Though I'd feel better if I knew for certain they didn't realize what their swords can't do. Maybe it doesn't matter. "The important thing is that we get down there and rescue your brother. I say we sneak in at night."

"It won't be so easy this time," he says. "They won't be drugged. Plus, they're sure to be on extra watch since they lost you. I have magic, which I can use. Maybe I should do this alone."

"Nonsense. I didn't have my powers last time we were caught. This time, I'll be going in with everything I can."

"I don't like it." He pulls my hand up to his chest, holding it tight. "What if something was to happen to you? It would be the end of life as we know it."

I put my other hand on his. "I don't want you going in by yourself. It's not safe."

"And it's not safe for you. I'm afraid we're at an impasse."

"What do we do, then?"

Without warning, he leans down and presses his lips to mine. We're kissing. *Kissing.* It's like nothing I could have guessed at. It's better than anything I imagined. I can't seem to get enough of his soft lips on mine.

He pulls away. "Sorry. I shouldn't have done that."

Ignoring his words, I pull him down for another kiss, longer this time. Fuller. Now I'm ready for it, it's even better. I disentangle my hands from his and wrap my arms around him so I can run my fingers down the back of his neck.

He reaches up and threads his fingers through my hair, knocking my hood from my head. It's a wondrous feeling, his lips against mine. I wonder why I hesitated so long when it feels so right.

His lips move from mine to my jaw as I gasp for breath. It's only moments before he's back on my lips, and I'm putting everything I have into the kiss. Every look I've wanted to follow through on. Every touch I've wanted to make happen. Every moment of joy he's brought me. Every good moment I've had with him.

Everything culminates into this second.

When we part, I feel colder without him, yet warmed from the inside. My heart beats wildly. I keep my fingers on the back of his neck, holding him close. "That's not what I expected," I say.

"Is that good or bad?" he asks, voice thick with emotion.

"Most definitely a good thing. I only wish there was time for more." My cheeks heat as I realize what I've said, but I don't let it get to me. There'll be time enough later to decide how I feel about this whole thing. For now, I want to enjoy it.

"We still have to figure out a way to save your brother," I say.

"I'll sneak into camp while you wait for me."

"I can't stay behind while you do all the work. What if something happens to you? I'll never know it."

"Nothing will happen, except me saving my little brother."

Despite his firm voice, I worry. He's strong, but he'd be stronger with me at his side. "I wonder if Saldor knows Neham's your brother," I say.

He blanches. "I hope not. I hate to think what it could mean for Neham if Saldor recognizes him."

"We'll have to hope for the best, then."

"The best," he whispers, dipping his head for another taste of my lips.

It's too short. I'd much rather kiss him for longer than send him off on a dangerous mission.

"Fine. I'll stay here," I say. "But I'm coming after you if you don't return by daylight."

"Fair enough." In his scowl, I can see the words cost him.

"And I'll make you a uniform and sword that looks like theirs. That way, you'll fit in better."

"Good idea. Now if only I knew where he was at in the camp."

"Let me make you a compass. That way you'll know for certain he's in the camp before heading in, and then you won't have to bumble around."

"If you can do that, it would be immensely helpful."

Without a word, I create a compass that's tuned into Neham. As it appears in my hand, the arrow swivels around until it points toward the direction of Saldor's camp. "That answers that question."

"He's there. I'll find him."

I hand him the compass and bite my lip, worrying about what awaits him. "Be careful."

"I will be."

CHAPTER 59

ONCE THE SUN GOES DOWN, I make Marric a proper outfit and a sword that looks like the useless ones I made before. Only this blade isn't useless.

He gives me another kiss and sets off. I watch him go until he disappears down the hill; then I secure the original sword I made him on the horse. The wait is going to be the worst part.

I crawl to the edge of the cliff to find out if I can see anything. Lights from the camp show the way to it in the darkness, but don't reveal anything useful. Still, I keep watch, not willing to miss out on what might happen.

It's then I get an idea. I'm going to create a distraction. The best one I can think of is simple—fireworks. I'll set off a bunch. They captured people's attention when I was with Pennington; I don't see reason why they won't this time.

I wish I had a way to communicate with Marric. Of course, there is no alternative to get a message to him. Even if there was, it could reach him when he was talking to the enemy, which would be disastrous. I'll have to go about my plan without telling him. He'll figure it's me.

I crawl away from the cliff and hurry to the west side away

from the camp. Marric should be coming at it this way. If I work quickly, I'll have the fireworks going off before he makes it there. Halfway between the camp and where I left my horse, I begin to create fireworks.

I make them brighter and more spectacular than any I created for Pennington, ranging their colors and adding lots of noise. When I have about twenty of them, I stop. If I'm to help Marric sneak in, I don't have time to make more.

I create a torch and then light them all, as fast as can be.

The night air is full of their noise and color by the time I get to the last one. Once that's done, I stick my torch in the ground and make a run for it. I hope I'm far from here by the time Saldor's men make an appearance.

My lungs burn as I run, reminding me I'm not accustomed to this sort of thing. The fireworks are still going off, but I don't look at them. I have no interest in them now that they've hopefully helped Marric sneak into camp.

I wish I thought of this sooner, but Marric knows me and what I did before. He's sure to recognize my work. Even if he doesn't, he's bound to make use of the opportunity.

Once I'm back to the cliff, I carefully crawl out onto the ledge and flatten myself against the ground. The camp below is doing what I hoped. Everyone's watching the fireworks, staring and pointing at them—not paying much attention to anything else.

A group heads toward where I set them off, though they aren't going at a fast pace. They must be more curious than uneasy. Clearly, they don't know who they're dealing with.

A worrying thought niggles at me. What if Neham is in the group sent to investigate the fireworks? What if Marric can't find him because I sent him on a task?

The thought eats at me, making me wish I could pace. But I refuse to move from where I lie. I won't give up my spot watching the camp.

Several minutes go by before the fireworks slow and then stop. It makes me wish I set more to go. They weren't nearly enough of a distraction. The group heading toward the fireworks hasn't even made it to them yet; their torches waver some distance from them.

As the rest of camp simmers down, I follow those torches. They get to where I let off the fireworks and then they stop.

I wonder what they'll think of not finding anyone there. It doesn't matter as long as Marric rescues Neham.

There are so many things to worry about. So many things that could go wrong. I wish I could create something to make time pass quickly, but there's no way for me to make such a thing. It's just as well I have no power over time, though. I'd probably change things so much, I'd mess it up beyond reason.

The flickering torches that investigated my fireworks are coming back toward camp. At least that's one thing not to have to worry over. They aren't coming for me. It's Marric who's in danger, just the way he wanted it.

I hate letting another person run into danger while leaving me behind. It feels cowardly and unhelpful. But his arguments were sound. I can run in to help, should it come to it.

The waiting gets worse, slowing more and more as time goes by. I can't gaze at the camp anymore. Nothing is visible from up here, and I'm tired of watching nothing happen.

I crawl away from the cliff until I can't see the camp before standing. It's unlikely that they see me in the dark, but I'm not taking any chances. I go back to the horse and pace. There's nothing for it. My nerves buzz like a bunch of angry bees.

Then I hear it—the soft crunch of footsteps. I grab the horse's reins, ready to run if necessary.

The next moment, two figures come into view. Marric is one of them, the other a little Marric who must be Neham.

Marric found his brother.

CHAPTER 60

"I'D LIKE to introduce you to my brother, Neham," Marric says to me. "Neham, this is Izzy."

"It's a pleasure to meet you," I say to Neham.

"And I you." He even sounds like Marric, his voice slightly higher.

"Did you have any trouble getting him out?" I ask Marric.

"I might have if it weren't for your fireworks. Brilliant idea, by the way, only dangerous. You're lucky they didn't catch you. I was worried about you the whole time."

"Sorry to cause concern. I knew it would work, though."

"And it did. Thank you." Marric puts an arm around his brother. "Neham and I are most grateful. I was able to sneak into camp while they were distracted and found him pretty easy. The whole thing went better than I expected, actually."

"Good. That's the way we like things." And it almost never happens. I'm ever so pleased it did.

"We should be on the move," Marric says. "I don't know how long it will take them to realize Neham is missing, but we don't want to be anywhere close when they do."

Marric switches swords with Neham, who still holds a sword

of no real use, and grabs his original sword. He leaves the useless sword lying on the ground. "It's too bad we can't ride to get away faster, but with the three of us, we'd need at least one more horse."

"We could have stolen one from Saldor," Neham says.

"But that would have cost us more time in his camp," Marric replies. "I wasn't willing to risk that."

We start walking toward the temple.

"This isn't the way home," Neham says.

"We have a stop to make first," Marric says. "Izzy has some important business that needs to be taken care of. You might end up journeying with us quite a ways until I can get you back home."

"Brusha has to be sick with worry," Neham says.

No doubt she is, for both of her missing brothers. "We'll send her word if we reach a town or find someone willing to take a message to her. She'll be overjoyed to hear the news that you're away from the army. What was it like, if you don't mind my asking?"

"Boring, really. We did a lot of training. Recently, we've been walking."

Something whistles past my right ear. I flatten myself to the ground and yell, "*Get down.*"

Marric and Neham aren't far behind.

"Well, well, well," says a familiar voice. Saldor. "If it isn't my old friends, come to return to my camp."

How did he find us? Better yet, how are we going to get away this time, when there's an entire army out there?

CHAPTER 61

"We'll never return with you," I tell Saldor in my firmest tone. "Never."

"I don't think you have much of a choice." He motions to the men behind him and the arrows pointed our direction. "I've missed having you around, Izlana."

"Izlana?" Neham asks. "Izzy is the goddess Izlana?"

Saldor chuckles. "They didn't tell you you're traveling with a goddess? Of course they wouldn't. She doesn't want to share her power."

"I only don't want to share it with the likes of you," I spit back.

"Don't be so hasty, dear one," Saldor says. "I'd hate for you to regret your words."

"The only thing I regret is not killing you when we had the chance." I should have found him when we escaped his camp and ended his life then, while he was knocked out. But I spared his life. I spared all their lives. Look where it got us.

"Harsh words for one supposed to be for creation instead of death. Trying to take over Daristona's job?"

"The goddess of death will come for you soon enough." Though not soon enough for our rescue. I have to think of a plan to get us out of here without losing our lives. It doesn't look easy, with the dozens of men Saldor has with him. I can't even see them all because it's too dark. They only seem to be on one side of us, and not surrounding us. That's something. Of course, with that many arrows pointing at us, they don't need to surround us.

"I see you lost your collar," Saldor says. "What a shame. I was hoping to utilize it. No matter. I'm certain we can find another way to persuade you. Two ways, it would seem from your traveling companions."

He's threatening Neham and Marric. I can't let him harm either of them, but what can I possibly do or create to stop him?

"Come, now. Let's go back to camp and discuss this like rational people," Saldor says.

"You're stupider than I thought if you think I'll come with you," I tell him.

He holds up a hand. "All I have to do is give the word, and these fine soldiers of mine will let loose an arrow into one of your companions. Is that what you want? To be responsible for someone's death?"

This can't be happening. There has to be something. Anything.

"I'm losing patience with you." Saldor makes a fist. "As soon as I drop my hand, one of your companions will die."

"Don't worry about us," Marric says. "Do what you have to."

"Brave words, coming from someone whose life I'm about to take," Saldor says.

It can't be. Not Marric. I can still feel his arms around me. His lips pressed against mine. I can't lose him. Not now, not ever. I don't know if we'll ever be together like I want, but at least there's our friendship.

"Last chance," Saldor says. "Come now and save your friends, or watch them die."

"If I come with you, will you promise not to hurt them?" I ask. Not that I trust him.

"They won't be hurt, as long as you cooperate. Any sign of rebellion from you, and payment will come from them."

"Very well." My heart feels as if it's going to leap from my chest; it's beating so hard. There's only one chance at this, and I have to hope it works, or I'll lose either Marric or Neham.

"Down," I yell.

I dive for the ground, pressing my hand to the dirt. Arrows fly all around, some coming awfully close. I hope they aren't getting too close to Neham and Marric. Hope they're still alive and well when this is all over.

Quick as I can, I call my power up and send it into the ground. There's a grumbling beneath us, as nature responds to my power.

"Get them," Saldor screams. "Get them now."

But it's too late. My power is already throwing up a blockage between us and them, in the form of a dirt wall. It's a sight to behold. It's tall and stretches for a mile in each direction, making it so Saldor and his men will have to go around, to chase us.

I turn to the others, neither of whom has an arrow protruding from him as they rise from the ground. "Run."

"Did she just..." Neham trails off, staring at me instead of doing as I asked.

"She did." Marric looks as awed at my power as Neham does.

"Now isn't the time," I say. "They'll be around it or over it as soon as they can. Maybe even through it. We have to go. Now."

Finally they listen and run with me, Marric taking the horse by the reins. I only hope I made the wall big enough that Saldor and his men don't have a chance to catch up with us.

CHAPTER 62

THE NEXT DAY we haven't rested at all. We've done nothing but try to escape Saldor and his men. It's exhausting, but we've entered a forest. That should help confuse them.

"Can we stop for a rest yet?" Neham asks, reminding me that though we've turned to walking, we've been on the move for far too long.

"Let's." I plop down on the ground, not caring how uncomfortable or dirty it is. Right now it feels like a little piece of the heavens came to join me.

Since Neham knows who I am, I don't bother to hide my creations. I make full water skins and food for us all and the horse.

Marric takes some and hands a portion to Neham, who stares at it like it might jump up and bite him at any moment.

I take a long pull on my water skin. The cool water is refreshing after such a hike.

Neham still stares at me.

I wipe my mouth, feeling a little self conscious. "Did I do something wrong?"

"I—I never thought I'd meet a goddess," Neham says. "And I never thought that she'd drink or get dirty."

Marric laughs. "Join the party, brother."

I shrug them off. They know little about my kind. Though I am rather dirty. What I wouldn't give for a bath... But we have no time for it.

"I still have to get to the temple of beauty," I say.

"We'll take you there, but you should know something," Marric replies. "On the way back to you, Neham informed me Saldor and his men were going to march on my sister's city. They're going to take it and use all the people they can in their war to make Saldor their kin, instead of taking a few boys at a time."

The thought makes me sick. "We should split up."

"No," Marric says. "I promised Idolo I would stick by your side."

"But I promised nothing to no one," Neham says. "I'll do it. I'll go warn the people that they're coming."

"It's not safe to be out on your own," I say.

"No offense, goddess, but I think it's safer than to be with you."

I think about this a moment. "Fair enough. I'll make you some food for your journey. You can take the horse, and it should only take a few days at most."

"I hope it's enough warning," Neham says.

Marric puts a hand on his brother's shoulder. "You'll be faster than a whole army trying to move. Are you certain you want to do this?"

"I am. I need to. Someone has to, and it's best if it's me."

"Tell Brusha I'll be along as soon as I can, but that I'm safe for now."

"I will."

The two brothers hug and slap each other on the back.

I wonder if I'll ever see Neham again. "One more thing," I say to him. "If you would, please keep my identity a secret. The less people who know who I am, the less danger for all of us."

"Of course, goddess." He bows to me before climbing on the horse. "I'll see you again soon, brother."

"Goodbye," Marric says.

Neham is off, looking braver than anyone I've ever seen.

Once Neham's out of sight, Marric looks to me. His gaze is comforting, like a familiar blanket.

"One thing is certain," I say.

"What's that?" Marric asks.

"We're going to need a lot more people if we're going to win the war against Saldor and Pennington."

EPISODE FIVE

Episode Five

CHAPTER 63

THE FOREST IS full of singing birds. It doesn't match my feelings. A fight is brewing on this world, and there is talk of one in heaven. It's hard to imagine how things will go down, even if I give it my best. The one bright note is that I'm with Marric. Though, even that's shaky.

We keep getting near each other as we walk, only to draw apart again. That kiss we had was something else. Something special. I don't know what his reasons are for wanting his distance from me, but mine are complicated.

I want to be with him, more than anything, but the problem lies in what happens if we're together. Will that make him my mate? I don't want him to be that. Our relationship is confusing, and I don't know what to do.

"Here's the temple of beauty," Marric says, pulling me from my thoughts.

I glance up. It's a thing of beauty itself, almost too much so. It's a gleaming white marble, sculpted to look like a flower. The entrance is at the base of the flower, and carved all around it is scrollwork.

"I suppose we should go in." I hesitate. After the last priest we encountered, I'm none too eager to meet the priestess. If it comes down to it, I may need my sword or power to thwart her. The priestess of beauty can't be anything like the priest of pain, though.

Marric stays close, though he doesn't take my hand as we continue forward. As we enter the temple, there are mirrors everywhere, showing my state of disrepair. I'm filthy. Covered with dirt. My clothes aren't any better, and even my hair has lost its vibrant white color underneath my hood. The only part of me that looks familiar are my eyes.

The room seems larger than it is with all the mirrors. The statue is of Dracia, her ebony skin apparent even in the statue. Her hair is thick and full, her eyes looking right at me.

"Where is the priestess?" Marric asks.

"I don't know." I glance around again but find nothing. "Hello?"

Still, no one shows up.

The statue comes to life, Dracia's skin smooth, her lips full, her curves fitting the goddess of beauty.

"Izlana," she says. "What are you doing here?"

By the tone of her voice and the way her words come out quickly, she's much more eager to speak with me than any of the other gods were, though her words come out stiff. I wonder why, since we were never close. "I'm looking for answers. How can I get back to the heavens?"

She glances around like she's looking for something before focusing back on me. "You can't return here. Not ever."

A dagger slices through me. Not go home? "What do you mean? I have to. I'm needed there, and wars are taking place here. It's not safe."

"You'll have to find some place safe to continue your work from the world."

"Charmina told me that there was a rumor of a war in the heaven. I'm needed to help stop it."

"You can't stop it. No one can. The best thing for you to do is go into hiding. If you return here, you'll be killed." With that, she turns back into a statue.

"DRACIA, come back. Don't leave me hanging." Despair rings through me. How am I going to get home if I can't find the way? Will I really die if I go home?

I glance at Marric. There's pity in his eyes, an emotion I can't stand to see directed at me. I turn back toward the statue. "Dracia, please."

Nothing.

I'm stuck on this world.

CHAPTER 64

MARRIC PUTS a hand on my shoulder. "I'm sorry, Izlana."

I shrug him off. "Dracia, come back."

A woman appears from behind the statue. Her beauty is outstanding, but it's not something I care about right now. "Can I help you with something?" she asks.

"You can call Dracia for me," I say. "I need to speak with her."

"Dracia never speaks to anyone, save for me."

I let out a growl of frustration.

The woman takes a step back, eying me like I've gone crazy. "I'm afraid I'm going to have to ask you to leave."

I rage, throwing back my hood. "Do you even know who I am?"

The woman looks at me closer, probably trying to see through the dirt. After a moment, she widens her eyes. She bows down to me. "Goddess, forgive me. I did not recognize you."

"That's plain to see," a bitter tone creeps into my words. "I need to speak with Dracia."

"Of course. I will leave you to her." The priestess hurries back around the statue and out of sight. I move around to see an exit hiding behind Dracia's statue.

I go to call out Dracia's name again when a hand touches my shoulder. I whirl on Marric. "What?"

His voice is soft against my harsh words. "I don't think Dracia is going to come back and speak with you. She said all she was going to say."

I feel myself breaking on the inside, and I work to keep my words from cracking. I need to keep them strong. Sure. "It can't be all. I have to return home."

"Maybe she's right. Maybe we need to wait until the war in the heavens is over."

I take a deep, shaking breath.

"Hey, now," he says. "It's going to be all right. I'll stay with you. We'll find some place to hide until you can return. Everything is going to be fine."

"No," I say. "I'm not going to stay where it's safe. We're going to war."

CHAPTER 65

MARRIC HURRIES after me as I storm away from the temple and into the woods. "What do you mean we're going to war?" he says.

"Exactly what I said." I don't bother slowing. "If I can't help the heavens, then I'll help this world. I'll save these people from Pennington and Saldor."

"How are you going to do that?"

These words slow me down, but I don't stop. "I'm not certain yet, but I'll figure something out."

"What if, instead, they harness your power again?" he asks, clear worry touching his tone. "Or worse, what if you die?"

The thought gives me pause, even as my legs continue to move. What will happen if I die on this task? Nothing good. But if I don't try, I'll never forgive myself as this world falls into disarray. I stop my hurried walk forward and turn to Marric. "I know this is dangerous, but it's something I have to do. I can't stand by while my creations are hewn down."

He sombers. "I'll go with you, then. Whatever you need, I'll be there."

This makes me want to break down crying. I don't, though. I stay strong and tough. "Thank you."

"Where do we go from here?" he asks.

"We should head back to your siblings. We know Saldor's going to attack that city."

"You really think you can stop him?"

"I hope I can." If not, this is going to be the shortest fight a god ever put up. What am I thinking? For all I know, this is the only fight a god ever put up. I mean, we argue over followers, to get the most, and we try to keep things the way we like it, but no god has actually come on the world to join a battle. I must be crazy to be doing so. Crazy, but right.

"And if you can't?" Marric asks.

"*Can't* isn't an option. We have to stop him and Pennington both. Otherwise, we're going to be in a world of hurt. This world was not meant to have a king. It was meant to be ruled by the gods."

"They haven't been doing a very good job of it lately," he mutters.

I stop and turn to him. "What is that supposed to mean?"

"Sorry. Forget I said anything."

"No. What did you mean? I must know."

"Really, forget it. You know me. I wasn't even a believer before I met you."

Realization dawns. "That's part of the problem, isn't it? We gods have been so busy fighting over followers that we've forgotten about the people that make up those followers."

His response is quiet. "Maybe so."

"Well, things are going to be different now." I start walking again. "I've been down here among you now. I know how much work it is to be a human—or at least I have some idea. I won't be ignoring you because I'm too lazy to get up at the moment. I'll be working harder than ever for my creations and will try to convince the other gods to do the same."

"I didn't mean to imply you aren't good at being a goddess. I'm certain you'll do a wonderful job at fixing things."

"Thank you," I say. "That means a lot."

The air between us becomes electrified. It tingles with anticipation. But no matter how much I want to reach across and take his hand, I can't bring myself to do it. I won't turn him into my mate, someone to be used at a god's will. He deserves more than that. I do too.

Humans have more rights than the gods do to live freely and make their own choices. Not that humans are perfect—far from it. But there's a lot we can learn from them.

CHAPTER 66

WHEN WE'RE a few hours out from the city, Marric stops. "I have an idea, and I mean no offense by it."

"What's that?" is my tired reply.

"If you're going to reveal yourself to the people, to help out..."

"I was planning on it."

"Well, then, maybe you should take a bath."

This makes me laugh. Hard. "Good point. I don't know a god who's been in such a state as I have. But do we have time for a bath when Saldor may already have taken over the city?"

"He either has or hasn't. A half-an-hour stop on our part won't make a difference."

"Very well." I create not one, but two baths full of warm water, each behind a privacy screen. "If I'm going to stop to get clean, you may as well do the same."

"I won't complain about that."

"I imagine new clothes are in order as well. What would you like?" I ask.

"Something like what I'm wearing now is fine. I think you should show up in white, though."

"Hmm." I'll have to give that some thought. I don't know if I should go for a dress or pants. A dress would look more the part, but pants would be more practical for fighting.

I hurry behind my privacy screen and dip myself in the tub of warm water as soon as I've undressed. The water feels good on my aching muscles. I'd love to stay in the bath all day, but people need me. I clean as quickly as I can and get out.

I decide on a dress, though it's not my first choice. It's white, with little frills. I add a white cloak to the mix. I've gotten quite used to having one around, and I'm not ready to give it up now.

Once finished, I step out from behind the privacy screen. Marric is here, waiting for me. His gaze don't leave mine. "You look beautiful," he says, voice hushed.

My face heats. "Thank you."

"Would you mind if I brushed your hair for you?"

I create a brush and it to him. "Just make it quick."

As he pulls the brush through my hair, he says, "I'm sorry I don't know how to make a fancy hairstyles for you. Sometimes I'd help Brusha with her hair, but I never did more than brush it."

"It'll serve its purpose as long as it's not flying away everywhere."

The strokes of the brush have me closing my eyes. It is nice to have someone taking care of my hair, especially when that someone is Marric. The moment feels intimate. Special. I don't want it to end any more than I wanted my bath to end, but all too soon, the movements of the brush stop.

"There we go," he says.

"Thank you." I turn to look at him and immediately drop my gaze. There's something in his eyes that I don't want to see. Can't see. Not now. Maybe not ever.

"We should go," he says.

"Let's get to it."

"It's kind of a funny thing to leave two tubs in the middle of the way," Marric says. "At least we're not on the road, where everyone would see them."

I look back at the privacy screens and tubs. "I do tend to leave a lot of stuff behind. Maybe we should start carrying it."

"Packing a tub? I think I'll pass."

I laugh. "Well, maybe not starting now, but in the future, we should take what we can."

We head toward the city in a quick pace. The hem of my clothes pick up dirt, but it's still better than what I looked like before. At this moment, I don't feel much like a goddess. I feel like someone pretending to have more power than she does.

It's a silly thought. I have enough power that I can create whatever I want. That doesn't change the fact that I feel like a fraud in my white dress and cloak. I don't know how I ever thought I was going to take on a whole army. What can I possibly do?

I need a plan, but nothing comes to mind. I don't know how to defeat an army without help. Even *with* help, it seems like a lot to hope for against a group of trained men. What's worse is some of these men were taken from the very city they're about to attack. I'm going to ask people to fight against their fathers and brothers and husbands. How can I ask this of them?

If only there was a way to win this without fighting. To take the day without bloodshed. But I don't know what that would be. I've never participated in a war or even studied one before. My studies were all on the power of creation, and what it can and can't do. Nothing to do with the unholy power causing the fighting.

And yet, here I am, about to go to war.

The city comes into view, and I can't help but gasp. There's an entire army at the gates, trying to get in—as we thought it would be. Soldiers who were helping the refugees now try to keep the army out, shooting arrows down at them. It doesn't change the fact that they are few against many.

I'm cut out for the task before me. I have to be tough against this opponent, using my full power if I'm to defeat them.

CHAPTER 67

"How are we going to get in to help the people?" I ask Marric. "The only way in is barred, not to mention the fact that we have to go through an entire army to get there."

"I don't know. We'll think of something."

"We'll have to make it quick. These walls may be keeping us out, but they're also the only thing keeping out Saldor's army."

We stare at the city, not knowing what to do.

"Maybe we should head around the city. We can figure out a way to get over the wall," Marric says.

"If the guards patrolling it don't shoot us down first." It's hard not to have a bitter outlook when I see what's before us. Still, I should be better than that. "You're right, though. Let's go down and try not to get shot."

"Sound plan."

We make our way toward the city, the long way. When we reach the edges of the woods closest to the part of the city not by the army, I stop Marric. "Maybe we should wait until nightfall. It might be more suspicious that way, but it also might help us not get shot at."

"Very well. It's not long until nightfall." He takes a seat nearby on a fallen tree.

I sit next to him, but not too close. Just enough to be companionable, but not so I'm tempted to touch him.

Who am I kidding? The temptation is still there, only easier to resist when I'm not too close.

The whole time we traveled, I was on edge, not because of the army sitting outside the city, but also because I don't know how to act around Marric since the kiss. Both are such tough subjects, I'm not sure which one I'd rather think on.

At least with Saldor, I know he's the enemy, and I know why I'm fighting him. With Marric, it's a bunch of unknowns. Where do we stand with one another? Am I going to have to leave him? Why did we have to kiss and make things so complicated?

I decide to think about the war instead of my relationship with Marric. It's easier to think about. Saldor's army may be defeated if they haven't figured out their weapons can't do more than scratch the enemy. If that's the case, and they're still using those faulty weapons, we may have a chance.

Only with my sword that aims true every time I swing, I know I will be able to defeat him. The problem is, he's got an army backing him, one that looked like it had hundreds if not a thousand men. If I'm surrounded, even with my weapon, I'll be rendered useless. Plus they have bows and arrows. They'll shoot me down before I can move.

I could make my own bow and arrow, but I can only shoot one person at a time. I cringe at the thought. I don't really want to shoot anyone. Not that I have ever wanted to slice anyone through with my sword either.

"What are you thinking about?" Marric asks.

I shift on the log so I'm facing him. "How are we going to defeat an entire army?"

"I don't know."

"That's what I'm trying to figure out. It seems like an impossible task."

"You're a goddess; it can't be impossible."

I sigh. "I appreciate your faith in me, but I'm the goddess of creation, not the god of war."

"You still have more of a chance than the rest of us."

"What are you talking about? You're strong. Not only are you the smartest person I know, but you also have magic on your side."

"Magic that I'm still uncertain how to use."

"You figured out how to undo my collar. I'm sure more is waiting inside you."

"I don't know."

"I think it is. You obviously have a lot of power. You just need to learn how to harness it."

He rests his hand on the log, close to me. It's hard to think of anything but that hand. I want to take it in my own. To feel his own skin against mine. But then I'd be giving into something I'm not sure I can allow myself to have.

He notices me staring at his hand and whips it away.

What's his problem? Why is he so uninterested in me after that kiss? I'm about to ask when he says, "I think the sun is low enough that we can make our way to the north of the city."

He's right. It's gotten quite dark. "Right," I say. "Let's go."

We head out to what may possibly be our deaths.

CHAPTER 68

WE CAN'T SEE anyone patrolling the top of the wall, but when we stop and listen closely, we hear the faint slap of footfall.

"We're gonna get caught," Marric whispers when the footfalls fade.

"Have a little faith," I reply.

We walk right up to the wall. I don't know how they haven't spotted me in my bright white dress and cloak. The thought worries me, but we have a more pressing matter—how to get up the wall.

"What if I create a ladder?" I ask.

"That would work. Let's hide until the next patrol passes, and then you can go ahead."

I do as he says, and the two of us flatten ourselves against the wall. It seems like forever before we hear a sound. Then there's the light tapping of feet.

My breathing comes in more rapidly. They could shoot us down without a thought. There's danger in trying to help.

I listen to the *pat, pat, pat* of someone passing until it's too far for us to hear.

"Go now," Marric says.

Without a word, I create a ladder tall enough to go to the top and set it where it needs to go. I put a hand on it.

"Let me go first," he says.

"I need to. If they stop to question us, I can prove who I am."

He lets out a soft growl. "I don't like it. But do it."

My heart pounds as I climb, but I'm ready to flash my eyes at them and demand they know I'm on their side. Once at the top, I hurry to move out of the way for Marric to come up, and then I head to the left.

"Wait," Marric says. "We can't leave the ladder here, for Saldor's army or spies to find."

I turn, to find him hoisting it up. "Don't fall," I say.

There's a prick at my back.

"Marric," I say.

He turns his focus from the ladder—almost all the way up now —to me, and drops the ladder. Teetering precariously, he manages to catch it before it falls back down. I reach out to grab him, but the point behind me presses harder. Ignoring it, I take hold of Marric's arm. No way am I going to sit here and do nothing while he falls.

"What do you two think you're doing up here?" A female voice comes from behind me.

"If you let me turn around, I promise to explain everything," I say.

"You can do your explaining fine from where you're at."

I sigh. She's right, but it's hard to talk to someone you aren't looking at. Plus, she can't see my eyes. See me for who I really am. "We're here to help," I say.

"You two? What good can you do? And how do I know you're not sent from the enemy?"

I go to take my hood off, but what I presume to be a sword presses harder into my back.

"Don't move a muscle," she says. "Explain yourself."

"If you'd permit me to take off my hood and look at you, it'll help a lot."

"You likely have magic you're trying to use against me," she says.

"I don't have magic, but he does."

A second person appears out of the darkness. A male, on Marric's other side. His sword is drawn. Marric goes for his own sword, but I stop him. "Let them do what they want with us. They'll soon understand we're on their side."

He nods.

I doubt they'll believe I'm a goddess right away, and I can't create anything without moving or scaring them, so I go for a simpler answer. "Marric here used to live in the city. His family still does. His brother Neham was supposed to come warn the city Saldor's army was coming for you. Did he make it?"

"We were warned," comes the female's reply.

"You can ask his family who we are. They'll recognize us."

This seems to convince her. "Come with me. Jesfu, continue to patrol the wall. Make sure no one else comes up. And take that ladder from him. We don't want to leave it down there for anyone to use."

The man takes the ladder from Marric and places it down the inside of the city wall.

"Move forward," the woman says.

We move past Jesfu, heading toward a round room at the corner of the city wall. There's a table with a lantern in the middle of it, several men and women in soldier garb gathered around it. They look up as we enter, eyes growing wide.

"What did you find?" asks a man with hair graying at the temples.

"These two climbed up the wall with a ladder. They're claiming they're here to help and that he has family inside the city."

The group eases, but the sword doesn't leave my back.

"If you'll permit me," I say, moving slowly to take off the hood of my cloak.

"Go ahead," the female says, sounding resigned. "But no sudden movements."

I take the hood of my cloak off, letting my white hair and emerald eyes be seen by all in the room. I hold out my palm and create a loaf of bread.

"I am Izlana, goddess of creation, and I'm here to help."

CHAPTER 69

Several gasps sound.

"It can't be," the woman behind me says.

I turn to face her. She barely gets a look at me before bowing. The others except Marric follow suit.

"You may rise." Once they're on their feet, I say, "I need your leader."

"I'll get her." A man bursts from the room.

The wait is uncomfortably silent. Everyone tries to sneak peeks at me without being too obvious about it. Except Marric, of course, who's avoiding my gaze.

When the door opens again, I'm past my patience limit, but I rein it in.

"Goddess," says a woman in full soldier gear. She gets down on one knee before me. "We are awed to be in your presence."

I'd rather they all be a little more toward normal than awed. "You may rise. What's your name?"

The woman comes to her feet. "I am Heslta, leader of this army."

She looks to be in her late fifties, with steel-gray hair and fine lines on her face. Truthfully, she looks more like a goddess than I feel. They probably think I'm forever young. "I have come to aid you in your battle against Saldor."

"We are most honored, goddess."

"Please, call me Izlana."

The woman's eyebrows raise, but she doesn't argue. "How can you help us, Izlana?"

"There are many ways." I almost admit I don't have a clue what I'm doing. But I clamp my mouth shut before my insecurities show forth.

"I never thought of how the goddess of creation could help during a war."

That makes two of us. "Before we speak of it, Marric here is most anxious to see his family. If you would allow him to go, that would be most welcome."

"Certainly. He's free to go to his home."

But he doesn't move.

I turn to lift one eyebrow at him.

"Forgive me." His voice is overly respectful, something I'm not used to coming from him. "Please give me permission to stay with you and continue to guard you."

I want to argue—to tell him I'm safe here, and that he needs to check on his family. But I know what Idolo told him. That in exchange for Idolo saving his life, Marric was to escort me through this world and to the heavens. It was a big promise, but one that wouldn't be marred if he were to go visit his siblings.

"There's nothing to forgive." I turn toward the soldiers. "I'm needed to go with him, to check on his family. When I return, we will talk about how I can aid you in this war."

"Excuse me, Izlana," Heslta says, "but I would prefer if a guard went with you. I know you're powerful, but with an attack happening on the city, it would give me peace of mind."

I want to roll my eyes. Everyone is so overprotective of me. Where were they when I first came to the world and had the collar placed on me? That was when I really needed them.

Instead of showing my frustration, I say, "Of course. And then they can lead me to your gathering place after we've checked in on Marric's family."

"Jelko," Heslta says, "guard Izlana with your life and take her to central command when she's finished."

A man steps forward. He looks to be in his twenties, with a line through his chin like a long dimple. "As you command." He points toward the door. "Marric, if you will lead, I'll take the back and watch for trouble from there."

With a nod, Marric shows us the way. I put the cloak back over my head and follow. We wind our way down some stairs and out into the city. There are people everywhere on the ground, trying to sleep. Maybe they *are* asleep, but I'd have a most difficult time sleeping under such conditions.

Seeing the people makes me all the more determined to help. There has to be something I can do. I wonder how many of them will help fight when it comes down to it. Will they all fight against Saldor's men? They'll have to, if they want to save their own lives.

The problem is Saldor's been training his men. There are obviously some soldiers among the city, but most seem like regular people. How will they hold up against Saldor's army?

It's then that I get an idea. Weapons and armor. How I can make them helpful? I'll have to make them carefully, though. Not like the swords I first created to always hit their target, but that fell into Saldor's hands. We can't have that happening. I still hope he doesn't realize what he has in them.

The streets are empty away from the compound. No people are about this time of night. If they're awake, they're hiding in their houses or those people who might be refugees. I wonder if those were the people we came across, sleeping on the ground.

It doesn't take long for us to reach Marric's house. Nerves hit me. I'm not sure how I feel about meeting his sister again, but I brought Marric back in one piece and helped save Neham. That has to mean something.

CHAPTER 70

MARRIC KNOCKS on the door again and says, "Brusha, it's me."

A moment later, the door bursts open, and Brusha rushes out to gather Marric in her arms. "I was so worried for you. Especially when Neham came back and told me you were going on, to help Izzy. Is she here, or did she make it home?" She looks around, and as soon as she spots me, lets go of Marric in favor of hugging me.

I stiffen in her embrace, not because it's bad, but because I'm unaccustomed to such contact.

"Izzy, you're safe too. I didn't know if I would see you again."

She doesn't seem to care that I'm a nervous wreck with her hugging me. She keeps on doing it until she spots the soldier with us and lets me go. "You two aren't in trouble, are you?"

"Nothing like that," Marric says.

"He's here for our protection," I say.

Brusha gives Jelko the eye. "Come in. We're not supposed to be out after dark."

The three of us follow her in the house, and Jelko shuts the door behind us and leans against it.

The children are all asleep, lying on the floor.

"I hope we're not disturbing you," I whisper.

"Nonsense," Brusha says, though she too is whispering. "I would have been more disturbed had you not come. I've been so worried about you."

Neham sits up. "Marric? You made it?"

"I did. Izzy is with me."

Neham scrambles to his feet. "I'm grateful you're both safe. I told Brusha all about how you saved me."

"Though it's beyond me where you found fireworks to set off," Brusha says. "That was an ingenious plan."

I share a look with Marric. I think he's thinking the same thing as me—we need to tell her who I am. After all, the whole army is about to know, which means the city will soon find out.

"My full name isn't Izzy," I say.

"Oh?" Brusha sounds like she's wondering why I'm bringing this up.

I swallow, hoping she still likes me after I tell her. "My full name is Izlana." I pull back the hood of my cloak, so she can get a good look.

She gasps and gets down on her knees. "And I hugged you like you were a human. I'm so sorry, goddess. Can you ever forgive me?"

"Please, get up," I say. "You don't need to treat me any different than you did before."

She rises slowly and looks from me to Marric, as if something dawns on her. I'm not sure I want to know what.

"We're here to help stop the war on this city," I say.

"That makes perfect sense. How did you get in here?"

Marric relays the tale to her. It sounds less frightening than it felt. I'm sure he's trying to make his sister not worry so much.

"And I have to stay with Izlana," he continues. "I've been charged with being her escort until she's safely back in the heavens."

Brusha's eyes widen. "You're what?" She gets a hold of herself and whispers, "Forgive me. I didn't except my older brother to ever have such a task."

"It's all right," he says. "I'm surprised by it myself."

"It explains a lot too," she replies. "I had this crazy notion when you first visited that there was love brewing between the two of you. Now I see it's duty."

My whole body freezes. *Duty.* Is that what I am to him? No, it can't be. Not with that kiss. But then, if that's not the case, why hasn't he tried to kiss me again or even take my hand? Not that I've made it easy on him. I don't know that's what's best for us anyway, but that doesn't explain why he hasn't tried.

No one speaks.

"I seem to be putting my foot in my mouth," Brusha says. "I'm sorry, goddess."

"Please, call me Izlana or Izzy." I'm saying that all too frequently.

"Izlana, then. *Izzy* seems too informal for a goddess."

Informal is something I could very well go for.

Marric and Brusha discuss the children and the state of the household for several minutes. While they chat, I take the time to make a few nicer things for them, like a large bed, a window that's not broken, lots of blankets and more food.

After Brusha and the others thank me, Marric says, "We should be going. We have people waiting for us."

"I should have realized," she says. "Thank you for taking the time to let us know you're all right. Both of you." She gives me a meaningful glance, but I'm not sure what it means.

"With any luck," I say, "we'll be seeing you again soon."

"I truly hope so." She wraps Marric in another hug, and then hesitates before I find myself in her embrace as well. "Stay safe," she whispers.

I think I've found a friend.

CHAPTER 71

JELKO LEADS us to a small building. Inside, there's a table and some chairs, which everyone is seated around. When they recognize me, they get up from their seats and bow.

"Please be seated," I say.

Heslta comes over to me and grabs a chair. "You can have a spot by me."

"Thank you."

Jelko gets a chair for himself and Marric, and they sit nearby. I wonder what they're thinking. Especially Marric. He's not trained for this sort of thing, but he acts like he knows what he's doing.

Without preamble, I say. "I will make armor and swords for your army."

"That is beyond what we hoped for. Thank you so much. Some of us already have weapons, but more are definitely needed," Heslta says.

I look around the room, taking in the gazes of those gathered. "The weapons and armor I make will be for everyone. They won't be regular. The armor will be tougher than anything a human can make and strong enough to resist the sharpest blade and hardest blow. The weapons will be special as well, designed to always hit their mark."

There's a scratch of a seat moving behind me. I glance back and see Marric shaking his head.

To ease his concern, which I think is probably about the fact that we will have dangerous swords for anyone's use, I add, "These will only work for those with a good heart and the intention of saving their homes and families. If they are used by someone with ill intentions, they will be worse than useless."

That wipes the smiles from their faces. It makes me wonder if I'm doing the right thing, creating such items for these people. But these caveats should prevent anyone from becoming power hungry.

"That is most generous," a man says. "Will you be able to create enough for all our people?"

"I can."

"We are many," another man says.

"It's not a problem," I reply. "How many do you need?"

"Around three hundred," Heslta answers.

So few, compared to Saldor's more than seven hundred? I hate to think what he could do to this city if these weapons don't work.

A crashing noise reverberates through the city. Screams sound. More crashing.

I jump to my feet, though I'm slower than most of those in the room. We all head for the door, but someone pulls me back. Marric. He's got his arms around my waist, holding me close.

For a moment, I think it's a strange time to choose to be intimate, but then I realize he's holding me back from rushing headlong into whatever danger looms outside. Jelko is close by too, but everyone else has left the room.

"Let me peek outside," I say.

"Only a peek." Marric releases me.

I head for the door as another *crash* makes my heart jump. When I look outside my breath gives out. The city is on fire.

CHAPTER 72

THE CRASHING CONTINUES for a long time as fireballs keep coming at us. I convince Marric and Jelko I'm no safer in a building than running around the city, helping. They concede but keep close to me.

When I see how many of the buildings are on fire, I thrust both arms up in the sky and let rain pour down. It doesn't take long for me to be soaked through, and it helps with the fires.

"That is..." Marric doesn't finish his thought.

"Not enough," I reply. "The houses are still burning. There's more I can do."

We form water bucket lines with others in the city. It seems like everyone is awake and working to keep the city from burning to the ground. The night sky looks nothing like it should, with flame balls flying through the air. They lessen in frequency but don't stop, continuing to haunt the night sky.

My arms ache as I create yet another bucket of water to pass down the line. It doesn't matter how much they hurt, though. I need to do this. I want to do it from the front of the line, where I could be more immediately helpful, but Marric and Jelko insist I need to stay farther from the flames to remain safe.

It's almost dawn before the catapult stops sending its dangerous ammunition, though it's much longer than that before we stop our water-bucket lines and survey the damage.

As we walk along the streets, I realize we're heading toward Marric's home, and I quicken my pace. Marric seems as much in a hurry as I am.

"I'm sure they're fine," I say.

He nods but doesn't give any other response. It's just as well. There's no telling they're actually fine. But I can hope.

When we reach the house, my stomach sinks to my feet. There's no house to get to. Only a pile of ash.

I freeze, not believing the sight before me. Marric has no such problem, jumping straight into the ashes.

"Careful. They may still be hot despite the rain." Though that's not what stops me from jumping in after him. The fear of what we'll find does that well enough.

Heedless of my warning, he digs through the rubble with a strength I haven't seen before from him. When he comes out, it's with a look I can't read.

"Well? Are they..." I can't finish the thought.

"They aren't here."

Tension rolls off me. "Where can they be?"

"We'll find them, wherever they are."

It hits me then that just because they weren't in the house when the fireball struck, it doesn't mean they're somewhere safe.

But they will be. They have to be.

We trudge through the city, devastation everywhere. It's clear Saldor has the upper hand in the battle. For now. I won't let it stay that way.

We come to the refugee part of the city, by the wall, only to find everyone up and about. Not as many people as I'd expect, but with as many as were throughout the city, it's no surprise. Everyone's doing what they can to help the city along.

My chest is an ache of worry over Marric's family. If I'm so concerned about them, I can't imagine how he must feel.

The city is a cacophony of misery. As we move through the refugee camp, we find an area they've set up to be a mobile hospital. The sight of people's burns has me avoiding their gaze. I can't stand to see their pain.

"We need more bandages," a woman yells.

"There are none," a man replies.

I quickly create an armful and bring them to the woman, along with a salve that should help ease the burns.

"Thank you." She doesn't give me a second glance, but I feel better knowing I helped in some way.

"Is there anything else you need?" I ask.

"More hands to help."

I don't know what to do about that, so I lead Marric and Jelko back toward the refugees.

"Does anyone have experience with the wounded?" I yell several times as we move throughout the people.

"I do." A woman comes up to me. "What do you need?"

"They need help over at the makeshift hospital."

"I'll do what I can." She hurries toward where I point her to.

We find several more people to send the way of the hospital, but there's still no sign of Marric's family.

"I'm sure they'll turn up," I tell him.

He nods but doesn't say anything.

"Forgive me, goddess," Jelko says. "We should get back to headquarters before they worry about you."

That's a nice way to say they're already worrying about me. I can't blame them. They're future is largely riding on what I can do. We will take Saldor's army down.

CHAPTER 73

I HAVE Heslta send runners to see if they can find anything about Marric's family, but with the scouts only familiar with Neham, I think Marric and I will likely have to find them.

I get to work, making the weapons and armor I promised. It takes a while because of the number of pieces, and the others send them out to those in the army as soon as I make them.

While I work, Marric paces the room, looking out the window and then at me like he can't decide where he needs to be.

I don't blame him. "Maybe you should go find your family."

"I will, when the city is safe."

I want to argue, to tell him there's time, but the truth is, the sooner we take care of the threat, the sooner his family will be safe. If they're still alive. The hard thought makes my chest want to cave in on itself.

I focus on the task at hand, trying to not to think of how Marric must be feeling. Once I'm finished, I ask, "What's the plan from here?"

"We're going to attack," Heslta says. "We can't wait around for them to throw us more fireballs or anything else they come up with."

I put my hand on the hilt of my sword. "Where do you want me?"

"Not going to happen," Marric whispers in my ear. "They have enough manpower without risking you."

"Can you give us a minute?" I ask.

"Certainly." Heslta ushers everyone out of the room.

Once they're gone, I say, "They'll be strong if they see me fighting with them. It will give them courage." At least I think it will. Maybe I'm overestimating my influence.

"As much as I believe you're right," Marric says, "I don't think that it's a good idea. What if something happened to you?"

"I can make me armor like theirs—strong enough to keep me safe."

"What happens if that fails? If a sword hits you where the armor doesn't cover?"

This sobers me. "You can't keep me from fighting. The city needs me."

"Isn't there a better way you can assist?"

"I can't think of one. Can you? I'm willing to do something else if we can think of it."

His silence is answer enough.

"I hate to think of you in danger," he says.

"You do?" My hopes rise. Maybe he cares for me after all. So much time has passed since the kiss we shared, and there's been no sign of affection. Maybe this is his way of saying he has feelings for me.

"Yes—well we both know the world is doomed if you die."

My hopes trip and tumble into a sea of loneliness. "Right. And that's one less fighter they'll have."

"Two. I'm not leaving your side. Though they need the help, someone has to protect you."

"Fine." As grateful as I am for his protection, I wish there was more feeling behind it. "But I'm watching from one of the walls, in case they do need me. I'll find a way to intervene if it comes to it."

"Fair enough. Would you like me to get the others?"

"Please."

He calls them back in.

Once everyone is seated, I say, "If there's no objection, I'll watch the invasion from the wall. We should do it sooner rather than later."

"Agree," Heslta says. "We should attack as soon as we can gather our soldiers.

"Are they well trained?" I ask.

She shifts in her seat. "They are city guards or volunteers. I'm not sure how they will do against trained soldiers."

I wave the concern away. "With my weapons and armor, they should be a match for Saldor's men."

"If you think so, goddess, I'm sure it will be fine."

With someone who trusts me behind us, I know my instincts are right. We will squash Saldor's army.

CHAPTER 74

WE DECIDE to rest while we have a little time. When dawn hits, I take the opportunity to make armor for Marric and me.

"This should protect you from almost everything," I say as I hand it to him.

He solemnly takes it. "Thank you. I'll protect it from falling into other hands."

"That would be wise, but it will only work if you're the one wearing it."

"You've gotten wise, I see."

"Unfortunately. Experience is a hard teacher."

Jelko already wears the standard armor I made for the army. I put mine on, and we climb the wall, where we wait for the soldiers to storm out the front gates and attack Saldor's army. It's a nerve-wracking wait, with Marric on my right and Jelko on the left.

The light from the rising sun kisses the armies below us, making them appear much greater than they are. I hope our little battalion can take on Saldor's men without problem. There's so much that depends on things I can't control, I hope the things I did control make a difference. That the weapons and armor I provided the people of the city with do a just job, and that Saldor's men still have their swords that do no harm. Not that I want the others killed. Our men have been ordered to incapacitate without doing any major harm whenever possible.

Heslta gives the motion, and the gates open.

There's a flood of men running toward the encampment that's not so far outside the city that we can't see.

"This is hard to watch," I say, just above a whisper.

Marric moves to take my hand, then stops himself. It leaves me wondering why he doesn't want to touch me. Why he doesn't want to do anything but protect me, and only because of his promise to Idolo. I wish there was more there, but now's not the time to think on the tangle that is my love life.

Our army is about halfway to the camp when Saldor's men begin to stir. At first it's a little movement, but it quickly erupts into a flurry of activity.

The army is still going for them. I wish we could shoot arrows from the city wall to back them up. But it's too far. An arrow would never make it.

"Here it comes," Jelko says.

The first wave hits the camp with a smash. They quickly overrun the unsuspecting men. Our army looks good against theirs. We should have gotten here and done this sooner. The weapons and armor I provided our people with are doing their job. We could have saved the city from burning if we were able to attack last night. Marric's family and hundreds of others might not be missing.

By the time our forces reach the middle of the camp, I'm certain we're going to have an easy victory. It's hard to make out the details from back here, but I see well enough to know our soldiers are wiping the land free of Saldor's army. Not killing them, but stopping them from reigning down on the city. Some that are fighting on Saldor's side turn and fight against him as our army approaches.

A pang goes through me. I hope the enemy isn't seriously injured, just enough to be taken out of battle. They are fighting their brothers in some cases. Some aren't fighting for Saldor's cause, but because he forcefully conscripted them into his army.

My heart hurts for them. They're fighting because they have to, not because they want to, while my people are fighting to protect their freedom. They have a right to be fighting. I hope injuries are kept to a minimum.

Then something changes about the battle, and my heart grows cold. A couple of Saldor's men are bursting their way through the armor, tearing through it so bad, I wonder how they're doing it.

Then it hits me. The swords Saldor took from us. These men must be using them to get through the crowd of soldiers. With the limitations I created on the swords for the army, these men are cutting through them, finding their weaknesses. Destroying good people.

This is my fault. And I'm going to fix it.

CHAPTER 75

BEFORE MARRIC or Jelko can stop me, I turn and head for the stairs. I race down more quickly than I've ever moved before.

"Come back," Jelko shouts.

"*Izlana*," Marric calls.

"I must help," I say over my shoulder and put on an even faster burst of speed. I won't be able to run long at this pace, but it should be enough to get me where I need to be.

I weave my way through the streets and out the front entrance, where I pass several soldiers standing guard. If they were looking my way, they could have stopped me, but since they were turned outward, there is nothing they can do.

After running some ways, I reach the back of the army. I try not to look at the ground so I don't see the dead and injured as I weave my way through the people. It's slow going. I'm afraid Marric or Jelko will soon catch up to me and make me go back.

"Coming through," I call. "Let me through."

The crowd parts, leaving me room to rush forward. I continue to yell. The further I get, the more fighting there is, but no one stops me. Until I get to the front lines. Then I stop myself.

A giant of a man wields one of the swords I created to always hit its target. Between that and his size, he's hewing men down like they're nothing. Their armor can't withstand the swords I made to cut down everything.

I break out in a sweat, but pull out my sword anyway.

As soon as he sees me, the giant laughs. "What have we here? Lindpo, do you see this?"

A smaller man, no less threatening, wields the other sword I made to always hit its target. "She's a feisty one; I'll give her that," that man says.

Hoping my armor will stand up to their weapons, I say, "You will harm no more of these men." That is, if I can get them to focus on me.

Marric and Jelko appear at my sides. I wish they hadn't followed. I don't want anything to happen to either of them, but I can't let their presence distract me.

"We will do whatever we want," the giant says.

"I'll get the girl," Lindpo says. "You get the two men."

This is stupid. I'm not about to let us fight these, the toughest men, on our own. "Attack," I yell, hoping the message gets across to the army around us.

Lindpo comes at me, sword aiming straight for my guts. In order to block it, I aim for his sword. There's a resounding clang as our swords meet. Just like I wanted, my sword hits his, but while I expected it to knock it out of Lindpo's hand, it breaks the blade.

The tip of the sliced off blade continues forward as if by magic. Or rather, by my power. It hits me in the stomach. There's a growing pressure as the sword tip tries to get to me and my armor fights back.

Lindpo laughs as I try to whack it away but nothing happens. Someone captures his attention from the back, and I look up in time to see him cut into his opponent.

I cringe. Ignoring the pressure in my stomach, I aim my sword for Lindpo again. The jagged end of the broken blade continues forward. I am determined that he's no match for me, but as I step forward, his sword cuts through my armor and into me.

Overlooking the pain, I aim for his sword arm. My blade connects, and I close my eyes so I don't see the carnage my sword creates.

When I open them again, Lindpo is howling, his sword on the ground. I pick it up. The giant has already fallen under Marric's sword. The rest of the army swells around us as they take down Saldor's men.

I put a hand to my stomach and glance down to see my armor seeping blood. "Marric." My voice is faint even to my own ears, yet he manages to hear me.

"Hang on," he says. He lifts me in his arms and runs back toward the city. "Just hang on."

"I'm sorry." The pain is ripping across my stomach. "I had to save them."

"I know you did." He holds me tight, and for the moment, I can pretend that he's holding me tight because he cares and not because he has to.

We get through the city wall. I feel dizzy. My head wobbles until it's against Marric's shoulder. I let my eyes close once. Twice. Blackness consumes me.

CHAPTER 76

I WAKE to a burning stomach and wish it would stop. I'm lying on something soft, at least. I flutter my eyes open, and find Marric at my side, face buried in his hands.

"Marric." My voice is dry and cracking.

Swift as the wind, he raises his head and grabs my hand. "You're awake."

I nod. "Water."

He pours a glass from a side table. Putting an arm beneath my shoulders, he helps me half-sit, which aggravates my stomach. Still, I'm able to get a drink, and then Marric releases me back onto a soft pillow. I try not to wince at the pain, but it's pretty severe.

"Thank goodness I don't get sliced by a sword every day," I say.

"It was a close one. The blade didn't hit any vital parts—you just bled a lot, which is why you've been out."

"How long have I been asleep for?"

"A day. We went to battle yesterday morning."

"Did we win?" I know it will be an affirmative.

"Only thanks to you. That giant and his comrade were slaughtering our men. I don't think we would have won if you hadn't stepped in."

"Not that she should have," Jelko says, coming into the room. "You nearly got yourself killed. I didn't know a god could bleed. What would we do if you died?"

"Luckily, it didn't come to that," I say.

"But it could have," Marric whispers. "We were so scared for you."

"I'm all right now." I have the urge to take his hand, but I stifle it. We can't be together. "What happened to Saldor and his men?" I ask.

"The men that don't want to work for Saldor any longer were given amnesty. Those who were for Saldor have been locked in prison. Saldor is also in jail for the time being. They're still deciding what to do with him."

I roll onto my side, swing my feet over the bed, and pop myself up without too much damage to my stomach. It hurts, but it's nothing I can't handle.

"What are you doing?" Marric asks.

"I'm going to deal with Saldor. He needs to be taken care of."

"He can wait until you're feeling better."

"I feel well now." Though lying back down does sound nice. "I can't let this wait."

He sighs but stands to go with me.

"Jelko, will you lead me to Heslta?" I ask.

"I will."

I follow him at a pace much slower than my usual. We go to the main headquarters, where Heslta is talking to a few other soldiers.

When she sees me, she dismisses them. "What are you doing up and about?"

"We need to take care of Saldor," I say.

"I should've realized it would be about him. What do you consider a fair punishment?"

"Fair? I don't know. I'd like to have him executed, but that will give more power to the god of war." Which is the last thing we need. Ramco is powerful enough without us adding more followers in the heavens. "Let's talk to him."

"All right. Jelko, fetch Saldor. Izlana will be safe with me and Marric."

Jelko nods and heads out the door.

"What do you believe is going to happen if you talk to him?" Heslta asks.

"I'm hoping to get an insight into what he's thinking. Get to know him better, so we know how to handle him."

"Is there another option, besides putting him in prison the rest of his life?" Marric asks.

"I don't know. There aren't a lot of options, but I'm hoping for something," I say. "Maybe someone can take him in and teach him how to be better. Of course, he won't change if he doesn't want to, but there's always hope."

"What if instead of having someone live with him, we find one or more people to visit him in jail regularly? Then we'll be safe, but he'll still have the opportunity to change." Heslta says.

"That's a wise plan." I carefully sit in a chair beside her.

Marric takes the seat next to mine.

While we wait, I ask, "How many casualties did we have from the fight?"

"Twenty-three deaths, sixty-seven injuries." Heslta takes on a reverent tone. "It appears that all of those came from the two of Saldor's army who had those swords."

I cringe, wishing I never made them. "What happened to the swords?"

"I had my men bury them in a deep pit in the forest."

I nod. I hope they're buried deep enough and those who buried them won't look for them, but they're taken care of for now. I can't do anything to destroy them. Hopefully, time and rust will do that.

The door creaks open, and Jelko walks in, face pale.

"What is it?" I ask.

"Saldor. He took his own life."

CHAPTER 77

THE NEXT DAY, I'm lounging in bed, where Heslta, Jelko, and Marric insist I stay. I'd argue with them, but my stomach hurts enough to make me let it go. Jelko is outside the door, where he's vowed to continue keeping guard. Marric is with me, like he always is. I wish there was more I could give him, but I'm not sure he'd accept it. There's been no indication he's the least bit interested in me romantically since that kiss we shared. A kiss I'll always remember.

My main concern now is his family. They're still missing, and he won't go searching for them without me. I'm determined to go look in a few hours, after I've rested some more.

"Why do you think Saldor took his own life?" Marric asks, startling me from my thoughts.

This isn't a topic I want to switch to, but since he brought it up... "I think he wanted to be a soul of Ramco's in the afterlife. That's my best guess, anyway."

"What's the point of being a follower once you're no longer living?"

"He likely knew he wouldn't be much good to Ramco in this

life. Having him as a follower in the afterlife gives Ramco more power."

"That's the last thing we need."

"I know, but it's only one person."

He shakes his head. "More than just him died in the fight."

"Not all of them would go to Ramco, though. They'll go to whomever they believed in the most."

"I hope the god of war doesn't get many souls, then. He's fearsome enough without them."

"Tell me about it." I haven't forgiven him for getting me into this mess to begin with.

There's a knock on the door.

"Come in," I yell.

The door opens, and in comes Brusha, followed by her siblings.

"*Brusha*," I call out. "You're alive."

Marric bounces to his feet and hurries to take them all in a giant hug. "I thought I lost you."

"No. We were trying to find shelter, to hide. Somewhere safe. We were lucky to decide that, or we would've been in the house when it was smashed. We thought you might be worried after it was destroyed. I heard the goddess was staying here and figured you'd be with her." She gives me a wink.

I laugh, though there's not much joy in it. "He's determined to keep his word and protect me until I'm back in the heavens."

Brusha gives him a sharp look but doesn't say anything.

"I'm grateful you're all safe," I say.

"And we're grateful you're safe," she says. "People are telling wild stories of how a goddess took on two giants with swords that couldn't be defeated. How you almost died in the process of saving us."

"That's an exaggeration." My cheeks are heating.

"But not much of one," Marric says.

"Thank you for your sacrifice," Brusha says. "We appreciate you keeping our city free."

"It's what I'm here for." Though I'd like to be back in the heavens, I have a feeling I should take Pennington out before I go. He's much worse than Saldor, and he has the things I created for him while he held me. Plus, he has magic and knows how to use it. It's going to be a hard battle against him.

I glance at Marric, wondering what he's thinking. He's carefully avoiding eye contact with me. I've got to find out what that's about, too. I can't traipse across this world with a bodyguard who won't look at me. There has to be something I can do to regain the camaraderie we had before the kiss. Something to get back our friendship.

Whatever it is, it's certain to not be easy.

EPISODE SIX

Episode Six

I'M TIRED. I feel it like an ache in my bones. But there's so much to do. I'm healed enough from being stabbed in the stomach that I should be on the move, but I hesitate. I don't know how I'm going to defeat Pennington. Not with his magic, even against my power. They are two very different things.

Besides, I hate to take Marric away from his family. I could try to leave him behind, but he'd come with me, no matter what. I wish it was because he cared about me, though it's probably best that he doesn't. I can't give him a real relationship.

"You're thinking hard about something, goddess," Heslta says.

"Too hard," I reply.

"Want to talk about it?"

There are other more important things I should tackle. "I need to ask a huge favor. Can I borrow your army to attack Pennington?"

Her mouth forms a thin line. "As much as I'd like to say yes, I can't leave my city unprotected."

"But if we don't defeat Pennington, your city may not be able to stand against him."

"I wish you were wrong, but I can't chance it." She drums her fingers against her leg. "How about we compromise? I'll see if I can get some volunteers to go with you. This way, you'll have help and my city will still be protected."

It's better than nothing. "Sounds fair."

"I'll go look for volunteers," she says. "Unless you need to talk about something else?"

I think about telling her how I feel about Marric, but I can't disclose to her how it can never be. Mates aren't supposed to be talked of, outside of the gods. It's all too messy to explain, anyway. "I'm good."

"If you're sure…"

Marric comes in the door with two plates of food. I eye him, wishing there was something more for our relationship. But we're stuck with being friends.

Heslta surprises me by walking over. She bends down and whispers in my ear, "He's a good man. Trust your instincts."

If only it were that easy.

She says goodbye to us both and leaves.

Marric hands me one plate. "Roast chicken and vegetables today. Pretty good fare."

"I like duck better, but chicken is pretty good," I say.

"What were you and Heslta talking about?"

"Fighting Pennington. She's going to see if anyone is willing to help us, but she wants to keep the majority of the army here."

"I can't blame her."

"Neither can I, but we need men. Last we saw of Pennington, he was strong and had ample help. People who believed in him, unlike Saldor. And what's worse, unlike Saldor, he has weapons that will actually work."

"It's a tough task," Marric says.

One I'm not sure I'm up for. "There's something else."

He stops eating. "What's that?"

"I feel like I need to find another temple. Maybe try talking to Charmina again. I don't want to leave this world at the mercy of

Pennington, but despite what Dracia said, I believe I should return to the heavens."

"If you think that's best, we can find a temple." His voice holds a note of something. Hesitance, perhaps?

"Is there a problem with that?" I ask.

"Not at all. I'm happy to serve you however you need."

That's what it comes down to—him serving me. I can't be all right with that notion, but I don't know what else to do.

CHAPTER 79

I FINISH PUTTING my armor on. Though I doubt I'll need it, one needs to be cautious. My white cloak is ragged and dirty, and long since abandoned. I create a new one, midnight blue this time, and put it on with the hood up. I've missed having it up. It's become like a friend to me.

I strap my sword to my side. Everything I have is ready to go. Despite all the things I create, I don't have a lot with me. What I do create, I leave behind. I've spent the last week helping create houses and shops where ones burned down, and providing food.

In addition, my presence seems to give people hope, though there's still much that needs to be done. What's more, the war in the heavens may still happen and bring everything crashing down around us.

Such a cheery thought. I open the door of my room and find Jelko waiting for me.

"Are you ready, Izlana?" he asks.

"I am."

"Marric's already down. He said he'd be waiting for us."

I give a nod and lead the way. This is a fairly safe place, or

Marric would be at the door. At the bottom of the stairs, Marric's chatting animatedly with a beautiful redhead.

Hurt pokes at me. He looks more engaged with her than he's been with me in a long time. What does she have that I don't, besides being human and gorgeous?

Instead of going over to him, I make my way through the tables of people and to the outside. Jelko is at my side, surveying our surroundings, but my thoughts are still on Marric and the way he looked at that red head.

I move forward.

"Where are you going?" Jelko asks. "Don't we need to wait for Marric?"

"He can catch up when he's ready." My feet kick up dust as we go, negating the bath I had this morning. I try to keep from stomping, but it's difficult to rein my feelings in.

Jelko hurries after me. "We really should wait for Marric."

I ignore him in favor of seeking out Heslta. She should have our group of volunteers ready to go. My feelings are a jumbled mess. I don't know what to do. I can't have them going off like this. I need to be in control, especially with how I need to lead a group of men and women against Pennington.

"Izlana, wait." Marric's voice comes from somewhere behind us.

I pretend I don't hear it.

After a few seconds, he catches up. Between huffs for air, he asks, "Where are you guys going in such a hurry?"

"To do our job." I almost spit out, *'instead of idling with a girl'*, but I refrain.

"Well, I found out some information that'll help with that."

When he says nothing further, I ask, "Which is?"

"Pennington's at his castle. He's gathering followers who are eager to join him. His army's been attacking cities and people who don't agree with him."

This stops me. "So do we go after him or his army?"

"Both, I would think," Jelko says. "We'll send the city army after his army, and we three will go after him."

"Do you think we'll be able to get to him without men behind us?" I ask.

"We might have a harder time getting to him if we have larger forces. There's more of a chance to sneak in if only the three of us go."

I tug on my hood, wondering if I'm too well known since Pennington took me out and about at times. There's a quivering inside me at the thought of going back to him. This time, I'll have my power on my side; it should be enough to stop me from worrying. But it's not.

"It's a good idea," Marric says.

"It's risky," I say.

"If we can't do it, we can always collect the army and come back," Marric says.

"Fine." I walk again, going toward the army's headquarters. "We can try it that way, but I'm not holding my breath for it to work."

He and Jelko are silent the rest of the way. When we enter headquarters, Heslta is speaking with someone she dismisses once she sees us.

"Are you ready to go?" she asks.

"Yes," I say. "But there's been a change of plans." I describe Jelko's idea.

"It's worth a shot," she says. "I know just the person to lead the army. He'll do a fine job at it."

"Tell him to start around Pennington's castle." Stupid building I had to create for him. "As they near it, they're sure to find men Pennington sent out to harass those who don't want to follow him."

"Will do. Is there anything you need before you go? I have horses waiting outside for you."

"Anything else we need, I can create. But thank you."

She bows. "It's been a pleasure working with you, goddess."

"I've enjoyed my time with you as well." My throat tightens at the thought of not seeing her again. Though we aren't close, she has a sound mind and would be a good partner in this endeavor, but she needs to stay and lead the people of her city.

With goodbyes from Marric and Jelko, we're off. As I look ahead, I can't help the tiniest bit of fear that creeps in. I have a feeling it will continue to grow the closer we are to Pennington. I don't want to go back to him, but we have no other choice.

CHAPTER 80

THE RIDE IS hot and dusty—more so than I remember it being before. The seasons are changing again. A time with no rain is coming to this part of the land. Where we're going, they'll still have the occasional shower. More, if Pennington uses his magic.

His magic. What are we going to do about it? I wish we could put a collar on him, but even if we did, we'd have to get close enough to put it on. It'd be a dangerous possession, anyway. I'm proof of that. If Pennington got free, like I did, we'd be right back to where we started.

"How far is the nearest temple of love?" I ask.

"It's past Pennington's house," Marric says. "Unless we backtrack, there's one about two days' ride from Pennington's."

"Two days will become four. We can't wait that long." Though I hope the heavens can.

"I agree," Jelko says. "Every day it takes us to get to Pennington is another day his power grows."

"That's one thing we can't have." I push my horse a little faster, and the others follow my lead.

Though my cape is warm in the sun, I'm grateful for the shade it provides. I don't want to deal with a sunburn on top of everything else.

"Maybe we should dye my hair before we get there," I say. "Does either of you know how to do that?"

"I do," Marric says. "I used to do it for my mother all the time. We can do it tonight when we stop."

"Do you think that'll be enough to hide my appearance?"

"It'll be a start. Your eyes are still vivid, but with your hair dyed, you'll be less noticeable."

"Does it wash out?" I ask.

"The dye?"

"Yes."

"How often you wash it will determine how long it stays," he says. "Maybe a couple of weeks. Maybe more, since your hair is so white."

Good. I don't want to give up my hair for long. "What color should we dye it?"

"I'll try for a dark brown. It'll be hard to get color to stick to your hair, but doable."

We ride along, chatting on and off throughout the day, mostly about nothing. Food we're eating. Animals we're passing, like a small herd of deer. The weather. It's a long ride, made longer by the fact that I'm not riding with Marric. I miss the way I leaned into him and felt his strength. It bolstered me.

Now I have to settle for looking at him, but I don't want to do too much of that. He can't see me stare at him all the time. Instead, I keep my focus mostly forward.

There's still a hint of daylight peeking over the horizon when we stop.

"We should make camp here," Marric says.

After we set up and eat the dinner I make us, I ask Marric what he'll need to dye my hair.

"I'll need black walnut powder and black tea. If we leave them in your hair long enough, they should give it some color. We can repeat it tomorrow night if needed, to make it even darker. And if you'll make me some lemon juice, oil, soap, and water, I'll be able to clean my hands afterward."

"You sound like you did this more than once for your mother," I say.

"It was my job to keep her from looking her age."

I want to give his hand a squeeze. Instead, I create the items he needs.

He gets to work making the dye. When he's finished, he says, "Go ahead and take your cape off, then lean back so I can get to your hair."

As I'm taking off my cloak, Jelko says, "I'm going to go scout the area ahead. I won't be long."

"In the dark?" I ask.

"I need to make certain it's clear."

"Be safe."

"I will."

I sit back, laying my head near the bowl Marric worked the hair dye in. He reaches up and pours the liquid over my hair and brushes it in. I close my eyes. It feels nice. And then he puts his hands in my hair.

This feels good. Oh-so-good. It seems like this is the first time he's touched me since the kiss, and all I want to do is reach up and kiss him again.

Ignoring the feeling, I take the time to enjoy the feel of his fingers running through my hair. The way his touch makes peace settles in my heart and relaxes me. It's almost like being in the heavens again, but somehow even better.

He continues for longer than I expect. Hair dying sure takes a long time, for which I'm ever so grateful. His fingertips gently massage my head. It is the perfect moment. I can close everything else out. Pretend there's no Pennington. No war in the heavens. No me being a god and him being a human. Just this perfect, unaffected moment.

"You two are still working on the dye?" Jelko's voice startles me out of my moment. "I thought you'd be done by now," he says.

"Almost," comes Marric's gruff reply.

Marric's massage isn't as easy to enjoy with Jelko staring at us. Marric doesn't wait long before rinsing my hair, anyway.

As soon as he's done, I towel dry it. "Thank you for your help, Marric."

"Yup." He doesn't look up from cleaning his hands.

My heart patters pitifully. This is going to be a lengthy journey.

CHAPTER 81

THE NEXT DAY passes without incident. We don't talk much—just ride our horses under the hot sun. I wonder what I look like now that my hair is dark, but I don't want to conjure a mirror to find out. After all I've seen, it seems wasteful to create things just for me that aren't necessary. What's the point of worrying about my looks out here with no one around? I want to look good for Marric, but it doesn't matter. Even if I were the most beautiful creature in the world, I doubt he'd pay me any notice.

We add more dye to my hair when we stop for the night, but it's not as nice as before. Marric is quick to work, not lingering over separate strands of my hair. I can't enjoy it when I know he doesn't care. He's doing a job.

Jelko seems to sense the tension in the air, and he keeps quiet even at times when I expect him to say something. We're all sober with the task ahead.

The next several days go on more like the same. We pass a few people on the road, but no one pays us any mind, and we pretend not to pay them any attention either.

When the city comes into view, we stop, our three horses making a line across the dirt road.

"His castle is in there?" Jelko asks.

"It is." And so much more. He had me make him not just a castle but everything he'd need to become king. I don't know if I'll ever forgive myself, though I had no choice.

"Maybe we should leave the horses here," Jelko says. "Not many of the travelers we saw had horses."

I pat my horse on the neck. She's been a good animal. "I agree. We shouldn't do anything to draw attention to ourselves."

"Which means you need to leave your cloak behind," Marric says, "and keep your gaze down."

I hate looking submissive, but he's right. My eyes are too recognizable. "What do you think we'll find in the city?"

"It's hard to know," he says. "I'm thinking we'll find a lot of Pennington's followers. If they don't follow him, they're going to meet an unhappy end, from what we've heard. Doesn't mean there won't be sympathizers to our cause. They'll not admit it out loud."

"Just like we shouldn't admit what we're doing out loud," Jelko adds.

I take off my cloak, fold it up, and hide it in some shrubbery. We grab the small packs we've started carrying around so as not to leave much behind, and then we take off from our horses, not tying them up.

I glance back at them.

"They'll be fine," Marric says. "Someone will be along to take care of them, happy to have free horses no doubt."

"You're right." But it feels wrong leaving them behind.

We walk the rest of the way up the dusty road until it turns to cobblestone. The uneven rocks beneath my feet aren't comfortable, but at least we're not kicking up as much dirt. Some time after that, we reach the walls of the city. Guards are speckled throughout the entryway.

My nerves grow taut. I keep my head down, watching the feet of those around me. There aren't many other people entering the city with us. It's too bad, because that would help hide us better.

Marric stays on my right and Jelko on my left. We move in

between two guards, only before we get through, the guard on the left stops us. "What business do you have here?"

Oh, nothing much. We're just here to take down your boss.

"We're looking to buy things at the market," Jelko says.

"Do you plan on staying long?" the guard asks.

"We may stay overnight. Maybe two or three nights, if things go well."

I'm grateful for Jelko's quick answers, but they do nothing to ease my nerves. The guard shifts his stance, moving closer to us. Creation forbid I have to bring out my power or sword now. That's not a good, unnoticeable way of getting in.

"Very well," the guard says. "You may pass, but know we don't take nonsense in our city. Pennington wouldn't hear of it."

"Of course," Jelko says.

We move forward, and I let out a relieved breath.

"Wait a second," the guard says behind us.

I freeze, every part of me ready to fight if it comes to it. I hope it doesn't. Did they figure us out? Is that why he's calling us back? My fingers tingle to grab my blade. I'm ready to, at a moment's notice.

Jelko turns. "Yes?"

"You dropped this." The guard hands him something I can't see.

"Thank you," Jelko says.

We walk on, trying not to hurry, but I feel like running. Once we're out of ear shot, Marric says, "That was a close one."

"Too close," I say, fingers still aching for my sword. "Let's not do that again."

"I'm afraid we're going to do a lot worse in the hours and days to come," Jelko says.

I heed his words. He's proven himself a sound voice of reason. I'm forever grateful he was the one to guard me and not someone who didn't care. Not that I can't handle worse. Saldor was fairly easy to overtake, despite my wound. Pennington will be harder, I think.

"Where to now?" I didn't get to explore the city before when Pennington had me, so nothing is familiar.

"We should head to the market," Marric says, though we don't plan on buying anything. "There should be good gossip there, if nothing else. We can learn a few things before we go storming in."

"Let's go," I say.

I follow Marric through the streets with Jelko at my side. It's comforting to have them both here, but my back feels exposed. We can't have them flanking my front and back, though. It would look odd for us to move in a line. Between the three of us, our armor, and weapons, we'll be able to take whatever comes. Unless it's Pennington.

I shiver at the thought of seeing him. It's not a memory I want to revisit. But this time, he won't have me under lock and key. This time, he will face my wrath. Just thinking about it has me striding faster.

The streets are clean—a nice, wide cobblestone beneath our feet —with houses on both sides. There are a few people about, either numbers growing gradually. They aren't smiling, but neither are they scowling. I wish I had the ability to read minds, so I'd know what they're thinking. If they are happy with Pennington's rule or not.

It strikes me then that maybe the people do want him to rule over them. Maybe they want a king. I shy away from the idea, but it keeps coming back. Is it right to take that away from them?

I'd like to think yes, simply because he's forcing himself to be a leader to a large group who don't want him. He's hurting people because they don't agree with him. He isn't the type of person I want to leave in power.

The street widens, more people milling about. Both sidewalks have stalls full of vendors selling different wares.

Marric pulls back to my side, so the three of us walk side by side. "Who should we speak with first?"

It's not like we know who the most gossipy person is. "We'll have to guess. Talk to them all, maybe."

Jelko rubs the back of his neck. "It's going to be a long day."

CHAPTER 82

JELKO'S PREDICTION IS CORRECT. It is a long day, with little information on Pennington. People are surprisingly tight-lipped about him. Not that we come right out and ask, but we use leading questions like, *How are the human leaders around here*?

No one seems to notice me. I keep myself small and unobtrusive, and it seems to work.

We're at one of the last vendors, the day winding down. I pick up a shawl from the table, fingering the fine material.

"Good choice," says a woman's cracking voice.

I don't look up, but try to gauge what I can about her without meeting her gaze. "You have lovely wares. I'd enjoy a scarf out of this material."

"It would be fitting for a lady such as yourself."

Jelko hands the woman some money. "We'll take it."

"Thank you, most gracious sir. Are there any other fine wares I can interest you in?"

I fold the fabric and place it in my pack. It's not that I need it, but buying something from people makes them more likely to talk.

"Have you anything that would be suitable for meeting with

Pennington?" I ask, hoping it's not too forward and won't give us away.

The woman claps her hands together. "You're meeting with Pennington? Why didn't you say so in the first place? I have just the thing for you." She's more open by far than other vendors have been.

She disappears behind the curtain at the back of her stall, and I use the opportunity to meet Marric's gaze. He's looks surprised as I am at this change. Maybe we didn't approach the others the same way? Or maybe this woman is a Pennington supporter.

Several moments later, she comes back with a material that shimmers in the fading light. "This will be perfect for meeting with him. He's sure to listen to you if you wear a dress made from this?"

"It certainly is pretty." I reach out and feel the softness that reminds me of the heavens. It almost makes me wonder if that's where they got it, but that's impossible. We wouldn't bring anything like this down here. Would we?

"Pennington had it delivered. He'd love to see someone wearing it; I'm certain of it."

"Who delivers it? Where do they get it? If you don't mind my asking…"

"A boy delivers it to me. He gets it from Pennington's resources. He gives it to me at a special price."

"We'll take it," Marric says. "How much?"

"Ten krats."

An awkward silence follows. That's a lot of money for a piece of material, no matter how grand.

"How about three krats?" Marric asks.

She pulls the fabric out of reach. "The price is non-negotiable." Her voice turns curt.

"We'll take it," Jelko says, "but only if you can refer us to a shop that will turn it into a dress for our fair lady."

"I'd love to." Her voice is warm again, like nothing happened.

Jelko pays her and gets information on a shop we can use.

"Tell me," I say, keeping my tone casual. "Have you met Pennington in person?"

"Only when I went to him to say my shop was failing and I needed help. That was when he gave me the material. It's much sought after and helps me remain afloat."

"Does he visit with the people often?" Jelko asks.

"Every afternoon, in the throne room of his castle."

I suppress a shudder. I remember that room all too well. But her story makes me hesitate once again. Sure, Pennington chained me up, but he seems to be doing good by at least a few of these people. What is his game? Is he still trying to win over the people while doing harmful things behind their backs? I have to find out.

CHAPTER 83

WE FIND an inn to spend the night. Marric wants us to take dinner in our rooms so as not to draw notice to me, but I insist we have it on the main floor. The place is busier than I'd expect for how few people we saw coming in this morning, but then maybe they all came before us or later in the day.

The owner brings us roast mutton, and I eat at a slow pace.

"Can you please eat a little faster?" he asks. "We need to get you to your room."

"Nothing is going to happen here. It's all fine," I reply, not bothering one bit to speed up.

"Fine until someone recognizes you," he mutters.

I put my hand on his, forcing myself to make the contact I want even though he doesn't seem to care for it. "We have a job to do. Whether you like it or not, we're here. We have to listen to the people talking about Pennington. Please don't be angry with me."

He sighs and puts his other hand a top of mine, spreading warmth through me. "I'm sorry. It's your safety that concerns me."

"I understand, but we can't let that stop us."

"But we will if it gets too dangerous," Jelko says, reminding me Marric and I aren't alone.

I take my hand from Marric's and miss him the moment I do. "You guys realize this whole thing is dangerous, right?"

Marric grunts. "This isn't the place to talk about it."

"We'll continue to ignore it, then," I say. "I'm all right with that."

Marric mumbles something under his breath and returns to eating. I do the same. Not like I can do much else; I certainly can't lessen the danger around me.

As time wears on, the inn gets more crowded. We wouldn't be able to have any sensitive conversations now, even if we whispered. There are too many people in this place that could overhear what we're talking about.

The plus side for us is we can hear everyone else as well. Problem is none of them seem to be speaking about Pennington or anything related to him.

I finally finish my plate only to have the owner whisk it away. Seems Marric's not the only one who wants me to go to my room.

With a sigh over the lack of learning anything useful today, I stand. As we're making our way through the crowd, the word *Pennington* reaches my ears. I stop, pretending to readjust my shoe, and listen carefully.

"He's looking for that girl still. Some say she's a goddess, others a witch."

"Whatever she is, she's caused a lot of problems."

I get a nudge from behind, and I hurry forward. It's not the news I was looking for, but it's good for us to know he's still looking for me. It makes me glad Marric dyed my hair. Will Pennington be expecting me to come back to the city? I sure hope not, but if I heard talk about him, perhaps he's heard talk about me.

I go to open the door to our room, and Jelko stops me. "Let me clear it first."

I nod, and he goes in. It's awkward, standing out here in the hall with Marric. I don't know what to do with my hands or where to look. The touch we shared earlier meant something to me, and I

279

want to tell him so. Unfortunately, there are too many things standing in the way.

"It's clear," Jelko says.

We hurry in the room, and Marric shuts the door behind us.

It's a clean room, though a little threadbare. It has a closet, a dresser, and a bed with a thin quilt. I take a seat on the bed hoping it's clean.

"Let's get something straight," Marric says. "You can't risk your life needlessly."

"Excuse me, but there's nothing needless about what I'm doing." I huff. "Besides, I thought you understood the dangers going in."

"Understanding them and dealing with them are two separate things. Next time I tell you it's time to go, you need to listen."

How dare he. "And next time I tell you I'm fine, *you* need to listen," I spit back. "I'm obviously right, since nothing happened."

"Yes, but you heard those guys. They're looking for you. Pennington is still pushing for your return. We should never have risked coming back here."

"I disagree. No one's recognized me yet. We'll be fine. We need to figure out how to sneak into Pennington's home."

"Not *we*," Marric says. "You're staying here."

"Ha. Not happening."

"Look," Jelko says, "I don't know what's going on between you two, but you both need to calm down. If you keep going at this rate, you'll have the whole inn know what we're doing here."

I clamp my mouth shut. What's going on here? Why are Marric and I so upset at each other? We usually get along so well.

"You know as well as I do that we can't risk Izlana's safety," Marric tells Jelko.

"And you both know Izlana is right here and will do whatever she wants," I say. "You knew there was going to be danger before we left."

"That was before we were here." Marric rubs his forehead. "It's not that I want to make it so you can't do anything. I want you to be safe."

I soften my voice. "I know you do, but there are things that have to be done. We don't know how hard Pennington will be to defeat. We need every resource we can find to fight him, including me."

"That doesn't mean I have to like it," Marric says.

"I don't like it either," Jelko says, "but I think she's right."

I know I am, but I'm not about to be smug about it. Well, maybe just a little.

CHAPTER 84

I'm grateful to get up in the morning. The men insisted I take the bed, which was probably better than the floor, but still hard and lumpy. I tossed and turned all night, trying to get comfortable and instead thinking about my fight with Marric.

I don't want to fight anymore, but I'm right. I'm needed. I also realize he's right—I have to be kept safe. I can't let anything happen to me. But how do we comprise?

Once we're back up from a quick breakfast of grits downstairs, I say, "What's the plan for today?"

"I've been thinking"—Marric sounds cautious—"maybe Jelko should visit Pennington in the guise that he wanted to meet him. He's never met Pennington before so he won't be recognized, and he'll be able to check the place out. Izlana and I can go to the dress maker's and see if there's any information to be found there."

Jelko looks to me for an answer.

"As much as I want to be in the action, I think it's a wise plan," I say. "We should be able to cover more ground this way." I turn to Jelko. "But you have to promise me you'll stay safe. That you won't do anything but observe while you're there."

He nods. "I can do that for you, goddess."

He hasn't called me that in a long time. I'm guessing he did now because he's following what he thinks are orders.

"I'd better get going," he says. "I hope to beat the crowd there." He walks toward the door but stops when he gets to Marric. "You'd better make sure not a thing happens to her."

"She's safe on my watch."

"I know. That's the only reason I'm comfortable leaving her with you."

"You two…" I say, exasperated. Though really, I'm touched by their caring.

With one final bow at me, Jelko leaves. His absence is immediate. Though he tries to make his presence unobtrusive, his quiet presence at all times has become a comfort for me.

"When should we leave?" I ask Marric.

"Maybe in another hour. It's still early."

"And what do we do in the mean time?" I have a few ideas that involve his lips, but I banish them.

He goes to the window, looking at who-knows-what.

Not the answer I was going for, but one I should expect with all we've been through lately.

"Maybe we should talk." His response surprises me.

I have a feeling I'll need to be off my feet for this. I move over to the bed and sit. "Talk about what?"

"Us."

That one word puts an arrow through my heart. "What about us?"

"We've been distant since…"

The kiss. I don't say it aloud. I wait for him to. He never does; he just leaves it hanging out there, tormenting my soul.

"Maybe this wasn't such a good idea," he says.

"We should talk about it. Things haven't been the same between us since we kissed." After a deep breath for courage, I add, "I miss things the way they were before."

"When we were friends," he says.

But that's not what I meant. I meant when there was this

tension between us, like something could happen. Before it actually did, and I realized it could never be. But how do I tell him that? I don't know if he wants to hear it.

"I have to be honest," he says, and I'm glad he can't see me cringe against the hard words to come. "I liked that kiss a lot more than I should have."

Air rushes out of me. Did he say what I think he did?

He grips the window seal tight, his hands turning white.

How do I respond to this? How do I admit I also liked it a lot more than I should have? I don't know whether to be elated or horrified. I feel frozen, like I can't move or breathe.

"I know we can never be, but I thought you should know that. Know that I care about you," he says.

The frozen feeling finally leaves, but I'm cold. Too cold. How does he know we could never be? He knows nothing about mates and gods. "Why do you say we can never be?"

He turns, and there's a fire in his eyes I've never seen before. I can't understand it. "Because you're a goddess, and I'm merely a human," he says.

"That's why you've been avoiding me? Because of that difference?" I feel my own fire kindling—one of anger and determination. It swells up within me until I have to act, whether it's a stupid move or not.

I jump to my feet, march over to him, and press my lips against his. At first he's hard, unyielding. But then he gives, turning soft and pliable against me. And what a kiss it is. It sends molten lava through my veins, pressing me closer, begging me for more.

I wrap my arms around his neck, anchoring myself to him. His arms go around me, holding me. It's perfect. Everything about it is what I've always wanted and more. It's even better than the first time we kissed. Even more wonderful and magical.

I want to stay here always. To keep him next to me. With me. I want him forever and ever. But I can't have him. Not the way I want. The thought brings tears to my eyes that run down my cheeks as we continue the kiss. It hurts now, making me throb with grief.

I want to stay in his arms, but knowing I can't have him the way I want—a real, warm, connective way—I wrench away from him, sobbing.

CHAPTER 85

MARRIC PUTS a hand on my back, and I work to get my emotions together. As soon as I can speak without the threat of tears, I ask, "Is it time for us to get going?"

"Don't you think we should talk about this first?"

I turn to find him watching me with concerned eyes. "There's nothing to talk about," I say.

"Clearly, there is. We can't kiss like that and have you cry without talking about it."

I fold my arms across my chest. "Fine. You're right. We can't be together. Not because you're a human and I'm a god, but for other reasons I can't discuss with you. Happy now?"

His eyebrows wrinkle together. "No. I want to know your reason. Then I'll be happy."

"I guess we both have to be miserable, then." I hurry to the door and wrench it open. "Coming?"

He lets out a huff before following me out of the room. "You can't avoid this forever, you know."

Yes, I can. But I don't tell him that. I don't want to think about it any longer.

We walk through the streets, though I don't notice much of

anything until we come to a house with a sign in front of it that reads, "Dress Shoppe."

"This is it." Marric opens the door for me.

I go in, and he follows.

"How can I help you?" a woman asks. She has vivid-red hair and freckles smattered across her face, despite looking like she's in her thirties.

"We were told you could help us turn this into a dress." I pull out the material we purchased yesterday.

"Oh, the new fabric from Pennington. I'd love to make this into a dress for you. Come stand over here, and I'll take your measurements."

How does she know it's from Pennington? As she takes my measurements, I casually ask that.

"Everyone who's anyone knows. Ever since it showed up, it's been all the rage."

Guess I'm not everyone. "We're not from around here. Do you know where Pennington gets the material from?"

She finishes and leans in close. "The word is that he gets it from the gods."

I work to keep from gasping out loud. I was right. It *is* from the heavens. Why would a god give this to Pennington? What purpose could it possibly serve?

"Do you believe such rumors?" Marric asks.

She turns her attention toward him. "Where else would one find cloth such as this?"

"Good point," I say, hoping Marric will stop asking questions I know the answer to.

We talk for several minutes about what I want in a dress, and she promises to have it done within the week after we pay her. I hope we aren't here to pick it up by then. A week is an awfully long time to still be around when I have work to do in the heavens.

"Thank you for your help," I tell her.

"Certainly. I'll see you soon."

Marric and I don't talk on the way back to the inn. Once we're sequestered in our room, he asks, "What did you make of that the dressmaker's answers?"

"I have no doubt Pennington is getting the material from one of the gods. The question is, which one?"

"And why?"

"Without asking Pennington, I'm not sure we'll find the answer."

"We'll have to see what Jelko says when he gets back. If he has any news that can help."

The dress shop took all morning. I can only hope Jelko is back soon. Not just so I hopefully have more answers, but also so I don't have to be alone with Marric any longer than necessary.

"Izlana." The way Marric whispers my name, like it's a caress along my skin, has me backing against the wall.

"What do you need?" My voice is sharper than I intend, but I can't handle him getting close again only to have to push him away.

"Why won't you talk to me?"

"The gods have secrets." It's the only thing I can think to say.

He comes nearer, making me press against the wall behind me. "How many secrets do you have, Izlana?" He gently touches my lips with his fingertips, and I close my eyes with the action.

"I can't tell you." Though with how he's making my knees quiver, I want to tell him.

He comes closer so I feel his warm breath on my cheek. I wonder if he's going to kiss me again. Instead, he says, "I can't find a way around your objections if you don't tell them to me."

I try to clear my mind to form a response. "What happened to you not being able to be with me, since I'm a goddess?"

"That thought is lingering in the back of my mind, but with the way you kissed me, it's getting pushed farther and farther away." He cups my neck, bring his lips so near mine, and they brush each other. "I want to know your secrets so I can chase them away."

The door opens, and we burst apart. My heart beats furiously, like never before. All I want is to be back in his arms, feeling him close. Nothing else seems to matter. Which is dangerous. I focus my attention on Jelko, though my body is all too aware of Marric.

Thankfully, Jelko doesn't notice anything. Or maybe he does and doesn't want to say anything.

"What did you find out?" I ask.

"It's worse than we thought. Pennington is generous to some, but he executes anyone who crosses the line he thinks is right, even if they aren't in the wrong."

I put a hand to my mouth, trying to keep the contents of my stomach down. How could any person do such a thing?

"How do we get to him?" Marric asks.

"Pennington's castle is heavily guarded. Not to mention he has an entourage of guards. I don't know how we'll get in, not to mention close to him."

"We've got magic, my power, weapons, and armor on our side," I say. "There has to be something we can do."

"But what?" Marric asks.

"I know." But they aren't going to like it. "We're going to use me for bait."

CHAPTER 86

"No," Marric and Jelko shout at the same time.

I put my hand up to stop further protestations. "I know we can't endanger me, but I don't see how else to get him out in the open. We have to try this."

"I think it's too risky," Marric says.

"And I say it's my risk to take," I counter.

Jelko gives me a piercing gaze. "I agree with Marric."

"All right, then. How do you two propose we capture Pennington?" I ask.

Both are silent.

"That's right," I say. "There is no other way. Whatever we try will have us running from his guards at best. We need to try this."

"I don't like it," Marric says.

"Honestly, I don't, either." Just how much I don't like it we aren't about to talk about, though. "But I think we have to do this, for the safety of everyone else involved."

"It's asking for trouble, but maybe you're right," Jelko says.

That's probably as much of a victory as I'm going to get. "I say we spread rumors I'm at a specific place and wait to ambush him there."

"You know the problem with this plan?" Marric asks. "He's not going to come for you. He's going to send his guards."

"Then what do you propose?" I ask.

"Let's sneak in his home at night. I can get us in one of the upper story windows. Then we'd bypass the guards on the ground floor."

"What about the guards outside?" I ask.

Jelko taps his fingers on his chin. "We could create a distraction."

"Without separating?" I ask. "It's not like we have a lot of people on our side, and I hate to split us up."

"We could send a note to the army to sit outside the city," Marric says. "That should draw some of the guards away from Pennington."

"But if it comes to an actual fight, how many people will be hurt because of it?" I hate to think of how high that number could be.

"It's better than letting Pennington continue to reign," Jelko says. "We should do it."

"As do I," Marric adds.

I close my eyes, trying to think of another way—*any* other way—to get to Pennington. Nothing comes to mind. "Fine. Let's do it. But tell the army to be careful. We don't want unnecessary deaths on our hands."

"I'll send the note right away." With a bow to me, Jelko turns and leaves the room.

I hope we're making the right decision.

CHAPTER 87

IT TAKES a week for the army to gather. A week longer than I'd like but quickly considering the short notice. We're lucky they were in the area dealing with some of Pennington's men anyway.

I spent this time mostly in the room with either Marric or Jelko while the other goes out in search of information. Days with Jelko here are much easier than the ones I'm stuck with the man I think I love but can't have. Other thoughts are easier to deal with.

Even though we have time, we don't bother picking up my dress. Something about the thought of owning it makes me sick. Probably due to the fact that it comes from Pennington, and nobody knows where he got it from. Whichever god it was, I'm not happy. They know we're not supposed to give things to humans in exchange for favors. I have a feeling that's what happened, and if that's the case, I have a god in mind who could have done this. Ramco.

He's behind everything lately. I wouldn't put anything past him. What further lengths is he willing to go to so he can get what he wants?

The door to the room that feels like my prison opens, and

Marric enters, a solemn expression on his face. "The army is in position."

"That means we attack tonight." I jump to my feet.

"Don't be so excited," Marric says.

"I know you're worried about me, but I'm sick of this room. I don't want to dwell here longer than I have to. In fact, dusk is in an hour. We should start getting ready now."

"I hate to agree," Jelko says, "but she's right. We should get ready to go."

"Is everyone still good with the plan?" Marric asks.

I nod.

"Got it," Jelko says.

* * *

WE ARE in our black clothes to blend in with the night. We look like the most somber people to ever grace this city. That's how I feel. I don't want any lives lost tonight. Not even Pennington's, if it can be helped. He'd be sure to go to Ramco, to help him further.

We head out of the inn for the last time and down the streets, trying not to stand out. There aren't many people out on the streets this time of night, so there's not much to hide from. I hope none of Pennington's men stop to question us.

The air grows cooler as the night takes over the day. Not so cool I need a cloak, more like a nice break from the heat of the day.

Our steps are quiet as we move toward Pennington's castle. His sanctuary. The place I created for him, without choice. I wish I were the god of destruction—not that there is one. But if I were, I could take on Pennington and his monstrosity of a house with little problem. Instead, I have to figure out a way to make my power of creation work against him.

There's the sound of footsteps running toward us. Jelko backs us into a nearby alleyway, and we press against the wall, trying not to be noticed.

The footsteps near, until they pass, but there's a lot of them. A slew of guards. While this is what we wanted, I fear one of them will turn his head and see us. And if they know who I am, the whole plan will go by the wayside.

Marric takes my hand. I glance up at him, and he gives it a squeeze. His skin is callused from practicing with his sword, but I don't mind. In fact, I kind of like it. I don't know how he does it, but he distracts me from the people running by until they're gone.

And he takes my breath away. How does he manage to give me what I can't give myself?

We wait another minute, making sure the road is clear. I slip my hand from Marric's. As much as I want to keep hold of him, I can't have any distractions in what's to come.

We slide out onto the street and hurry forward. It doesn't take much longer to get to Pennington's. He's improved his place, though not in size. It's still gigantic, but the fence around it goes further out, taking up a larger area around it. The fence is made of stone and only about waist high. Still, it's one more barrier in our way.

Guards are still milling about. "What do we do about them?" I whisper.

"They're fewer than before," Jelko says. "We can make a loud noise over here and then come in from the other side."

"I'll set off one of my fireworks." It worked well the last time.

This is it, then. We are about to enter Pennington's domain.

CHAPTER 88

I HURRY to create several large fireworks with a long tail, so they won't go off right away. This way, we'll have time to get to the other side of the castle. Once they're created, I make certain Marric and Jelko are ready. They each give me a nod, so I light the fireworks with a flash of fire.

We hurry away from the area as quietly as possible. There's no sense drawing attention to ourselves early. We make it all the way to the other side of the castle, and the firework still hasn't gone off. Thankful I made it long enough, I get ready to jump the fence and run.

But it still doesn't go off. Nor does it a minute later. Did I create faulty fireworks? I've never created a failure before, so I doubt I'm starting now. Did someone find it and cut the cord before the fire reached the explosion part? If so, they're probably on to us.

"Maybe we should chance it and go," I whisper.

Marric shakes his head.

Jelko nods.

"Don't give me mixed answers," I say.

The next moment, the boom of a firework going off reaches us

—only it sounds more like a cannon, and there's a flash of light on the other side of the castle.

The guards run toward the sound. I jump on the stone fence and throw myself over it, grateful it's not taller. Jelko and Marric come over at the same time, and we all hurry to the castle. By the time we make it there, I'm panting for air. The long space we covered in a short amount of time was worth the run, and no one seems to have spotted us.

"How are you going to get us to the second floor window?" I ask Marric. I suppose I should have asked sooner, but I trust him. I could even make something to get us there, but if he's willing, it'd be good to let him practice his magic.

"Like this." He puts a hand on me and pulls me closer. If he weren't pulling Jelko in too, I would think he was looking for some romance at the wrong time. Apparently, I'm not focusing on the things I should be.

The next thing I know, we're moving upward, a clump of dirt lifting us to the second story window. I hurry to open it and climb in. The flight up was disconcerting, and I have no desire to stay outside longer than necessary.

Once we're all in the castle, Marric sends the bit of earth down, so it relaxes back where it should be.

I glance at him, letting how impressed I am show on my face. "That was very well done."

"Yes, well, I've been practicing when I've had time to myself."

"We've got to go," Jelko says, reminding me we're in Pennington's castle.

Marric leads the way, with me following and Jelko in the rear. We race toward Pennington's bedroom, where we hope to find him. If he's not there now, he will be sooner or later.

We get close to the hallway his room is in and slow when we reach the corner. Marric peers around and snaps back. He holds up one finger and mouths, "Guard."

We'll want to get rid of him but without alerting others. Jelko shrugs. Well then, I guess that leaves it up to me.

"Stay here," I mouth.

Before either of them can protest, I put my sword behind my back and walk around the corner, like I belong in this place.

"What are you doing up here?" the guard asks in a deep voice.

"I've got something for Pennington," I say, using my most sultry voice. I fail horribly, but it's enough to get me close enough to him to whack him over the head with my sword.

"Well done," Marric whispers.

"Too close for me," Jelko adds.

I nod toward the door. Marric puts his hand on the handle and tries to turn it. I'm surprised when he manages. The door swings open.

"I'm glad to see you decided to join me," Pennington says, sending a chill through me.

CHAPTER 89

How did he know we were here?

"The fireworks gave you away," Pennington says, as if he read my mind. "I'd heard about you using them before. I figured I might be seeing you when your army closed in on the city, but I have to say, actually doing so is a pleasure. Though the dark hair doesn't suit you."

Pretending to be perfectly calm, which I'm not at all, I say, "I can't say this castle suits you."

Marric and Jelko flank my sides, swords drawn.

Pennington ignores them, having eyes only for me. "It's been too long since we last met," he says. "I must say I'm curious to know how you got your collar off."

"Like I'd tell you." I spit the words out, letting my hatred fill them. "It's time to be done with your reign, Pennington."

"Why would you knock me off my rule? I'm becoming a great king. The people love me."

"The people that you don't force to do your will? The ones left because you haven't killed them yet?"

"Someone's been doing their homework. Should we see how

much you've been studying up?" The soft sneer he gives me makes fear crawl through me.

He raises his hands, palms facing us. The floor shakes beneath my feet. Next thing I know, the floor is falling out underneath Marric and Jelko. I don't know who to grab for, so I try for them both. Marric I miss completely, but Jelko's fingers brush mine before he falls. I rush to create a net that catches them before they call fall all the way to the ground.

"We'll come up for you," Jelko yells, maneuvering himself from the net.

"Stay there," I call.

Keeping an eye on Pennington, I start to create a ladder. I'm halfway done, when Penning pulls out a bow and arrow and shoots at me. I dive to the floor, my feet dangling off one of the holes and the half-made ladder falling through the other.

While on the ground, I make a second ladder, finishing it in time for Pennington to shoot another arrow.

I jump to my feet, as Marric climbs up. "I didn't know you were handy with a bow and arrow," I say.

"I heard about your swords. You didn't think I'd let you get near me with them?" He holds yet another arrow, ready to shoot me. As soon as Marric surfaces, Pennington changes his aim for him.

"Don't shoot," I cry. Even though we have armor on, he could still get him in the face.

"Ah, yes. I see we've grown feelings for the poor servant boy who helped you escape my clutches. All the more reason I should kill him."

"Don't. I'll do what you want. Don't hurt him." Not that I really will, but I have to buy time. I can't have Marric injured because of me. I need to distract Pennington. "Tell me where you got a hold of fabric from the heavens."

He chuckles, not easing up on his bow. "That's not the only thing I got. This arrow is from the heavens too."

Fear trickles through me. "We don't have arrows in the heavens."

"You mean you didn't. They're clearly there now, because I have one. Much like your sword, it can't miss its mark."

"Ramco." The name boils off my tongue.

"That's right. In exchange for giving him a war on the world, he's giving me all sorts of nice little prizes. Let's see how well this one works, shall we?"

"*No.*" I throw my sword, aiming for the bulk of his frame. He lets off the arrow at the same time.

I want to push Marric away, but everything happens too fast. Someone else beats me to it. Jelko. The arrow swivels to the floor, where Marric now lies. Jelko and I dive for him. Jelko is faster, and the arrow slices through him. He grunts, and I cry out, pain riddling me as much as if I were the one that got hit.

"Jelko, no." Pennington could be attacking, but I care more about my friend then him. I roll him over, and find the arrow went all the way through his armor to his chest to graze Marric. Marric's barely bleeding, but Jelko isn't having the same luck.

"What do we do?" I cry.

"It was a pleasure serving you, goddess." Jelko's final words are uttered with a stutter. Life leaves him, and I feel my power increase the tiniest bit—enough for one human to have joined me in the heavens.

Tears fill my eyes as I turn to take on Pennington. I'll do whatever it takes to avenge Jelko. Only it's too late. The sword did its job, and Pennington is gone.

CHAPTER 90

MARRIC, some people from the army, and I stand around, waiting for Jelko to be buried. I created the best clothes I could for the occasion, not only using the traditional funereal purple, but threading it with yellow to represent the sanctity of his life.

I can't help but think it's not enough. I never realized how much it'd hurt to be parted from someone I care about. Though I can see Jelko when I return to the heavens, it won't be the same. His life on this world was cut short. It's not supposed to be like this.

Marric holds my hand, giving me what little comfort he can. I suppose I should refuse it, but right now, all I want is someone to offer me that little bit of comfort. Even if it means later having to re-explain that we can't be together, I'll take it.

They finish laying Jelko in a hollowed-out tree trunk and get ready to lower it into the ground. It's sad, but he doesn't have any family here. We don't know if he even has a family. A note was sent to Heslta to tell her what happened, and she wrote back telling us to go ahead and bury him.

Letting go of Marric, I kneel beside the tree trunk and put my hand on it. "Thank you for protecting me and Marric with your life. You will never be forgotten."

I'll tell my child stories of Jelko's bravery and have her pass the stories to her daughter, and so on through the ages. I won't let his sacrifice be in vain.

When I stand, I realize everyone else followed my lead and knelt. I walk away from the trunk, letting them bury it. I can't watch this part. It's too much for me to maintain control of my emotions, and I'm not sure I want to be known as the goddess who cries, even at a funeral.

Moments later, Marric catches up with me. "Are you doing all right?"

"As well as can be expected, I suppose. I don't know what to think. Though I knew it was dangerous, I didn't expect anyone to die."

"I know what you mean."

"You do?" I stop walking to look at him.

"Yes. He died saving my life. I know that arrow would have run me through if he hadn't jumped in front of me. It's a hard thing, knowing you're alive because someone else died."

I almost take his hand, but I see the funeral crowd coming our way. I turn away from them and hurry forward, Marric following. "You can be comforted by the fact that he's not gone," I say.

"What do you mean?" Marric asks.

"He's in the heavens, of course. You should remember that."

"I do. It's not the same. Does he walk around the heavens?"

"There are parts of the heavens designated for those who've passed on to the next life. It's meant just for them. Even the gods don't dwell there. Though, the gods can ask mortals to join them in the rest of the heavens, it's rarely done."

"So you won't be mingling with Jelko when you return?"

"It may not be the norm, but I plan on speaking with him as often as I can. He was a good man in this life. He will be in the next, too."

We're both silent as the thought sinks in.

I watch Marric from the corner of my eye. I don't want to leave him—don't want to go to the heavens—but it must be done. Once there, I'll never return here. Never see Marric again. My heart aches at that.

Even if Marric dies believing in me and becomes one of my followers, I'll be an old woman by then. He'll return to his prime and want nothing to do with me. I may even have a child. I should, actually. Not that I want to, but I can't let the line of creators die off.

"You know what we need to do now?" Marric asks.

My thoughts are still on taking a mate. I won't let it be him. I won't let Marric be treated like that. But that's probably not what he's thinking of. "What?" I ask.

"Get you to the temple of love," Marric says. "Return you to the heavens."

I swallow past the thickening in my throat. "You're right. I need to return to where I came from." And try to stop a war.

EPISODE SEVEN

Episode Seven

CHAPTER 91

"How much farther is the temple of love?" I ask Marric, anxious to talk to the goddess Charmina. I hope she has answers for me. News that I don't need to hurry back. That the rumor of the war in the heavens was just that—a rumor. That I'm not needed at all, though my return would be most welcome.

What would I do if I weren't needed in the heavens? Could I stay here and create a life with Marric? No. I have followers who need me, and it wouldn't be fair to him. I need to let him go. To give him a life all his own. Let him be free to find true love with someone he can marry and respect, not someone who'll trample all over him.

"Izlana?" Marric calls me from my musings.

"Yes?"

"Is everything all right? I answered your question, but you didn't seem to hear me."

I sigh. "I'm sorry. What did you say?"

"That it's a two-day ride from here. It shouldn't be much longer before you have answers."

Answers. Just what I need. Only it means leaving him behind. "That's good," I say, but my heart isn't into it.

"Is something wrong? I mean more than Jelko's death. You seem more distant than sad at the moment." He goes to take my hand, but I snatch it away.

I can't have us connected this way. I've already led him on too much as it is. "There's just a lot on my mind."

He looks forward. "I get it. You don't want to talk. You could have said that, instead of being evasive."

"I don't want to hurt your feelings," I say.

"Is it about those secrets you keep?"

I don't say anything.

"I'll take that as a yes," he says.

"It's not that I don't want to tell you; it's that I can't."

"I get it." Though he's clearly unhappy about it.

"But you're not happy about it," I say.

"I don't wan— You hear that?" He stops, cocking his head. "More horses coming this way."

"And nowhere to hide."

"We'll be fine. Stay close." He shifts his horse to walk closer to mine and speeds up a little.

I follow suit, listening carefully as the sounds grow nearer. I put my hand on the hilt of my blade, just in case. We haven't had any trouble since I took care of Pennington, but it pays to be cautious. We thought about taking some of the army with us but decided we needed to move faster and with more stealth than they would afford.

When I glance backward, the riders come into sight. I grip the pommel tighter, ready for action. The horses and their riders pass us without a single look. I ease my hand from my sword. There's no telling what they'd have done if they wanted to fight, but thankfully, they were only passing by.

The tension between Marric and me is thick as we continue on. It makes me miss Jelko more, for how he came between us when needed.

The heat of the day lessens as the sun dips in the sky. I wish it were enough to pull out my cloak—I feel naked without it—but it's still too warm. I miss the heavens, where the temperature is always what I want. Never too hot, never too cold. Just right.

I miss the peace I had there. The joy I found in doing my duties. I'm anxious to get back, but I'm afraid it won't ever be the same.

"We should stop for the night," Marric says.

I'd rather keep going, to find my way sooner, but he's right. Without another word, we lead our horses to a clearing off the road.

I make us some chicken and dumplings for dinner, which we eat in silence. I want to reach out, to explain the mate thing to him, but it's forbidden. Not being able to talk about it leaves little room for conversation.

I pull my blankets down from the saddle. "Do you want me to take first watch?"

"No. I got it." He doesn't even get settled; he sits on the ground, staring up at the stars.

I trust him to keep a good watch. I put my blankets down to try to get some rest. It's not hard, with as exhausted as I am and having grown accustomed to sleeping on the road.

I quickly fall asleep.

Then, a hand is pressed against my mouth. "Move, and I'll slit you open," a craggy voice says.

CHAPTER 92

A BLADE IS PRESSED against my chest. I hold as still as can be, but my heart doesn't do the same. It beats wildly, out of control. Where is Marric? Did they capture him? Hurt him? I glance around but don't see anyone but my attacker.

He's got a thin mustache and beady eyes. He's thin, spindly, with long, dark robes. His dark gaze is focused on me. "You're going to come with me, no questions or comments, or else you'll get my knife."

Not daring to say anything, I nod my understanding. My sword is strapped to my side. If I can stand and get to it fast enough, I may have a chance to knock this guy out.

The spindly man follows me with his knife as I sit up and rise to my feet. I'm taller than he is by several inches. It should give me the advantage if it comes to a fight. Not that I'm trained in hand-to-hand combat without a weapon. Most of my skills come from my sword. If only I could get my hands on it.

"I'm going to tie you up, and you're not going to fight me, or my knife will be back where it started," the man says.

I nod, but of course I don't agree. This may be my only chance to pull my sword on him. He turns me around, and as soon as his blade is off me, I reach for my sword and aim for the air above his neck.

My sword is faster than his knife as he tries to pull it out. "Who are you?" I demand, pressing my sword into his skin.

He laughs, but it sounds more like a cry. "You don't know?"

Marric comes racing out of the woods. "I thought he had you for sure. That was some fast work."

"Where were you?" I ask.

"Bathroom break. By the time I saw him, he already had his knife on you."

"Next time you need to go to the bathroom, wake me up."

"Done. Please forgive me for not doing so in the first place." His voice has a pained quality to it.

"Apology accepted. Do you know who this jerk is? He seems to think we should."

"Never seen him before."

I press my blade deeper, causing a thin line of blood to flow. "Who are you?" I ask the man.

"My master sent me here," he pleads. "Don't hurt me. I'm doing what I was told."

"Who is your master?"

He shakes his head.

"Do you know who I am?" I add a threatening note to my voice.

He nods.

"Then you know not to mess with me," I say.

"Forgive me, but my master is much worse than you."

Realization dawns on me. "Ramco."

The man widens his eyes.

"That's what I thought," I say, trying to rein in my anger. "What did Ramco want you to do with me?"

He shakes his head again.

"Marric, cut off his hand."

"Wait, mistress. Wait. I'll tell you," my would-be attacker says. "He wanted you imprisoned in the temple I'm in charge of."

"You're a priest?" Marric asks.

"He didn't want me killed?" I ask, baffled.

"I don't know his plans, goddess. Just that he asked me to imprison you."

"What do you think his game is?" I ask Marric.

"I'm as clueless as you are."

With a sigh, I say, "Let's tie him up and take him with us."

"You want to bring him with us?"

"What other choice do we have?"

"We could…" Marric makes a cutting motion across his throat.

"No. Please, don't kill me," the man says.

"That would give him to Ramco on the other side. We don't want that. He'll have to come."

Marric's shoulders relax. "Good. I didn't want to kill him. I've got enough blood on my hands without adding more." He ties up the priest while I hold the sword to the man's throat.

Once he's tied up, I put my sword away. "How close is it to dawn?"

"It should be in about an hour or so."

"Why didn't you wake me for my turn to watch?"

He avoids my gaze. "I wasn't sleepy."

"More like you didn't want to make me watch." I want to be miffed at him, but things turned out well. I can only hope he doesn't get too tired as we journey through the day. "Shall we head out for the day?" I ask.

"Let's go. I can sleep on my horse."

Yeah, right. "What about him?" I point my thumb at Ramco's priest.

"We'll make him walk behind."

"Won't that take longer?" I ask.

"It would." Marric rubs his eyes, and I'm convinced he's going to need sleep sooner than he thinks. "What if you made a wagon?

312

The horses could pull it and carry us all. It wouldn't be as fast as straight riding, but better than the alternative," he says.

"Good idea."

I create a wagon, going a step further to make a confined space in the back. We lock the priest in there and hook up the horses. The journey before us isn't too long, but it'll be an uncomfortable one with a prisoner at our backs.

CHAPTER 93

THE TWO-DAY JOURNEY feels shorter than I expected, and it's not that bad. The priest never tries to escape and gratefully accepts food from me when I create it. The worst part is the hard bumps we go over.

The temple of love we get to is awe-inspiring. Beauty graces its spires as they wind their way together. The soft white of the walls takes on the glow of the sun. Like the last one, there are multiple buildings, connected with bridges over water. Trees and plants offer shade and beauty. It looks like a place lovers could take a stroll around.

I glance at Marric and then shake my head. No sense having thoughts I can't do anything about.

With a hope that this priestess of Charmina is nicer than the last one, I step off the wagon. "Stay here and keep an eye on him," I tell Marric.

"Are you sure you're all right, going on alone?"

I can tell he wants to come with me. "I won't be far. Not at all. And someone should stay with Ramco's priest. Besides, I need to do my talking alone."

"Very well. Call out if you need me, and I'll be right there."

Wishing he was coming with me, I head toward the middle building. I can see the faint outline of a statue in it. Before I get to the entrance, a woman appears. She's a dark-haired, dark-eyed beauty in her thirties.

"How can I help you?" she asks.

I look straight at her so she can see the vivid color of my eyes. "I'm Izlana. I'm here to talk to Charmina."

She bows low enough it eases my worries about her some. "Please, come in, goddess. She has been most anxious to speak with you."

With any luck, this means I won't have to spend hours calling to her before she finally appears. The priestess leads me to the temple but doesn't follow me in.

"I'll wait here," she says.

"We have a prisoner we'd like off our hands. Maybe you want to speak with my escort, Marric."

She nods. "Very well. I will speak with him, but there's no promise I can keep your prisoner."

It's worth a shot.

I enter the building to find the statue of Charmina on a pedestal shaped like a heart. I open my mouth to speak her name when her statue comes to life.

"Izlana, what has taken you so long?" she demands.

"I've had a war to fight."

"All your war did was make Ramco stronger. You should have returned to the heavens as soon as you got the collar off."

The reprimand hurts, but I don't let her see it. "I did what I had to do. Besides, I don't even know how to get back to the heavens. I need you to tell me where an entrance is."

"I can do that, but know you're coming into a fight the likes of which the heavens have never seen."

I swallow past the thickening of my throat. "Has anyone died?"

"Not yet, but it's been close a few times. Ramco has become reckless."

"He sent a priest after me to keep me in one of his temples, but the human didn't have orders to kill me. Do you know what that is about?"

"I can't say that I do. I only know Ramco grows more fearless by the day. Some of the gods sided with him out of fear of losing their lives. We can't handle not having your help much longer."

I don't know what she expects me to do as the youngest of them all. I wonder if she forgotten I'm only seventeen. An untrained seventeen year-old at that. Things would be different if my mother didn't die at an early age, but the fact remains that she did.

"I'm not sure what I'm supposed to do," I say, frustrated.

"We need you to help balance things out. Besides, Ramco wanted to get rid of you before he started this war in the heavens. There has to be a reason why."

Not one I can think of. "Fine. How do I return to the heavens?"

"There's an entrance, not far from here. My priestess will guide you."

I want to ask her another question, but she's already turned back to stone. I grind my fingers into my temples. "What are we supposed to do with the prisoner?"

But the statue doesn't answer. Charmina's gone into her own world, where things are full of love. I don't know how she's dealing with this war when it's so against her nature.

I turn to look outside. I'm not prepared for the things to come.

CHAPTER 94

"SHE SAID I was to lead you to the entrance to the heavens?" the priestess of love asks.

"That's right."

"What about him?" she points at Marric.

Marric and I lock gazes. There's so much I still want to say to him. So much I want to do with him. I'm not ready for him to be gone from my life. I'm not sure he's ready to leave me, either, though it'd probably for the best if he did. We can't be together the way I want.

"I'm coming with you," he says.

My heart warms at those words.

"And the prisoner?" she asks.

"Can the wagon come with us?" I ask.

She shakes her head. "Not the way we're going."

"Let's leave him here," I say. "I'll give him enough food and water to survive on, but we can't have him slowing us down."

"It should only take a day for me to come back," the priestess says. "Let's move him over to the shade."

We take care of the prisoner and get started on our journey. It doesn't feel like the last time I'll be on the world. It feels like any other journey I've taken with Marric, only this time we have a priestess with us.

We move through the woods by the temple on an area that doesn't look like a path. After half a day of traveling, we come to a mountain.

"Mount Hovon," Marric says. "I should have realized it's the mountain of heavens. Of course, even if I'd figured it out, we wouldn't have managed to get here sooner."

I agree. "We have to climb it?"

"Only partway," is her reply.

We follow her up the side of the mountain, to where the path becomes windy and narrow. Once we've gone up a ways, we reach flat ground. The area around us looks like a mini canyon, with the top open to the sky above. The way through is so narrow we have to walk single file, with the priestess in front and Marric in the back.

I feel stifled. Stuck in an area I can't get out of. I want to run ahead or hurry back, but both ways are barred by people. It's just as well; I need to stick with my guide. Though at this point, I'm wondering if I need her. I have a feeling the end of this pathway is where the heavens is.

Despite wanting out of this cramped space, I realize these are the last moments I have with Marric. The thought has my feet slowing and my throat closing up. My eyes burn mercilessly. It's not fair that I have to leave him behind, but nothing ever is fair.

"Are you all right?" Marric asks, putting a hand on my shoulder. Though he whispers, the sound echoes, making the priestess stop.

She turns to look at me, studying me for longer than I'd like. "It's up ahead," she says.

When she continues on, I give Marric's hand a squeeze and follow after her. What feels like an hour or so later, the way opens up into a small clearing, surrounded by steep slopes on all sides, except for the narrow passageway we came through. Across the clearing from us is a gate that looks all too familiar, though it's different than the one I used before.

It's the gate home.

CHAPTER 95

"It looks like nothing but a rusty old gate," Marric says.

I glare at him.

"Sorry," he says. "I expected a little something... more."

"I'm sure you did," the priestess says.

The way beyond the gate looks like you'd expect the other side of the clearing to look—more plants that narrow off into another path through a canyon. It doesn't look like home, but my heart feels it. This is it—the way that's going to part me from Marric. To take me from this world I've lived in for months and months, to the home I grew up in.

It'd be a happier thought if my mother was there, but I'll have to deal with this the best I can.

"I suppose it's time, then," I say.

"Past time, if you ask me," the priestess says.

I give her a dirty look.

"Any mortal who passes this gate dies," the priestess says.

Which isn't exactly true. A god can claim a mortal as their mate, and then they can come through. Or so I've been told. It's not like I've had a chance to test it.

"Since you're done with my services, I'm going to head back. Can you find your way without me?" she asks Marric.

"Go ahead. I'm going to need a minute, but I'm sure I can find my way back."

The priestess gives me a small bow and is out of the clearing.

Marric and I avoid eye contact. It's a little unsettling, how much I want to be with him, yet how much I know I can't. It's like neither of us wants to admit it. It's not what I planned when I knew I was coming to the world. I didn't expect to fall in love with someone.

I love him. It's a fact. But what do I do with that fact?

"Is it true that I'll die if I walk through this gate?" Marric disrupts me from my thoughts. "Because I'm willing to do anything it takes to go with you. I feel like you still need my protection. And maybe you don't. I've seen how capable you are. I'm not willing to let you go alone if I can help it."

"But Idolo said you only have to see me off to the heavens."

"That's why you think I'm doing this? Because of my promise to Idolo?"

"Well, yes." I didn't want to let myself hope there was more to it.

"Idolo has nothing to do with why I stayed with you all this time. It was a coincidence that he asked me to come. I did so because I wanted to. Because I care about you. I…"

"Yes?" I press closer.

"I love you."

My heart races and then trips and stumbles as I realize what this means. He loves me, and I love him. We could be together, were it not for the fact that I'm a god.

When I don't speak, he says, "You don't have to feel the same way. I didn't mean to spring it on you. It's only that this is probably the last chance I'll have to see you. I don't want you to leave without knowing how I feel. And if you know of any way I can come with you, I'll gladly do whatever it takes to stay by your side."

Do I admit that I love him? Do I tell him how much he means to me? Do I tell him there's a way he can come with me?

"But I can also go," he says, taking a step back.

That decides it. I can't let him leave me, even if having him stay is selfish. "There is one way."

His eyes light up. "What is that?"

"Gods take humans for mates. It's not nice, like your human marriage. A mate's more like a slave, really. But any mate can come through the gate to stay in the heavens. You wouldn't be able to return to this world. You wouldn't be able to do a lot of things without my permission. And you could never tell another human about mates."

"This is one of those secrets you've been keeping from me, isn't it?"

I nod. "I shouldn't be telling you now, unless you're to become my mate."

"I'll do it," he says.

"Don't be so hasty. You may be okay with this, but I still need some adjustment. I can't stand the thought of you being my slave. I'd rather have what you humans have."

He takes my hand. "But if it means we can be together, isn't it worth it? I know you. You wouldn't treat me badly. You'd take care of me, and I'd be able to take care of you."

"I don't know. Mates don't even usually stay with their god. They're treated even worse than the humans who pass on."

"But would you treat me that way?"

"You know I wouldn't. That doesn't mean it will never happen, though. What if the other gods influence me to treat you like a mate should be treated? Even if they don't, you'll never be my equal, like I want you to be. Not to mention we have no idea what we're getting into. There's supposed to be a war going on. Something unprecedented."

He puts a hand on each of my cheeks, looking me close in the eyes. "I don't care how bad things are. I want to be with you."

"I want to be with you, too."

He moves in until we're kissing. And oh, what a kiss. All the heartache and worry I've felt over the past few months bury themselves in a wave of joyous splendor. I push everything I have into the kiss while pulling him in closer.

As the kiss deepens, I know this is where I want him to be. Here, with me. Anywhere I go, he needs to be with me. Not as my mate, but as the man I love.

His kisses move from my lips to my cheeks and my eyelids. His breath is warm as he whispers, "I love you with everything I have."

Then his lips find mine again. I'm hungry for him, like I'll never get enough. And it doesn't feel like I will. It feels like any moment he could be ripped away from me. I don't trust this to last. Don't know it will be what I think it will. But, oh, how I want him to be with me always. I want to at least try.

When we part, we're both gasping for air.

"Let me come with you," he says.

"I want you to be more than my mate."

"We can worry about that later. For now, we can tell everyone I am, and I can stay with you. Keep you safe. Keep us from being parted."

"What about your family?" I ask.

He hesitates. "Would you be able to give them everything they need?"

"Not only their needs, but I can take care of many of their wants too."

He's quiet a moment. "Let's do it."

I rest my forehead against his. "All right. I'll tell everyone you're my mate. But know you mean much more to me than that."

He kisses my forehead. "Being with you is all I'll ever need."

CHAPTER 96

MARRIC and I hold hands as I look at the old gate. It looks as if it's been there since the beginning of time. It probably has.

"Are you ready?" I ask.

"Yes."

"Then, Marric, I make you my mate, for now until the day I die."

"Which I hope never happens," he says.

"There's a lot we need to talk about."

He gives me a sharp look. "Does that mean you're going to die?"

"Not any time soon, but gods grow old like humans and at the same rate. We keep on going by having children. One child for each god or goddess, and that child is always the same gender as its divine parent."

"You weren't kidding about having a lot to talk about."

"Doesn't it make you feel better to know we can grow old together?" Though I'd feel better if we were able to marry.

He kisses the back of my hand. "It does."

I grin until I look back at the gate. There aren't many places I want to go right now, and I dread going home as much as I want it. But I'm needed. "Shall we?"

"Let's."

I open the gate, and we walk through together, with his hand in mine. Closing the gate behind us, I give a little sigh of relief. Though I've seen mates in the heavens before, so I know they can make it through just fine, it makes me feel a lot better to have Marric alive and well on this side of the gate.

He lets out a deep breath. "Glad to know I'm not going to incinerate upon coming into the heavens."

I laugh, though it's not funny. I need the release. "I was thinking the same thing."

"We are in the heavens, aren't we?"

"We should be, but I'll know for sure once we're out in the open. I hope it's not as long a walk as it was getting here."

As we continue forward, I revel in the feeling of his hand in mine. He knows my secrets. He knows I love him. I can't wait to show him the heavens. To let him see my home. How lovely it is. Though who knows what it's like now that I've been gone so long and there's war brewing.

The narrowness of the canyon doesn't bother me as much as it did on the way in. There's no one before me, and I'm free to move as quick as I like. Though I still can't walk side by side with Marric, I keep my hand behind me, so he can hold onto it.

Coming home is magic. I wonder what part of the heavens we'll end up in. I hope it's close to my domain, so I can take him right there without any wandering eyes spotting us, or worse, people stopping us.

The canyon soon opens up to the heavens. Beautiful green hills. Trees speckling the area. Flowers all around. In the distance, a waterfall cascades down a mountain, creating a river that runs through the grassy area. The sun is shining, and it feels like the perfect temperature.

"This is the heavens?" Marric's voice is hushed.

"This is it," I reply. "We've come out by Ityos's area. The god of nature."

"It's beautiful."

"It is. Ityos is always working on making it better, too. There's a bridge up ahead that we need to cross to make it anywhere else in the heavens."

"Is your area very far?" he asks.

We stroll through the fields, hand in hand. "No, it's not. But I'm wondering if we should go to Charmina first. She seems willing to tell me things. And now I'm in the heavens instead of the world, she should be more forthcoming."

His hand tenses in mine. "I'm not sure about meeting another god."

I give his hand a squeeze. "It'll be fine. She's nice. Besides, if you're going to be here for a while, you'll have to get used to the gods."

"You're right. It's not something I'm accustomed to."

"You'll do great." I only hope I do as well. There's so much unknown with what's to come. At least Marric is by my side.

When the bridge comes into view, a person's standing on it. Once we get closer, I realize it's Charmina.

"That's the goddess of love," I tell Marric, quickening my steps.

He hurries along until we reach the bridge. Charmina is wearing an alluring red dress, her lips painted just as red. Her sapphire eyes sparkle. "Izlana, you finally made it."

I didn't expect her to meet us here, but it's fortunate she has. "We have so much to discuss."

She takes in Marric and the fact that we are holding hands. "I see you picked a mate while you were on the world."

The word *mate* makes me tense, but now isn't the time for arguments. Besides, if I want to keep him here with me, he needs to be my mate, even if I don't like it.

"This is Marric," I say.

She waves a hand. "His name doesn't matter, darling. I thought you knew things like this."

I clench my jaw. What right does she have to say such things? That she's been a goddess longer than I have doesn't give her permission to treat him in such a way.

"I'm so glad you arrived. There's much that needs to be done," she says. She reaches out and snatches my hand.

"What are you doing?" I ask, confused.

"Sending you where you need to go. You didn't really think I'd be on your side, did you?"

My heart sinks. What have I gotten us into?

CHAPTER 97

A MAN I haven't seen before comes at us, while Charmina holds me close, a dagger to my throat. If I could move fast enough, I'd get my sword. I know Marric would too, but with a blade at my neck, there's not much anyone can do. He grips my hand, not letting go. It means a lot that he's staying with me, but at the same time, I fear for him. What will happen to him? What will happen to us?

The man closes in on Marric, puts a dagger to his throat, and yanks him away. I'm grateful I made the swords to only be used by Marric or me; I don't know what these two would do with them. What destruction they would render.

"You're on Ramco's side," I say.

"Very good. And now he's going to reward me for imprisoning you here instead of his plan to leave you on the world where you could do damage." Charmina pushes me forward, across the bridge. There are footsteps behind us, so I assume Marric and the man follow. "You always were a quick one." She snickers.

I have an urge to stomp on her foot, but I ignore it. There's no point in getting my neck cut off for a moment's satisfaction. "Where are you taking us?"

"You're going to Ramco. We won't bother taking your mate there. He can go to our dungeon."

"There are dungeons in heaven?" I've never heard of such a thing.

She laughs again. "Oh, you poor, sweet, innocent girl. There's so much your mother never taught you."

Because she never got the chance.

"I've changed my mind," Charmina says to the man who is probably her mate. "Let's bring her mate and let Ramco decide what fate shall befall him."

The thought makes me fear more for Marric than sending him to the dungeons would. I can only hope we find some way out of this.

The way through the Ityos's area is pretty and serene. When we switch over to the area of Beazle, the god of festivals, it's more like a carnival no one's at. I have fond memories of playing here as a child. Of parties and gatherings held here. I hold out hope that Beazle will show up and stop Charmina and whatever plan she has, but the place remains desolate.

We go through Yaral's area, but there's no sign of the goddess of art. Just statues and beautiful works of art. I know her home is like a work of art too, filled with paintings and more sculptures and all sorts of things to behold. Her area is as abandoned as the previous two. Either that, or she's hiding.

Maybe they're all hiding from what's happening. Maybe no one has the courage to stand up to Ramco. I can't count on anyone for help, but I don't know how to help myself.

I've failed.

The world and the heavens are going to fall into chaos, and there's nothing I can do about it.

CHAPTER 98

By the time we get to Ramco's territory, my nerves are taut with frustration. I want out of this situation, but I don't see how. This isn't how I planned to meet Ramco.

His area is full of destruction and more like a wasteland than any place I'd want to live. I don't know why I was so caught up in being his friend. How could I not see he is not someone I want to be around?

When we get to him, there's an addition to his area I haven't seen. A throne. It's much taller than him and made of ornate gold and velvet, made by some previous goddess of creation that earned the god of war's favor. Plus it's raised upon a pedestal. He's made himself a king over the gods, but I will never bow to him.

Charmina gives him a nod, about as much of a bow she can do with her dagger still at my throat.

"Well done, Charmina." Ramco's voice is rumbling and deep, like a mountain ascending from the ground. He's thickly built and only a few years older than me. His eyes flash their light-brown topaz in my direction.

His parents died around the time mine did, mates always dying when their god does. I thought he was sympathetic to me and what I went through. Instead, he trapped me on the world and created a reign of fear.

He stands at his full height, even taller than usual because of the pedestal. "Why, Izlana, have you worked so hard against me? It's like you're the goddess of peace instead of the goddess of creation."

"I won't let you ruin everything my ancestors and I worked to created, either here or on the world."

He waves a hand, dismissing my words. "I tried to lure you in, to get you on my side, but when you refused, I locked you down on the world. I was certain you would stay trapped there out of my way, but no, you had to get out of your imprisonment. I tried trapping you again, but I think I will enjoy having you here where I can torment you. You may have temporarily thwarted me on the world, but it won't last once I'm in power here in the heavens."

I try not to let my sinking feeling show. "What could you possibly hope to gain from taking over the heavens?"

"You're not very bright, are you?" He takes a step down, but I still have to look up to see him. "I will have domain over everything, both the heavens and the world. What more could one want?"

"Love. Care. Respect." Each word comes out of me full of passion.

"Better to be feared than respected." He circles around to Marric.

My heart stutters. What is Ramco going to do to him? Nothing good. I should never have brought him here.

"And this must be the young man I've heard so much about," Ramco says.

"Funny," Marric says. "I haven't heard a thing about you."

Ramco's smile tightens. Without warning, he slugs Marric, making him jerk backward.

"Leave him alone," I shout. "He's innocent in all this."

"Not from what I hear," Ramco says.

"It was all me," I say. "All of it."

Ramco moves back over to me and squeezes my chin. "Don't worry. I'll deal with you. It would have been better for you if you'd let my priest capture you, but I must say, I'm happy to have you here, where I can punish you myself. Charmina did well."

He lets go and shoves my head to the side. Ramco laughs and takes my sword from its sheath. He saunters over to Marric and takes his as well. "I've heard great things about these swords. I'll make sure to put them someplace safe."

I smirk, grateful no one else will be able to use them. But then reality sinks in. I'm in a world of trouble. "What are you going to do with us?"

"You'll be taken to my dungeons. Separate cells, of course. I've found I need special ones for gods. Pitiful humans don't have near the power of escape we do. He can take refuge in my souls' area. They'll be sure to treat him as they should. Take them where they belong." Ramco sits back on his throne, my sword on his lap and Marric's at his side.

Charmina yanks me away from him, making more liquid drip from my neck. I wince at the pain, but I'm more worried about being separated from Marric.

I wish I had words of comfort for Marric, but all I can say is, "I'm sorry. I didn't mean to bring you into this."

"Shut up." Charmina jerks me the opposite direction than her mate takes him.

Will I ever see him again?

CHAPTER 99

THE PIT IS like nothing I've ever seen before. Granted, I've never seen one to begin with, but it's not how I pictured it. There's a hole in the ground just wide enough for me to fit through with a ladder next to it. Charmina places the ladder for me to use, and it's a long, long way down. Once I reach the dirt at the bottom, she pulls the ladder up and disappears from view.

It's stupid of them to leave me here when I can create another ladder and crawl out. Only, it feels strange in here, like it did when I was wearing that collar. Like my power is held in a tight little ball I can't access. Whatever they did to this pit, it's affecting me, and I don't like it.

The pit stinks of must and feces. It makes me want to gag. I stand where I am, in the light, not daring to explore the pit farther. I can tell it's not big, just about long and wide enough for me to lie down or maybe do a little pacing. The depth is the real issue. If I had my powers, it would be nothing, but without them, I'm at a loss.

Despite feeling their absence, I try to summon my powers forte, to create a ladder, or anything. My powers roil like they're trying to obey my command, but there's nothing they can do. I'm like a caged human.

I hunch down, trying not to sit, but wrapping my arms around my legs. It's hard to think of anything except Marric. What type of prison did they take him to? Are they punishing him because of me? It's against the rules to treat a mate so, but we're obviously playing outside of the rules now.

Why did I ever think I could defeat Ramco? Whether he trapped me on the human world or here in the heavens, I'm at his mercy.

The day passes, giving me less and less sunlight until it's dark. At least it's still the perfect temperature. I fear the creeping things that could be in this hole with me. I don't want them to climb on me.

My legs ache with my staying hunched over, only touching the ground with my feet. I give in and sit on down. It's hard and probably filthy. It's difficult not to, especially with the smell. I don't want to know what I'm sitting on.

It's hard not to despair at a time like this. How can I not? What hope is there? Desperate, I feel my way around the pit while sitting on the ground, looking for something that might offer a way out. Nothing. Just dirt walls and worms. I don't want to think what else.

Maybe I can dig my way out, making a slopping path upward. It might take a while, but it'd be worth it. I go to the closest wall and try to dig, but despite being made of dirt, it doesn't budge. I'm stuck down here.

CHAPTER 100

"Izlana." The whisper startles me awake.

When did I fall asleep? It's still night. The voice belongs to a female. Charmina? But why would she be whispering? I don't know, and I'm not about to answer and make things easy on her.

The voice comes again, louder this time. "Izlana."

Definitely not Charmina. "Venza?" What is the goddess of rage doing here?

"Good. You're here. I've been searching for you since the rumor you were back in the heavens started. Watch out. I'm sending a ladder down."

I jump to my feet and brush myself off. Then I put my hands up in the air to catch the ladder. It brushes my fingertips, and I assist her in lowering it to the ground. Hoping this isn't some sort of trick, I hurry to climb up.

At the top, Venza helps me out. "We need to move. Now."

"What about the ladder?" I ask.

"We won't need it again. And don't talk."

"But Marric—"

"We can't help him."

What does she mean we can't help him? The thought of it

consumes me as we run over dry landscape that's so hard we leave no footprints. There are so many other questions I want to ask. What is she doing? Why is she helping me? Is she helping me, or is this another part of Ramco's plans for me? If so, he's not thought it through. My power returns, raging through me. It wants to be used, to show its worth, but I hold it back. There's no reason to use it yet.

We come to the end of Ramco's land. The ground turns softer, and we dodge trees. I'm not exactly sure in the dark, but it seems like we're in Sen's area. He's the god of health, and it smells like herbs, so I'm almost positive this is it. Which is bad. He hates anyone being on his property.

Halfway through his area, Venza pulls me to the ground next to a bush. I'm about to ask what is going on when I hear the clomp of someone walking around. They're whistling, a solemn tune that sends a shiver through me. With them making noise, I doubt they're looking for us, but there's no reason to show ourselves.

Next thing I know, Sen jumps out at us. "What are you doing in my area?"

"We're just crossing through," Venza snaps.

"No one passes through my area. No one."

"But we need to. You must know what Ramco's doing."

He crosses his arms. His features are hard to see in the dark, but I'm certain his expression isn't happy. "I don't give a pig's foot what Ramco's doing. As long as he leaves me alone to my plants and my work, everything will be fine."

"He's trying to make himself our king," I say. "Sooner or later, that will affect you. Please, let us leave."

Silence follows.

I scramble to my feet, and Venza does the same. We stand there waiting, my worry growing with each moment. What punishment is he considering? Should I create another sword to protect us from him, or would that force his hand?

"Fine," he says. "Go through my lands, but just this once. If I ever catch you in here again, payment will be made."

"We understand," Venza says.

Relief fills me, but it doesn't take long to run again and feel the panic that goes along with it. It's hard in the dark, and I trip more than once. Venza stops and waits for me each time, until we finally slow to a jog. It's still difficult, but not as tortuous as running.

When we make it out of Sen's lands and into Venza's, I exhale with relief.

"Don't relax yet," she says through her panting. "It's not much safer here. We have to keep going."

We run more, but I feel free to ask questions. "How did he spell the pit like my collar that was on the world?"

"I don't know for certain," Venza says, "but I have my suspicions that it's one of his newly acquired souls."

"Pennington."

"Exactly."

It makes me simmer. Pennington caused enough trouble on the world; he doesn't need to bring it in the heavens as well. But if he's got Ramco backing him, he can do just about anything he wants except live again. None of the souls can return to the world.

We come to a small brick house, suitable for humans more than the god of rage, but it's what she likes. She takes me in through a side door but doesn't light any candles.

"Do you want me to create some light?" I ask.

"No lights," she says. "It's still not safe."

Is it ever going to be?

She leads me through her narrow kitchen to a closet, moves a rug out of the way, and lifts a panel of the floor.

"In you go." She motions me down.

"Another pit?" I glare at the dark space below.

"Unfortunately, but I promise you you'll be secure in this one."

That's only somewhat reassuring.

"What about Marric?" I ask again.

"I don't know how to help him. We were lucky to help you."

"There has to be something."

"I don't know. We'll think about it."

"Why did you help me?" I have to know before I know if I can trust her or not.

"Because we need every god we can get on our side. Too many have turned to help Ramco. We need each and everyone we can get willing to fight against him. Besides, the same reason he went after you in the first place. Your powers are strong."

They don't feel strong. "I don't know how to use them properly."

"But you're figuring it out. And the more you do so, the more scared Ramco will be of you."

"How many gods are on our side?"

"Not enough. Look, I know you have a lot of questions, but right now you need to get in there."

I lower myself down into the pit anyway, trusting her because it's what my gut says to do.

The pit isn't very deep, and I have to duck once inside. Venza covers the hole back up, and I feel I've made a big mistake.

CHAPTER 101

A LIGHT FLICKERS. A candle. A face appears above it.

"Dracia?" What is the goddess of beauty doing here?

"I told you not to return here," she says. "You would be much safer if you stayed on the world."

"What are you talking about? There was fighting going on down there. I almost died, and a priest of Ramco tried to kidnap me."

"Would that he'd managed," Seifer, god of deception, says, his voice booming in the darkness.

Several more candles are lit, and I find myself surrounded by half a dozen gods.

"Are you all hiding from Ramco?" I ask.

"We were waiting for Venza to bring you here," Dracia says. "We have to get you out of the heavens, but Ramco has his follower and souls watching all entrances to the world."

"I can't go back to the world until this one is settled. And especially not without my mate. Are you going to rescue Marric as well?"

No one answers. They exchange awkward glances. Finally, Dracia says, "We didn't know you were going to bring a mate with

339

you. You shouldn't have. He could have done his job on the world well enough. As it is now, we don't have the means to rescue him. Ramco's souls are watching him."

"Why weren't they watching me then?" I ask.

"There were some, but Venza probably scared them off. That was the plan. Ramco is going to come looking for you," Dracia says.

"We'll attack then," I say, determined to free him.

"We can't attack his souls."

"What do you mean?" I ask.

"Your mate's cage is in the middle of his soul's area. They're guarding it. You know that's one of the few places we can't go."

My heart drops. I feel sick all over. They're right. There's no way to rescue him from that.

CHAPTER 102

THE OTHERS TALK in hushed tones around me. I don't care what they're saying. I failed. Miserably so. Marric is lost to me forever, and Ramco is going to take over the heavens. Dracia was right; I should have stayed on the world.

She comes over to me, her candle held tight. It's easy to see why she's the goddess of beauty, but right now her full lips are turned downward. "I'm sorry things didn't go better."

I keep my voice low. "I feel like all is lost, and after I worked so hard for it to come together, too."

"There's still hope. There's always hope."

"It doesn't feel like it." I sigh. It feels like the world is weighing on me. "How did Ramco become so powerful?"

"He's been planning this for a long time, I think. Gathering his supporters close. Doing what he can to lessen those of us who aren't with him. And it's worked, except for you. You're so young and innocent. He probably thought by killing your parents he ensured you wouldn't have the guidance you needed to be strong enough."

"He killed my parents? My mom?"

"I assume so. He's killed several others."

Rage pulses through me, wicking away my sorrow. I clench my fists. "Someone has to make him pay for this."

"Who? No one has nearly as much power as him. You're the closest, but he's doing his best to make it so you're not able to stand against him."

"I don't care." Determination fills me. "I will defeat him."

I will stop the war in the heavens, and I will find a way to rescue Marric.

EPISODE EIGHT

Episode Eight

CHAPTER 103

THE SPACE under Venza's house is dark and damp. I wish I could get out, but it's not wise until I develop a plan. There has to be a way to save Marric from being in the midst of Ramco's souls. Something I haven't discovered yet. And then we can deal with Ramco.

I wish I had enough room to stand, so I could pace. I'm now alone in the dark space I shared with other gods earlier. Everyone else left to avoid Ramco's suspicion that they're doing something against him. It's colder in here without them, not literally but in a lonely sort of way. It does give me more time to think without seeing the pity in their eyes.

Most think I should go back to the world. That's the last place I want to be right now, not with out Marric. I refuse to leave him alone to deal with this. I wonder what he's going through. What he's doing. If he's given up on ever being rescued.

I hope my love is enough to sustain him.

I can't go in after him. Only a god can go in the area of their own souls, in addition to mates and souls.

The hatch to the underground room opens, letting in faint light that still has me blinking. A shadow moves over it. Venza comes down and brings a candle and a plate of food.

"I thought you could use something to eat," she says.

"Thank you." I'm not hungry, but I force myself to eat. I'll need my strength for whatever's to come. "Can I ask you a question?"

"Certainly."

"Why aren't you, the goddess of rage, on the side of war?"

She sighs and sits down across from me, placing the candle between us so shadows skirt across her face. "By all rights I should be, but all I can feel for him is rage. It seems that in taking over the heavens, those of us against him will likely be losing our powers. If he can create here, it could have a bigger affect than anyone will ever know. Who knows what this will mean for the heavens and the world? My anger remains directed at him. I can't join in causing our downfall."

"That makes sense. I wonder why others joined him? Do they not want to exist anymore?" The thought baffles me.

"I believe they think that by supporting him, they'll be spared."

"I can't imagine that happening with Ramco in charge."

"Me neither. If most of us go down, we'll be taking the rest with us." There's venom in her voice. "I'd best leave you to eat. I'll keep the candle here as well. There are blankets and pillows over there." She points to a corner.

"Thank you. For everything."

"Just don't go telling anyone else that the goddess of rage is a softie."

If I weren't so depressed, I would laugh.

She departs, covering the hatch as she goes.

I pick at my food, not paying attention to the taste. It quells hunger pangs I didn't realize I had. Once I'm finished, I set the plate by the candle and move to the corner. I find a blanket and pillow and lie down. I'd rather pace, but I need to get my rest in if at all possible.

Sleep doesn't come. Too many thoughts race around my head. I don't know how much time passes; it's impossible to tell in the dark, but it feels like forever.

I eventually drift off, but a sudden banging above me wakes me up.

Venza's voice is muffled, but I can hear he say, "What do you want, Ramco?"

What's he doing here? I crawl to my candle as quietly as I can and blow it out. The stomping overhead draws nearer, and softer, lighter footsteps that I recognize as Venza's follow.

"What do you think?" Ramco's voice is threatening.

I hold as still as can be, hoping he doesn't know about the hideout under here.

"I'm not the god of mind reading," she says. "There isn't one of those."

"Don't play with me. Where is she?"

"Where is who?" To her credit, her voice is strong and unwavering, unlike mine would be at this moment.

"I know you've hidden Izlana. Where is she?"

"I thought Izlana was on the world."

There's pounding, followed by Ramco saying, "You know she's in the heavens. Where did you hide her?"

"I can assure you, if Izlana is indeed in the heavens, I know nothing about it." Venza's light pattering heads away from me. "Now if you'll excuse me, I have work to do, and you have no right to be here."

"I have every right to be wherever I want. And I'm afraid you're going to have to come with me."

She laughs, but it doesn't sound humorous. I hunch there, undecided whether I should get out and help or let her handle it.

"You'll have to catch me first," she says.

The door slams above. Ramco gives a curse, and his heavy footsteps hurry toward the front of the house. There's a *bang*, and then all is silent.

CHAPTER 104

It's silent for a long time. I want to go after them, but without a plan, I'm afraid I'd end up captured again.

I can't leave Venza to face Ramco alone, though. I hope she ran from him fast enough. If he was dumb enough not to bring anyone else with him, she might have a chance to get away.

That doesn't help me, though. Do I leave? Is my hideout compromised? Is there some good I can do out there, or am I of most use staying out of the way? With my power, I have the ability to live a full lifetime anywhere I like, as long as I'm hidden from Ramco. But I don't want to spend the rest of my life in hiding.

Maybe I should move. If Venza is caught, she may give away my location, however unwillingly.

It's decided, then. I make my way to the hatch and push it up. It's heavier than I expected, but I manage to move it. There's the sound of the rug sliding off as I tilt it upward. I climb out and put everything back where it was. No sense leaving it open for anyone to find.

I creep to the door and listen. My heart races, nerves getting to me. There's no sound other than the usual chirping of birds. Who would have thought the goddess of rage would have birds in her area?

I open the door softly and look outside for signs of trouble. No one in sight. Just lots of trees. I slip out and close the door behind me.

Staying close to the trees, I sneak my way through Venza's area. I have to cross several more areas, but remain alone the whole time. Everyone is fearful of Ramco. There's nothing they can do against him so they hide. I don't want to be like that, but then, I don't want to be recaptured either. Then again, won't there be more we can do if we band together? Part of the reason they rescued me, I'm sure. I have to find a way to join those against Ramco and hope they haven't all been captured.

The brisk walk feels good and reminds me of being on the world. I finally make it back to my area, but what I see there stops me in my tracks.

It's been burned to the ground.

Everything. Nothing is left except ash and soot. I take a tentative step forward, tears threatening to fall. I grew up here. I lived here almost my whole life. My mother, and occasionally her mate, took care of me here. She made certain I had a happy childhood. She created things for me to play with. Even the tree with the swing on it is gone.

A tear spills over. I rush to brush it away. My toe hits something. I glance down to find my symbol has made it through everything. A bronzed circle with a flower in the middle and leaves coming out of it at different angles. I brush my fingers across it, wishing more than this had survived.

And then I think of my follower souls. I still have my power, so they can't have been destroyed. I don't know how one would even do that, but I worry for them regardless.

I run through the ash, no longer caring about my things. I hurry down hill and I see them off in the distance. The closest town I created for them is in one piece. My breath leaves me in a whoosh.

I don't slow my pace. They sense me approaching, as they should, and come out of their houses. Seeing them all well brings me great relief.

I stop, and they bow to me. I bow back, wanting them to know how much I appreciate them. Their eyes widen.

"Is anyone missing or hurt?" I ask.

They look to one another as if someone might have suddenly disappeared. Or maybe they're putting off telling me bad news.

"No one, goddess," a man named Brenzor says.

"Thank your souls," I say, glancing over everyone that's here. I know them each by name. They are my souls, and I take that seriously. "Do you know when my area was burned?"

"A day or so after I got here." Jelko comes forward.

I rush to him. Unlike others who look different than they did on the world, Jelko looks the same. He must have been in his prime when he died, which gives me more reason to mourn his death.

"I'm so sorry you're here," I tell him.

"Don't worry over it, goddess. I died doing what I was supposed to. It was my pleasure. And now I can serve you from here."

His words move me to the point I want to cry again. "It is I who should serve you. What do you need?" I turn to the rest of those gathered and raise my voice. "Any of you?"

After a moment of silence, a woman named Sisha says, "We only want to serve you, goddess. You've given us so much already, with these homes and lives that are much like we had before we became only souls."

There's a lot I can learn from these people. "If that changes, please let me know—if you have any want, the smallest at all. I'm sorry I've been away for so long."

"It's all right," Sisha says. "Jelko told us what was happening. We've all been concerned over your safety and are glad to see you well."

"As am I. But the danger's not over yet." I explain the situation to them, ending with, "I need to get Marric out and defeat Ramco. I think there's a way you all might be able to help me."

I hope it works, and no one gets hurt.

CHAPTER 105

"I'D LIKE it if you would all infiltrate Ramco's soul area and release my mate, Marric. I don't know how he's locked up there or where exactly he is, but I'm certain that if you work together, you can find a way to save him."

"We'll leave immediately," Jelko says.

"Thank you so much," I say. "Could I hide in one of your houses until your return?"

Everyone in the crowd raises their hands.

Jelko says, "Let's put you somewhere in the center, where you'll be the farthest from any harm. Maybe we should leave a few souls with you, just in case."

I nod. "I agree with staying near the city, but I'm afraid you're going to need every soul with you. I don't know what's going to happen while I'm here, but no one should know where I am. Plus, Ramco can't enter this area. Only his souls can, and I hope they'll be distracted by you."

"Very well, Izlana," Jelko says.

"I have one thing I'd like to give you before you go." I create a key and hand it to Jelko. "This key will unlock anything. You may not need it, but if Ramco's smart, he'll have Marric locked up somewhere."

"I would as well." Jelko pockets the key.

The escort me to a house, and when I go in, they leave—one crowd, moving en mass. I've never had all my souls leave this place at once before, but nothing bad will happen. I hope. I'll still have my full power. They're already dead, so it's not like they can die again. Neither can Ramco's followers.

But something can happen to Marric.

The thought makes me shiver. I don't want anything to happen to him. I want him to come back in one piece. I need him at my side.

I can't keep worrying about him; it's entirely unproductive. I take in the house around me. It's got a clearly feminine touch, with flowers in the windowsill and frilly curtains. I'm sitting on a comfortable wooden bench. Everything here was made by me.

The souls that were previously here when other goddesses of creation were alive disappeared when their goddess died. I always assumed they went wherever gods and mates went when they died. But after my mother passed away, I decided to make this area all it could be. Mother made it nice, but I wanted it perfect.

I've created a few things for other gods' soul areas because they asked nicely, but usually I only make things for my own area. I want my people to be happy. Not all gods feel the same way. The god of death has nothing but darkness, where his souls wander for all eternity. I feel bad for those whose main belief in life was in him and for those who feared him.

I fiddle with the armrest of the bench. How are my followers? Are they faring well? Are they getting Marric out of Ramco's area? I wish I could have gone with them to help.

I can't believe Ramco or one of his followers burned down my area. I can create things again, though. Even make it look like it did before. But such a thing will take time I'd rather devote to those on the world who need my attention. I'll have to do it a little at a time.

But first, I have to take care of Ramco. I stand and pace the room, wondering how he can be defeated. Could I create a cage that would hold him? I'm not certain my powers are that great, but even if they are, how could I get him in the cage in the first place?

My pacing becomes more frantic. Not only do I not have a plan for defeating Ramco, but my souls have been gone too long.

I glance out the window but see nothing but houses I've created, green grass, flowers, and sunshine. It looks like a lovely day, but it's not. It's a horrendous one, full of too much waiting and not enough options.

I move to continue my pacing, when a noise stops me. It sounds like... pounding? Yes, pounding. And it grows louder.

Hurrying to the window, I wonder what it could be. I look out. It's souls, running this way from the direction of Ramco's area. Did my souls succeed?

I scurry out of the house, anxious to meet them. The pounding grows louder as they approach. The first faces come into view, but I don't recognize them. How can I not recognize my own souls? I should know them all.

I take in more of them and realize I don't know them at all, but they look fierce. They're angry, with scrunched up faces, some letting out a battle cry. War. Ramco's souls. They're here, and they're coming straight for me.

CHAPTER 106

I JOLT BACKWARD, only to bump into the wall of the house. They're growing near. I turn to run, but they're almost here. I'm not going to make it. They're going to catch me. What will they do to me?

I shudder, keeping close to the wall of the house even as I move. I won't let them surround me.

They're coming. My breath comes in short gasps.

They're going to get me. The first few are only feet away now.

What do I do?

An idea blossoms. I stop running and concentrate on my power. Two feet away, I create a bubble big enough to hold me and that only allows air in. The souls closest to it run into it, but bounce off. I jump.

They crash into it again, smashing their bodies against the clear bubble. I don't know how long it can last against such a force. They bang their fists against it, screaming at me to come out. It makes me want to sit down and put my hands over my ears. Instead, I focus on making a second bubble, smaller than the first. A backup, in case the first one breaks.

"Get out of there," a woman yells at me.

"We'll get you, no matter how hard you try to hide," another yells.

A man bangs his fist over and over on the same spot. I should have made it soundproof, winged, and steerable, in addition to unbreakable.

One soul stands staring at me, while the rest clamor on. Saldor. As expected, he's a follower of Ramco and is giving me an unnerving stare. It's worse than the noise and screaming. Like he knows they'll break through, and he's waiting for them to do so. Then he'll take me away. Maybe to Ramco's area, so Ramco can throw me back in his pit. And this time, there'll be no one to save me.

The bodies press in all around, continuing to shout and hit the bubble. There has to be something I can do. It can't go on like this forever.

Another thought hits me. A worse one. If they're here attacking me, did my souls fail? Were they imprisoned themselves? I don't know how you could imprison so many souls at once, but there has to be a reason Ramco's souls came back instead of mine.

I push up on my tiptoes, looking across the crowd gathered around me. There are several dozen at least, but they can't be all of Ramco's souls. They're intent on doing his bidding, though.

I cross my arms and stare them down, trying to think of a way out of this. The loud noise makes it hard to think and even harder to concentrate. I don't know how much focus I can give the problem at hand.

I try to focus my breathing, to help me pinpoint my thoughts. The thumping against the bubble fades. At first I think my breathing's pushing it to the background, but then I realize something else is drawing their attention away.

I reach up on my tiptoes again to see what it is. I can't tell for certain over the group of souls, but something's gleaming in the light. I don't see anything, but Saldor moves away, pushing his way through the crowd.

Screams sound again, though these are of fear instead of wrath. The souls part and run in different directions.

And then I see him. Marric. Holding aloft the sword I made him and coming straight for me. I don't know what a sword can do against souls, but the look on his face is fierce enough to scare even me. He doesn't pay any mind to those running from him. There are others following him. I recognize them. My souls freed his, and now they're coming to save me.

CHAPTER 107

MARRIC PRESSES his face against the bubble. "Are you all right?"

"I'm fine. You?" I study him, looking for injuries.

"Not a scratch. Just time spent in an awfully small cage. How do we get you out of here?"

"I... I don't know. I made it in such haste, I only thought about how to make it unbreakable. The only thing that can get through is air."

He jostles his sword. "I bet this can get through, but I hate to have it shatter and hurt you."

"What if you cut a circle in the bubble, large enough for me to get out?"

"We'll try it." By his grimace, he doesn't like the idea.

The souls are watching with concerned expressions, but none step forward.

Marric lifts his sword and slashes through the bubble, making a perfect circle.

I slip out and rush to him. "I thought I'd lost you forever."

"Your people saved me."

It was souls that saved him, but I don't correct him. Instead, I press my lips to his. The souls around us cheer, and my heart feels content. We end the kiss quickly, mainly because of the souls around us, but we stay wrapped in each other's arms.

I never want to leave. I want to stay by his side forever. We've been through so much together, to be parted in such a horrific way, and I'm ecstatic he's back. But we need to do something to make sure he's never taken away again.

When we pull apart, our hands remain linked. I look for Jelko and spot him in the middle of the crowd. As soon as we make eye contact, I ask, "What happened?"

The souls shift to make room for him to come forward.

"It wasn't what we expected—that's for sure," he says. "We went into Ramco's area to find all the souls gathered around a box that was barely big enough for a person and two swords. They fought us, but we managed to beat them. Nester picked up the swords, and I unlocked the box with the key you gave me." He holds out the key on his open palm.

I take it from him, only because we need to be careful with such objects. I do trust Jelko. I trust all of my followers. "What happened next?" I ask.

"As we lifted the lid to the box, some of Ramco's followers took off running, while others attacked us again. Nester gave Marric the swords, and he flashed them at the souls, which was enough to get them to scatter. We returned here, and the rest you saw."

"I'm glad things went so well."

"They weren't as easy as he makes them sound," Marric says. "I heard them fighting with Ramco's people for a long time. It sounded like quite the feat. I thought for sure they were going to lose from all the ruckus."

I look over my souls. "Thank you all so much. This is important work you've done, saving my mate and returning the swords. Without you, I don't know how we would ever get Marric back."

As one, they bow to me.

"Here's your sword." Marric hands me my blade, and it feels good to have it back in my possession.

I slip it in a hastily created sheath.

"What's the plan now?" Marric asks.

"We need help defeating Ramco," I say. "This isn't going to be easy, but it will be possible if we convince the other gods to help us."

"No sense dallying, then," Marric says.

"Right." I give proper goodbyes and many, many thanks to my souls. "I'll be back to visit as soon as I can."

And I head straight for Dracia's area.

CHAPTER 108

I GO to Dracia because she's the one I know best of those hiding under Venza's floor. Since Venza ran away, I'm hoping to find her here. Or at least find directions on where to go.

The area is beautiful, like Dracia, but it's a different kind of beauty. Instead of grass or a field, or some sort of natural landscape, her grounds are pure white marble. Instead of trees, she has intricately designed mirrors. I suppose that, being the goddess of beauty, she likes to look at herself a lot.

We search through the entire area, looking behind mirrors and finding a large spot with brightly colored pillows, but there's no one around.

"Do you think she's been taken by Ramco?" I ask Marric.

"I don't know."

If I knew where the pits Ramco stored me in were, I could see if he had other gods trapped there, but it was dark when I came out. I don't remember much except running. Plus, it's a dangerous thing to be snooping through Ramco's territory without any idea if someone is there to save.

"We should try Seifer's area," I say, heading for it. It's only one area over, so we have to make it safely through the forest of mirrors, and hopefully we can find Seifer.

"The god of deception?" Marric asks.

"Yes."

"He doesn't sound like the type of god we should be running to."

I pick up my pace at the mention of running. We don't have a lot of time. Ramco could show up at any minute, like he did at Venza's. "I wouldn't think so either, but he was at Venza's with the rest of the group, waiting for me. I think he can be trusted."

"You think?" His tone is uncertain.

I take his hand and give it a squeeze. "We have to try. I don't know where else to turn."

"Very well."

We pick up the pace more until the marble abruptly turns to a wooden floor, shining in the sunlight that won't last much longer. Soon, it will be night.

In front of us stand about a dozen doors on a wall, each one different. One is made of wood, another iron, one carved stone. I don't know how I'd even be able to move the last one. Whatever they look like, they're all probably traps.

"Which door should we choose?" Marric asks.

"It's not a door at all we should choose. I don't know what would happen to us if we did, but he is the god of deception, so it can't be good." I get on my hands and knees, feeling the floor and searching at it as I go.

Marric gets down beside me. "What are you doing?"

"Looking for another way in."

"You think there's a hidden way?"

"I'm sure of it. Keep looking."

We crawl all over the floor, looking for anything that might be different. Something to give us a clue as to how to get in Seifer's dominion without using the doors. But it all looks the same. What's worse, the sun is going down, making it harder to see.

Once it's fully dark, I stand. "I don't think we're going to find anything now."

He stands as well. "Do you think we should try one of the doors?"

I glance at them, wondering if I could be wrong. Maybe I'm making this too hard, and one of them is the way in.

"Let me try something." I create a horn that only Seifer can hear so that others won't be alerted to our presence. I blow on the horn, not a sound made.

The darkness is overtaking us now. I could make a candle, but the light would bring more attention to our spot than I'm already bringing it.

"I was wondering how long it would take for you to call for me," Seifer says, seemingly appearing out of thin air. "Come quickly. This isn't a safe place."

CHAPTER 109

WE FOLLOW Seifer through a hidden door and shut it after us. I knew there was a hidden door somewhere, but I would have never guessed it'd between the other doors.

The whole place is like a maze. We move through bushes and what look like dead ends that turn out to have small secret paths by them, until we come to a cave that's a tunnel system with seven branches coming off it. We take the second one from the left, but partway through the tunnel, Seifer pulls up a hatch that reveals stairs.

As I climb down the stairs, I say, "You have quite the system set up in your area."

"It works, as long as no one tries to burn it down like they did to yours. The cave would stay in place, but everything else would go."

"How long did it take you to build this place?" Marric asks.

Seifer stops and gives him a once over. "Mate, it's been here for ages. Every new Seifer adds to it, making it more elaborate."

He turns and continues to lead us through the mess of mazes. When we finally come to a cozy room with several chairs, a table, and a bed, he stops.

"Now," he says, "what did you need? It's dangerous meeting you like this. You should have waited at Venza's instead of going after your mate."

"Didn't you hear about Venza?" I ask. "Ramco invaded her home, and she took off. I hoped she'd be here."

"What about him?" He indicates Marric with a tilt of his head. "How did your rescue him?"

I give him the short story version, and then ask, "Have you seen Dracia? She seems to be missing too."

"Why would I be hanging out with the goddess of beauty?" Seifer looks at me as if I've lost my mind.

I take a seat on one of the chairs without it being offered. I have to try a different tactic that I hope will work. "We need help. Ramco's too strong for me to fight alone. Please, will you help us gather the others and fight against him?"

He turns around and puts his hand on the wall. Whatever he does to it, it starts to open like a door. For an awful minute, I get this image of Ramco bursting out of the opening. Instead, Venza, Dracia, and several other gods come into the room, which seems to be growing smaller.

I jump up. "You hid them this whole time?"

Seifer shrugs.

I go to Venza. "I'm so glad you escaped. I didn't think you'd be able to when I heard Ramco after you."

"And I'm glad you did. I was afraid you'd still be there when he set fire to my area."

"He did it to yours too?" My heart aches for her.

She nods, blaze burning in her eyes.

"I'll help you rebuild it after we get this settled." I turn to the rest of the group. "For now, we need to come up with a plan of action against Ramco."

CHAPTER 110

Plans come and go late into the night, but no one has any worthwhile ideas.

"He's got too many gods on his side," I say. "We're a pitiful bunch against them, even with our powers."

"But a determined bunch," Venza says. "And we're fighting for our homes, souls, mates, children, and followers. There's a lot of power in that."

She's right, but it's hard to see when it feels like there's no chance for winning against him yet. "Who's his strongest ally?" I ask.

"Probably Tybalt," Seifer says.

The god of pain. Of course. I shiver thinking of my last experience with him. "Maybe if we can find a way to take him out, Ramco won't be as strong when we attack."

"But how will we get him alone?" Dracia says, reminding me we're not really fighters, but gods who usually only serve one purpose.

"They're sticking together more and more," Seifer says.

Marric slips his hand in mine. The comfort is reassuring at a time like this. I think about making the others special armor and swords like Marric and I have, but I don't think it's a good idea. They could be turned against me at some point. As much as I want to trust those with me, I can't. Not after what Charmina did.

"Maybe we're making this too hard," I say. "What if we attacked him head on? If we can take him hostage, the others will surely back off. Once we get him, we can imprison him in one of his own pits."

"Or they may attack us worse," Seifer says.

"They may. But if we don't try, I'm afraid we're all going to fall when he comes after us and our areas one by one."

"She's right," Venza says. "We have to strike now, before he gets any stronger. Before he weakens us more or has more gods follow him."

"I agree," Dracia says.

There are more murmurs of agreement.

"Fine," Seifer says. "We can try it. But I'm not holding out hope this is the way to defeat Ramco. Sooner or later, someone is going to have to release him from his pit. We'll have to constantly guard it, too. Not to mention the fact that he needs a mate and an heir to carry on his god line."

"We'll worry about that when the time comes," Venza says. "We can do this."

Their support means a lot. We can win this.

CHAPTER 111

GETTING out of Seifer's area is a feat in and of itself. I'd never be able to do it if he weren't leading the way. We whisk our way through other gods' areas, sticking to the ones we know are on our side as much as possible. The nine loyal to us are all gathered, readying to fight. Seifer says Ramco has eleven gods on his side so far, which makes me worry. What if we don't have enough power to stand against him? Or worse, what if he steals some from my side? How can I be certain they're loyal to me? I'll just have to trust they are.

As we approach Ramco's area, Marric whispers to me, "No matter what happens in the coming hours, know that I love you."

"I love you too." The thought fills my heart until I realize what I'm dragging him into. "You should stay behind."

Stubbornness squares his jaw. "If you're going, so am I. I've got good armor and a good sword. Plus, there's always magic on my side."

"I'm not sure magic can save you from the gods." Though the combination of all those elements does make me feel a little better.

"I can do this. We can do it. Together."

I give him a quick peck on the lips, butterflies floating through my stomach. "Just promise me you'll try to stay safe, okay? You're the biggest target out there, since killing you will have little repercussions for the heavens but will devastate me."

"I'll do what I can."

Grateful I created steadfast armor and a sword that always pierces its target, we continue on, hurrying to catch up to the others.

It isn't much longer before Ramco's barren landscape comes into view. I don't know why it's such a boring, raw place, but it must make him happy.

We hurry forward, our swords out now, ready to fight until incapacitated or imprisoned. Or win against Ramco. I wish I had more confidence going in. Venza sure seems to. Her eyes are bright with rage, her mouth already snarling, though we have yet to enter the battle.

Dracia is in the back, holding her sword firm, but looking less secure. Seifer's expression is inscrutable. Others are somewhere between Dracia and Venza.

We're coming up to the pedestal. Why aren't they trying to stop us yet? What have they got planned? I can see the pedestal, with gods around it. It's hard to tell which from here, but they're more than the eleven we thought Ramco had. They're fifteen. Almost all the remaining gods are on his side, while we only have nine.

We'll never defeat them, but we can't turn back. We at least must try to defeat Ramco, even if the odds don't look good.

CHAPTER 112

"WHAT HAVE WE HERE?" Ramco laughs. "Someone trying to knock me out of power?"

He's on the throne, the other gods surrounding him. I pay no attention to them for the moment. My focus is on Ramco.

"You can't take over the heavens," I say, letting my voice carry. "We won't allow it."

"It's too late for that. I've won, just by you being here."

"You think you can take us, but you can't. We'll never stop." Though I'm quite certain he can take us.

His laugh this time is big and boisterous, and fills the air with his mirth. "Soon, you'll all be dead."

Fear rushes through me. "You can't kill us. The world will fall apart, which will make the heavens fall apart as well."

"We'll see about that."

He snaps his fingers, and those surrounding him surge forward. We're after Ramco mainly, but anyone else who gets in our way will share his fate. It's not a fair fight if they're trying to kill us and we're trying to capture them. I don't know how we're going to survive.

Charmina comes first, aiming straight for my heart. Others are already fighting. I block her, aiming for her sword. My blade is swift to carry out my will, saving me from getting stuck through. Not being able to aim for her is tricky business.

I move so I'm a little closer to Marric in case he needs my help. Charmina moves right along with me, attacking with a vengeance. I have to follow carefully but quickly in order to maintain proper blockage. I don't know how to incapacitate her without risking killing her. Marric must be having the same problem, because he's grappling against the god he's fighting.

Swords clang through the air. The ground is hard beneath my ever-moving feet. I thrust forward, aiming for her sword. It hits with such force, it reverberates in my arm. She attacks, and I parry.

"This is getting old," I say through heated breaths. "Why don't you give up?"

She drives her blade forward, but I halt her before she hits my stomach. My heart pounds in my ears. I focus on her blade, blocking it once, twice, three more times.

"The only one giving up today is you." She pushes toward me, and I retreat.

"Where did you learn to fight like this?" I ask as she takes a moment to catch up.

"Don't you know? Ramco's been training us."

That explains why her moves are so quick and precise. It looks as if the others are struggling with the same thing—enemies well-trained in combat. We should have practiced more. Done something to prepare ourselves better for the fight.

"Why are you so determined?" I ask her between the clanging of our swords.

"Because Ramco is going to make all of us fighting for him powerful. He will rule over the heavens, and we will be just as strong as him."

That's not a comforting thought. We continue back and forth, with Charmina always having the edge and forcing me back. A second god joins her, pure glee in his gaze. Tybalt. I don't want his sword to catch me. He'd delight in giving me a most painful death; I'm certain of it.

As our swords fly, my arms weaken. I need to rest if I'm to have a chance against them, but there's no time for a break. The others look as hard pressed as I feel, swords whipping around and Marric's magic flaring.

It's not a fight we can win. I want to yell retreat, but I can't give up. I want to win or die trying. Only, if I die—if any of us die—the consequences will be severe.

Tybalt lifts his hand in the air and pinches his fingers together. Pain flares in my arm, like someone stuck a knife through it. I suck in a mouthful of air, trying to combat the pain while still keeping my sword up.

"You didn't think you were the only one with tricks, did you?" Tybalt makes a fist and thrusts it forward.

Though he doesn't hit me, pain ricochets through my chest, as if a hammer slammed into it. Air is pummeled out of me, and my blade wavers. My grip loosens. I'm going to lose my sword. I tighten my grip on the hilt at the last moment, my heart beating furiously.

An idea hits me as I tighten my hand. What if the accuracy of the sword includes the hilt? If we can aim it at their heads and knock them out, maybe we can at least end this fight. Though it will leave me open to attacks while I'm trying. It's worth a go.

Hoping it works, I aim the hilt of my sword for Tybalt's head. It connects with a thud at the same time there's a stinging in my shoulder. Tybalt falls to the ground, but Charmina has a pleased expression. Blood drips from her sword. My blood.

I block her advance once more, then aim for her head as well. She stumbles back and then races forward. I dive to the ground and put a block of dirt up in front of her, just enough to trip her. I jump to my feet as she falls to the ground.

She glares up at me, already trying to get to her feet. I have to do something fast. I force out my power of creation, making a bubble around her and Tybalt both, so they can't get out of it.

Charmina bangs her sword against it, but it's too late. She's trapped. I should have thought of this sooner. I have to get used to fighting if we're going to win.

I check my wound. It's dripping but isn't deep. I rush to help Marric with the god he's fighting, Daristona the god of death. With two against one in our favor, it works well. I wait for an opening and thump him across the head, then create a bubble around him. With another enemy down, hope kindles within me.

Without a word to Marric, I head straight for Ramco. No one stops me. They're all too busy fighting for their lives.

As I approach, Ramco pulls out his sword. I don't bother messing with him. I aim straight for his head with the hilt of my sword. If I have to go down with him, so be it.

Before I reach his head, he blocks me with the flat of his sword, making my hand ache. I tumble back several steps. "How did you do that?"

"You think you're the only one who can create weaponry? I'm the god of war. Weapons are my specialty."

He pounces, coming at me with his full strength, bent on killing me. I'm no match for the god of war. My weakened arm goes numb as I try to block his attacks. I can't win against him.

I can at least get some answers and maybe distract him long enough to come up with a plan. "Why did you kill my mother?"

His blade flashes as a grin appears. "Because of how strong she was. I couldn't have her getting in my way, just like I couldn't have you getting in my way. Of course, you're weak and untrained. It's easy to defeat you."

I try not to slump at this pronouncement even though it feels true. "Why are you so intent on taking over the heavens? Isn't your area and power enough?"

Our swords *clang* together.

"No. I want it all. I want to rule both heavens and the world. I will reign over all."

I shrink back further and further. His expression grows more gleeful, in a savage way. I can't think; I react, my sword doing all the work. Soon that's not going to be enough.

I have to find a way out of this, but with my waning energy and with me getting ever closer to the rest of the gods fighting, I can't come up with something.

With one last stroke of hope, I aim for the middle of his blade, telling my sword to break it in half. My sword flashes forward, connecting with his. Our blades clang together before biting into each other. Not only does his sword break in half, but so does mine.

For a moment, he scowls, but then his grin is back as he thrusts his broken blade toward me. As it pierces my stomach with burning pain, Marric comes into view behind him.

Marric raises his sword high above his head and brings it rushing down straight onto Ramco. The world around me darkens. As Ramco falls, so do I.

CHAPTER 113

My head spins. I'm lying on soft ground. Something warm touches my hand. I try to blink, but it's hard. After a couple more tries, I open my eyes all the way. Everything is blurry at first but gradually comes into focus.

"Marric?" I ask.

His face hovers nearby, looking down until he hears my voice. Then he looks right at me. "You're awake."

"What happened?" I ask.

"You took two nasty cuts. Second wound you've received on your stomach without the first fully healing first," Sen, the god of health, says coming into view behind Marric. "You should take things easy."

"You're helping me? I thought you wanted me off your area."

"Only when you came uninvited." His scowl makes me think I'm not really invited now either.

"You've been out for two days," Marric says. "Sen has been working tirelessly to make sure you survived."

"Thank you, Sen," I say, my voice croaky.

He shrugs me off. "We couldn't have the goddess of creation dying. It would ruin everything."

I give a small smile. "Thank you, anyway. I appreciate still being alive."

"Just don't overdo it now and ruin all my hard work."

"I'll make certain she takes it easy." Marric gives my hand a squeeze.

Sen leaves out a door I didn't notice till now. I realize I'm not on the ground but in a cot, Marric sitting by my side. The walls around us are made out of logs. Sen's house? It seems logical.

"You passed out from your injuries and lack of blood," Marric says, bringing me back to the present. "You'll be weak for a while, but Sen assured me that you'll live."

"Good to know. But what happened to the rest of the gods? Is everyone all right? I thought I saw you kill Ramco, but that can't be." Being without the god of war sounds nice right now, but I can't help wondering what type of consequences it will have in the long run. I cringe to think of it.

"Everyone on our side is fine. There were some injuries, but no one died."

I wait to hear more, but he doesn't continue. "What aren't you telling me?" I ask.

He glances down again.

"What's going on?" I ask when he still doesn't say anything.

He drops my hand.

"You're scaring me." More than I'd like to admit.

He stands and turns his back to me. "I killed Ramco."

I suck in a breath, but I'm not wholly surprised. I thought I saw him aim for Ramco. But it's not the first time he's killed someone in battle. Why is he acting so strange? Is it because he killed a god instead of a human? No one knows what happens to gods and their mates when they die.

I want to sit up, to go to him. I try, but the burning across my stomach doesn't allow it. "It's all right. We'll deal with what we need to," I say.

"You don't understand."

"Then tell me, so I understand."

He whirls around, face contorted with rage. "When I killed Ramco, I became the god of war."

He storms out of the room, leaving me confused in his wake.

CHAPTER 114

S<small>EN FINALLY LETS</small> me leave his home after a week, claiming I'm not entirely healed but fit enough for the heavens. I've been worried about Marric since he stormed off. Not once have I seen him since, though I've asked about him. I need details. An explanation. But mostly, I want to comfort him. Comfort myself. If he really is the god of war, he can no longer be my mate.

We can no longer be together.

As much as I wanted him to be more than just my mate, at least then we could be together. I'd come somewhat to terms with it. Now he can't be even that. There has to be some mistake. I've never heard of a human becoming a god before.

I don't know where to find Marric, so I go to Venza's, hoping she has news. Her place is rebuilt, though only shabbily, like she didn't have enough time to do it all. It's something I could help with, given time and motivation. Right now, I just want to curl up in a ball and never come out. Instead, I knock on her door, and she lets me in.

"I figured you would be by sooner or later," she says.

"I don't mean to disturb you." Well, maybe I do, but not for long. "I was wondering if you know where Marric is."

"You mean the new Ramco?"

"So it's true?" I sink down on the nearest chair. "How can it be true?"

"No one knows. It's never happened before, but when Marric killed Ramco, all of Ramco's power shifted to him. He has control over Ramco's souls and his power from the belief of the followers on the world. No more magic though. It's gone."

"I can't believe this. I have to talk to him. Do you know where he is?"

"Last time I saw him, he was in Ramco's area."

I shiver. I don't want to go back there, but I need to if I'm going to connect with him. There's one more thing I must know before I go to him. "What happened to those fighting with Ramco?"

"They're all alive. Once he fell, the others stopped fighting, as you said they would. Some, like Charmina, seemed upset by his death. Others were relieved. They've been sent back to their own territories. We haven't had any problems from them since, though we've been watching them just in case they start amassing forces again."

"That's something to be thankful for. Do you think it will stay that way?"

"Without a leader, I do. If someone brings them together again though, who knows what could happen?"

"So the question is will Marric bring them together?"

"Yes."

I put all my conviction behind my words. "He will never start a war in the heavens. It goes against who he is."

"Who he is has changed considerably. He's a god now. Of war. This must have affected him more than you can guess."

I think of him running off instead of talking to me. Anything is possible. There's no way of knowing without speaking to him. "I have to go."

"I figured you'd say that."

I stand. "I want you to know how much I appreciate all your

help with this. You've been a life saver. We wouldn't have been able to win the war against Ramco without you."

"Why, then, do you seem so sad?" she asks.

I roll my shoulders. "Marric and I can never be together now."

"What do you mean?"

"Well, he's a god. Only humans are mates."

"Yes, but didn't your mother tell you? Gods can marry."

"What?" I jump to my feet. Did she say what I think she did?

"Human mates are what most gods choose, but gods can marry. They have two children instead of on —a boy and a girl. One to take over each of their powers, when they come of age."

My jaw drops. "You're certain?"

"I'm positive."

I pull her into a hug, not caring that she's stiff against me. "Thank you so much. You don't know what this means to me."

Once I let go, she gives me a gruff, "You're welcome."

"I'll talk to you soon. We're going to become friends; I just know it." I rush out of the house, heading straight for Ramco's area.

CHAPTER 115

THE PLACE LOOKS as we left it—dry and desolate. If Marric is the new god of war, I hope he changes the decorations soon. It's miserable here. Which is probably the point.

I find Marric at the bottom of the pedestal on which he defeated Ramco. It's hard, being here. Lots of memories of fighting and waging war. Memories I wish I didn't have to return to. But I can't stop them.

Marric doesn't glance at me. He stays there, hunched over, almost curled in on himself. He's never looked so defeated, even when things were at their worst.

"Marric?" I keep my voice soft, as I sit beside him.

He scoots over, creating a distance between us that yanks at my heart. "What do you want?"

"I just want to be with you. That's all."

"Haven't you heard? I'm the new god of war. No one wants to be around me. Not even me." He's never sounded so bitter before. So utterly discouraged.

I put a hand on his shoulder, grateful when he doesn't pull away. "I know this is hard—not what either of us planned for—but we can make it work."

He jumps to his feet, finally facing me. His eyes. I didn't notice how they changed when I saw him at Sen's. I must have been too sick to pay attention. Their old hazel wonderfulness that I loved to stare in has been replaced by Ramco's brown-topaz color. It takes everything in me not to shudder at the sight.

"I'm not who I was," he says. "I'm a god who causes destruction in his wake. One who can never be with the woman he loves. One who'll make the world rue my rule."

I stand and go to him slowly. "I'm not sure where to start. There's so much we need to go over. First, I want you to know I still love you, no matter what happened to you. I found out gods can be married, so we can still be together."

The anger in his eyes dissipates and turns to hope before he grows bitter again. "Why would you want to marry the god of war?"

"Because I love him."

"But I don't want to be the god of war," Marric says. "I don't even like fighting."

"Which is why you'd make a good god of war. Fighting should be minimized, but sometimes, you have to fight for what's right. As the god of war, you can do that."

That hope in his eyes is rekindled. "I didn't think of it that way. Do you really believe so?"

"I do." I hurry to press my lips to his, to give him confirmation that this is good and right. He freezes for a moment before returning my kiss. It moves me in a way I've never felt before. I want to be with him the rest of my life, and now it's possible. Not with him being an almost slave to me. This is nothing like having a mate, but a true partnership that will bring the right kind of war and creation to the world.

He cups my face with both hands and pulls away just far enough that we share the same breath. "I love you, Izlana. Thank you for always being there for me."

"I'm happy to do it anytime."

Our lips meet again, pressing together with urgent need. I pull him close, wishing we were already married. We've been through so much. I don't want to be without him for a minute longer than I have to.

When we break the kiss, we're left gasping for air. We hold each other, and I don't want to let go. I never want to let go again. Of course I still have duties to attend to, but I can spare some more time with him before I get to those.

"What are you thinking?" I ask him.

He presses a kiss to my forehead. "That being the god of war who wants to make as much peace as possible is a tough job."

"It should be. But remember, sometimes you need war, like when we had to take down Saldor and Pennington. Without that fighting, the people on the world would be oppressed by one or both of their rule."

"How did you become so wise?"

I laugh. "I'm anything but. I happen to have a few thoughts on the subject."

"They're thoughts I'll take," Marric says.

I lean my forehead against his. "The best news of all is that you can visit your family. We can, together. You wouldn't have had that freedom as my mate."

"That is the best news of all. They will be excited to see us for visits. Though they'll wonder why my eyes have changed."

"Tell them it's the trend in the heavens," I say with a laugh.

"Speaking of the heavens, should I change my name to *Ramco*?"

I think about it. I don't want him to; I hated the last Ramco. But there are other things to consider than my hate. "It may be the best choice if you're not going to tell others in the world that a god can be defeated and replaced by the one who kills him."

"I don't like the idea of being someone else."

"You'll always be Marric to me," I say.

"And we'll always be together."

"Forever and ever."

The heavens and the world have never looked brighter.

THE END

If you enjoyed reading this book, please consider helping the author by leaving a review where you purchased the book and / or on Goodreads. Even a simple one line review helps.

You can sign up to receive notification when Janeal Falor releases a new book, get prizes, and insights into her books at www.janealfalor.com with a Release Notification link on the side bar. Or talk to the author directly at janealfalor@gmail.com

BOOKS BY JANEAL FALOR

Mine Series

Mine to Tarnish (Mine Prequel)

You Are Mine (Mine #1)

Mine to Spell (Mine #2)

Mine to Fear (Mine #3)

Sacrifice of Mine (Mine #4)

Darkening Light

Ever Darkening (Darkening Light #1)

Savage Light (Darkening Light #2)

Elven Princess

Bound by Birthright (Elven Princess #1)

Bound to Endure(Elven Princess #2)

Bound by Love (Elven Princess #3)

Death's Queen

Death's Queen (Death's Queen #1)

Death's Queen (Death's Queen #2) Coming Fall 2017

Standalones

Goddess Ascending

A Genie's Heart

ABOUT THE AUTHOR

Amazon best selling author Janeal Falor lives in Utah with her husband and three children. In her non-writing time she teaches her kids to make silly faces, cooks whatever strikes her fancy, and attempts to cultivate a garden even when half the things she plants die. When it's time for a break she can be found taking a scenic drive with her family or drinking hot chocolate.

Connect with Janeal

www.janealfalor.com

janealfalor@gmail.com

www.ingramcontent.com/pod-product-compliance
Lightning Source LLC
Chambersburg PA
CBHW050025030726
47506CB00001B/117